The KING of the TREES

BOOK FOUR

The GREENSTONES

WILLIAM D. BURT

William D. Burt

"Once a Greenie, always a Greenie!"

FROM THE LIBRARY OF:

Jessie Castronovo

WINEPRESS WP PUBLISHING

Cover by Terri L. Lahr.
Illustrations by Becky Miller and Terri L. Lahr.

Packaged by WinePress Publishing, P.O. Box 428, Enumclaw, WA 98022. The views expressed or implied in this work do not necessarily reflect those of WinePress Publishing. The author is ultimately responsible for the design, content and editorial accuracy of this work.

ISBN 1-57921-671-4
Library of Congress Catalog Card Number: 2003105406

For all who long for love.

"God sees not as man sees, for man looks at the outward appearance, but the Lord looks at the heart."

1 Samuel 16:7b

Contents

Prologue

A dozen butter rolls, you say? Coming right up. Pardon my fingers; they're a bit greasy. That'll be five gilders. Oh, please close the door, won't you? The snow blows in, and that's bad for rising bread. No, I've never seen a colder Yuletide, either.

Dall? Dall! Drat that boy; he's never around when I need him. At times, having an apprentice is more trouble than it's worth. Still, he's just a lad. I must remember to buy him a toy dragon for Yuletide. He loves dragons. The woodcarvers here in Beechtown turn out some fair imitations, but they're nothing like the real thing, believe me. Dall won't know the difference, bless him.

I was once like him—blind as a bat and bitter at the world. By all rights, I should have drowned or hanged or fallen prey to the dragon long ere now. Dall! Where are you? I'll have to knead out the bread myself. Yes, it's tiring work, but I've got good hands, smooth and strong, and they do my bidding well. Nowadays, I need several more pairs. I did once, you know—not hands, but something better. That was in my Greenie days. Still and all, my eyes—and Gaelathane—were well worth the trade.

What's that? You haven't heard about the dragon and the green men? It's quite a tale. Most folks think I made it up. The brewery boys know better. Have a mug of mulled cider while I tell you my story. You might say I owe my life to . . . *Hoppy*.

CHAPTER 1

Hoppy

I am afraid your father isn't coming back."

Merryn jumped up, overturning a metal pan filled with curling quince peelings. They poured out like faded yellow rose petals, the color of her mother Milly's wispy hair. A plump woman with a pinched face, Milly was cutting up the cellar's last few shriveled quinces into a pot that *plop-plopped* on the stove, steaming the windows and filling the roomy kitchen with a spicy aroma.

"Why not?" Merryn asked. "Doesn't he love us anymore?"

Tears fell from Milly's red-rimmed eyes into the pot. "No, Hoppy, it's not that. Something's happened to him. He should have returned from his river voyage weeks ago."

Merryn blinked back her own tears. It seemed ages since Beechtown's brewmaster had found her wandering wounded and witless in a hop field. *Hoppy,* he had called her until he and his wife settled on "Merryn" as more dignified, but the nickname had stuck. "Hoppy" she would always be to her family and friends, although the townsfolk preferred a crueler version.

She plopped back on the floor and began chewing a quince peeling. In March, her father Hamlin had left for the North Country with a boatload of ale. Ordinarily, the trip took about a week. He always returned from his travels with knickknacks for Merryn and her brother Emory, such as wooden soldiers, sailboats, spin-tops and shiny porcelain dolls with eyes that blinked.

Now March had bowed to April, and no barge or boat had yet brought news of Hamlin son of Harmon from upriver. To ease the waiting, Merryn had busied herself with errands at the brewery. All the same, she often awoke mornings to a damp pillow. Each night, she saw her handsome, hazel-eyed father stepping onto the dock, his arms open to greet her. As she ran to him, though, he vanished like the Foamwater's fogs after a summer's sunrise.

Merryn's mother was stirring the bubbling quince sauce with an old wooden spoon. "There's no sense moping about the house and eating those quince peelings," she said huskily. "Here—" She fished in her apron pocket and handed Merryn a couple of shiny copper coins. "Take these and buy us some rye bread. The darker the better. I suspect Baker Wornick is lacing the white loaves with sawdust again, just to pinch a few gilders. I threw a loaf on the fire yesterday and it burned like a stick of wood."

"But Mother—" Merryn protested.

"No 'buts,'" said Milly firmly. "Just cover yourself well, and don't dilly-dally. You'll be back in less time than it takes Old Tom to drain his pint of ale." Old Tom was a one-eyed carpenter fond of spirits, pipe-smoking and darts, in that order. Rumor had it that he also supplied Baker Wornick with alder sawdust.

Sighing, Merryn took down her red long-sleeved smock and blue scarf from the clothes tree in the hallway. After arranging the smock and scarf to cover her arms, neck and face, she studied herself in the hall mirror to be sure only her eyes were showing. Then she slipped out the back door and followed the pebbled path bordering the garden, where only a few hardy kale plants had survived the winter. Merryn could hardly wait for warmer weather to arrive, when she would plunge her arms into the black earth, bringing out cabbages and cucumbers; onions and radishes; sunflowers and squash. "If Hoppy can't grow it, then it's not worth growing," Hamlin had often boasted, and it was true. Everyone knew Merryn had a green thumb. Perhaps if that was all she had, people would learn in time to accept her.

Her father's brewery stood at the back beside a stream-cut ravine, soaking up the wan April sunshine. She loved the yeasty smell that sweated out of the rambling, slate-roofed building, although she couldn't understand why anyone would drink the bitter stuff fermenting in the wooden vats inside. Skirting the brewery, she nimbly climbed down into the ravine.

One of the last wild, wooded refuges left in bustling Beechtown, this secluded valley with its alder-lined stream was Merryn's private retreat from the world's prying eyes. Here in birdsinging, rock-rimmed solitude, she could bare her sun-starved skin to the open air without fear of ridicule.

Removing her scarf and rolling up her sleeves, she gazed into the stream, whose kindly waters washed away all her imperfections, leaving only a sweet, rippling face hung with brown curls. Then a necklace of water weeds swirled up, spoiling the fairytale reflection. Framed in green, her face still looked oddly *right*.

Beside the stream sat Merryn's saddle-topped "sitting rock." Under its base in a natural cavity lay her most precious possession. She was about to remove it when a twig snapped and the undergrowth rustled. "Is that you, Emory?" she called out.

Wearing a sheepish grin under his mop of wheat-colored hair, her younger brother emerged from the bushes. At least, she assumed he was younger. Not even Merryn knew how old she was. As nearly as anyone could guess, she was a rather tall eleven or twelve to Emory's very short nine. She felt much older.

"Thought I'd find you here," he said. "Will you buy me something sweet at the bakery?" He stared at her exposed neck and arms, and she self-consciously rearranged her scarf and smock to cover them. Even here, it seemed, she had no privacy.

"Oh, very well," she said. "Please don't tell Mum I was down here. She thinks I dawdle enough as it is. She doesn't understand what it's like being me. You understand, don't you, Emory?"

Emory gazed at her with wide, blank blue eyes. Then he ambled back the way he had come. Merryn felt a pang of compassion for him. He had endured much for her sake. None of his friends would come near his home, and the older boys often taunted him on her account. A tear coursed down her cheek.

Quietly creeping up the ravine, she reached the stream's source, a spring gurgling cheerfully out of a rockfall. Merryn clambered over the boulders, straightened her scarf and shift and darted between two old brick houses bordering the square. Though the spring market was still weeks away, men were already at work sprucing up the place. Cutting across the square, Merryn had Baker's Street in sight when she heard shouts.

"Hey, Scabby! Wait for us! We want to talk with you!"

Merryn broke into a run, but before she could escape, her tormentors swiftly surrounded her. Their ringleader, a swaggering ne'er-do-well named Ort, stepped up to her and jabbed her stomach with a stick. She gasped in pain and doubled over.

"Just as ugly as ever," Ort sneered, his upper lip curling under a broken nose. "I'm surprised yer *keepers* let you out of the house. What happened? Did you break all yer mama's mirrors looking into them and now ye're gonna have to buy her new ones?" The other boys snickered and elbowed one other.

"Leave me alone," said Merryn sullenly. Her eyes scoured the square, but no one seemed to notice her plight.

"You're sick, Scabby," Ort said, hooding his flinty eyes. "You should lie down." He shoved Merryn backward just as another boy dropped to his hands and knees behind her.

Losing her balance, Merryn fell back and cracked her head on the cobbles. Fuzzy stars floated before her eyes. She had hardly caught her breath when the boys began kicking her in the face and ribs and beating her with sticks. She curled into a ball.

Whack! Slap! Merryn braced herself for the next blow, but it never came. She lowered her arms and opened a slitted eye. A pair of mud-spattered, green-cloaked legs stood before her. The legs squatted and a young man's pleasant face peered at her. "Those rascals are gone now. May I help you up?"

Merryn numbly nodded and took her rescuer's proffered arm. Once on her feet, she realized her scarf had been torn off in the scuffle. Never had she appeared in public without it. Burning with shame, she covered her face and neck with both hands.

"I believe this is yours," said the young man. He picked up a filthy rag that had been ground into the cobbles and handed it to her. After all that she had endured, the sight of her trampled scarf was too much to bear, and Merryn burst into tears.

"I'm sorry I wasn't here earlier," the stranger said. "For some reason, Beechtown has more than its share of street toughs. I've run afoul of them myself once or twice. Are you hurt?"

Merryn wiped her eyes on her sleeve. "No, I—I'm fine," she lied. Her body ached all over from the beating. "Thank you for helping me. What is your name, if I may ask?"

"Timothy," replied the stranger with a smile. "My parents live south of town. Why were those boys kicking you just now?"

"They don't like my looks," Merryn said miserably, her eyes flooding again. "Nobody does. That's why I cover myself." As she tied the tattered scarf around her head, Timothy regarded her with a mixture of amusement and sympathy. Then he gently removed the scarf, rolled it up and dropped it into her hand.

"I think you look better without it," he said.

Merryn stared at him, hardly believing what she had heard. Most people recoiled in disgust from her uncovered face. Then her gaze flitted around the square. Except for the workmen, it was vacant. "What happened to those bullies?" she asked.

Timothy drew back his cloak. A short sword in a jeweled scabbard was strapped to his hip. "They won't come around here again for a while," he said. "I gave them the flat of my sword." He burst out laughing. "Let's go visit some shops. I'm hungry!"

Ignoring the frank stares and scowls of passers-by, Merryn took Timothy to the bakery, where she bought two loaves of dark rye and some gingerbread for Emory. Timothy settled on a bag of sticky buns, which he shared with Merryn.

As the portly, flour-dusted baker bagged up their purchases, he remarked, "Have you heard the latest news on the river?"

Timothy stopped chewing on a bun. "What news?"

Wornick leaned over the counter, his sweat-limp hair plastered down. "Yesterday, a boat floated into town w' nary a soul aboard. Some vittles was missin'—spuds, bacon and mutton—but all the clothes and valuables was left. It ain't th' first time, either."

"Sounds like the crew jumped ship," Timothy offered.

Wornick snorted. "With all their supper laid out? There was leaves everywhere, too. Nobody knows what to make of it."

Thanking the baker, the pair returned to the square, where the sun-warmed cobbles were steaming like stony buns straight from the oven. Then a stiff wind sprang up and the daylight dimmed as ominous gray clouds streamed down from the Tartellans.

"I suppose I should be going," said Timothy.

"Please don't!" Merryn begged him. She trembled. Could she trust this young man with his easy manner and ready sword? "I want to show you something," she ended lamely.

"Really? What's that?" Timothy asked, arching an eyebrow.

"It's a secret. That's why I have to show you." Without waiting for Timothy's answer, Merryn dragged him down into the dell to her sitting rock and reached under it. Her treasure was gone.

CHAPTER 2

Spoiled Quince Sauce

Y ou should know better than to uncover yourself in public!"
Milly scolded Merryn. "What will people say? I've heard talk
that you're a changeling and should be burned at the stake.
Goodness gracious, child, where did you get all those bruises?"

Merryn sat in the kitchen, hugging her knees and weeping.
First her father had gone missing, then the bullies had beaten her,
and now this. Her most cherished keepsake had vanished, and
with it, the only clue to her mysterious past. She should never
have hidden it under that rock in the first place.

After searching the stream bank in vain for her treasure, she
had snatched up her sack of bread and sweets and bolted for home,
leaving Timothy to find his own way out of the valley. Drying her
tears, she now told Milly how the young stranger had rescued her
from the bullies. "He saw me uncovered, Mother, and he thought I
looked better that way! Maybe I'm outgrowing it, just as you used
to say. Maybe I'll be normal some day!"

Milly was briskly stirring more quince sauce. "The boy must
be blind," she muttered. "It's plain to see she's not getting any better, nor ever will. What man will have her like this?"

Whatever else was ailing Merryn, her hearing was still as sharp
as ever. Tears coursing down her face, she fled out the front door

and ran smack into Emory, knocking something out of his hand. He grabbed it again, but not before Merryn saw what it was.

"You! You're the one who stole my stone! Give it back this instant or I'm telling Mother!"

A cunning look came over Emory's face. "I'll tell her about your secret spot! Then where will you be?"

Fury kindled in Merryn's heart, and she flew at her brother, raking his arms with her long fingernails. "Thief! That stone belongs to me. Hand it over, or so help me—!"

"It's mine now, Scabby!" he threw back with a mean laugh. Darting inside the door, he slammed it shut behind him. Merryn heard the 'snick' of the lock, and with a wrenching sob, she sank onto the unforgiving earth. *Scabby*. Never before had Emory wielded that cruel name against her unguarded soul. At home, she was supposed to be 'Hoppy,' an endearing name that soothed away the pain of mocking eyes and muttered curses.

A bitter wind stung her face as fat, lazy snowflakes whirled down from a slate sky, reminders that winter lingered long in the shadow of the Tartellans. Merryn wished her father were home to defend her. In Hamlin's hearing, a drunken fisherman had once referred to her as "that scabby brat." Those careless words had cost the man his front teeth and most of his back ones, too.

Collecting herself, Merryn pounded on the door. Let Emory betray her if he would; she was going to have her stone back!

The door opened, letting snowflakes in. "Whatever has gotten into you?" Milly demanded. "You'll catch a cold standing out there in the snow; come in and warm yourself by the fire."

"Emory stole something of mine!" Merryn blurted out.

Her mother glanced back at Emory, who was toasting his feet by the stove. He shot Merryn a defiant look as she entered.

"Well?" said Milly, standing with arms akimbo.

Languidly, Emory got up and approached Merryn, making as if to return the stone. Abruptly, he spun around and opened his fist over the pot of burping quince sauce. *Plop*, went the stone.

Merryn screamed. Milly grabbed Emory by the hair and yanked so hard that the boy's feet flew out from under him. "What did you just drop into my quince sauce?" she hissed.

"Ow! Let go of me!" he yelled.

"Not until you tell me what's going on here," said his mother firmly. "Now—what—did—you—drop—in—my—sauce?"

Emory twisted out of his mother's grip. "She won't be needing it where she's going, and I hope she never comes back!"

However, Emory was already forgotten. Greenish steam was boiling out of the pan like some vile poison. Milly backed away from the stove, her eyes bulging and lips quivering. As the green cloud rolled over Merryn, she saw herself picking up the stone from a bed of bruised grasses. She had been pursuing something that was cutting a wide swath through the bushes. Green, coiling snakes writhed around her. Dizzy, she fell to the floor.

With a shriek, Milly hurled the pot of sauce through the window. As snowflakes billowed into the kitchen, Merryn floated away into a robin's-egg sky above many-eyed marshes.

"Merryn, wake up! *Wake up!*"

Shadowy forms hovered above Merryn like tree-reflections seen in her secret stream. Her mother's face swam over her.

"Merryn! Say something! Are you all right?"

Bully boys were beating her, their booted feet and heavy sticks thudding against her ribs. A coppery taste tainted her mouth. "Mother—" she croaked. Then the world spun into darkness.

When Merryn awoke again, she was lying on her own bed. Moonlight frosted the room, casting black spiders into the corners. Feeling oddly light, she stood on the bed and looked out the window. Her heart caught. Snow glistened over the slumbering landscape in mounded pillows and smooth satin sheets.

She loved the snow, from the first shy, wispy flakes of autumn to the fat, floating goose feathers of blustery winter. She loved its squeaky crunch beneath her boots; the way it whispered through the trees and melted on her tongue; how it wove lace around the windowpanes and graced every eave, twig and railing with its white-gloved touch. She loved the clean-slate, unspoiled promise of a fresh morning's snowfall, just begging to be sculpted into turreted castles and lumpy snowmen, unsigned love letters and miniature Beechtowns. She loved everything about snow.

Best of all, snow spelled *freedom*. No need to stick to roads and lanes; snow laughed at fences and gates and stony boundaries, making of all one great untrodden highway. Bundled in hat, scarf and mittens like every other mother's snow-child, Merryn could forget who and what she was, if only for a few hours.

Then she remembered her stone. Quietly, she pulled on her boots and stole through the house. Since the back door squeaked, she took the front. Sinking deliciously into the yielding powder with every step, she slogged around the side of the house. Upriver, on the snow-stacked bridge, hundreds of stolid, petrified batwolves wore comical white caps and nose-mittens.

Below the broken kitchen window, a hump in the white blanket marked the gravesite of her mother's pan of quince sauce. Digging carefully to avoid broken glass, Merryn unearthed the pot, dented on one side from its hard landing. Upending it, she dumped out a slurry of cold cooked quinces. Nestled amongst the golden, grainy fruit lay a smooth, jade-green stone, apparently unharmed. A pretty bauble she had thought it—until now.

This time she was taking no chances. Moonlight glinted greedily off the stone as she dropped it into the buckskin bag she wore around her neck. Her gem was back where it belonged, and there it would remain. Leaving the pot, she returned to her room.

The moon had hidden behind a bank of storm clouds when Merryn pulled off her boots and slipped into bed again. Despite her cold-nipped fingers and toes, a glowing warmth flooded her limbs as she thought of her precious stone in its pouch. Lulled by the hiss of snowflakes against her window, she slept.

The next morning, Merryn awoke to a pounding sound—and an awful itch. This was not the sort of itch that goes away when you scratch it. No, this was *the* Itch that begins all over your body at once and burrows down deep until you long to throw off your skin and scratch yourself to the bone.

She broke a couple of fingernails scratching her legs and arms and torso. Then she rubbed her back against the door jamb. Finding no relief, she struggled into her damp boots and trudged outside, where she rolled over and over in the refreshing snow, which soothed her raw sores and itchy skin. *Bam! Bam!* Armed with a hammer, her mother was nailing boards over the shattered window. As Merryn came near, Milly broke out in dimples.

"How are you feeling, dear?" she asked. "Shouldn't you be in bed? You gave your brother and me quite a fright. Emory says it was a lump of saltpeter he dropped in my sauce. I've warned you before to stay away from those mines up in the hills."

"I'm sorry, Mother," said Merryn. "I'm much better today. What did Emory mean when he said I was going somewhere?"

Milly's eyes turned brittle. "Let's go inside," she said.

Following her mother into the kitchen, Merryn ladled herself a bowl of quince sauce and settled on a stool. Her breath clouded in the chill air that poured between the hastily nailed-up boards.

"I've come to a decision," said Milly absently as she lit a lamp. Her eyes focused above the top of Merryn's head. "I am sending you away for a time. It is for your own good, mind you."

Merryn nearly fell off her stool. "Sending me away?" she repeated. "Why? What have I done?" She couldn't breathe.

In a rare gesture of affection, Milly touched her arm. "It's not your fault. You can't help being what you are—and our townsfolk can't help being what they are, either. You'll be better off upriver. I hear all sorts of odd lots live north of here, and they won't bat an eye over you and your scabby skin. Besides, that's where your father disappeared. I want you to keep your eyes and ears open for any news of him. Emory and I can manage without you for a few weeks. I'm sure it will be for the best for us all."

The blood roared in Merryn's ears. "Upriver?" Her voice sounded harsh and distant. "When?"

Milly blew on her cupped hands. "Your ship sails in a month."

Merryn jumped off the stool and ran to her room, where she threw herself on her bed and let the tears flow. Leave Beechtown? By herself? To be sure, the place held few warm memories for her, but it was all she had ever known. Besides, how would she get along without her mother and brother? Despite their faults, they knew and understood her better than anyone else.

April passed all too swiftly into May. Each day found Merryn at the docks, asking among the rivermen for her father. They all knew Beechtown's brewmaster, yet no one had seen him.

"'E's gone off, 'as he?" they would say, clucking their tongues sympathetically. "Poor lil' tyke, to lose yer dad so young." She would come away with a pocketful of sweets and a heart full of stones. Why hadn't her father come back to rescue her?

One morning when Merryn was preparing for another visit to the docks, her mother's voice bit through the bedroom door. "He's here, Hoppy. Come out when you're properly covered."

Merryn hurriedly dressed. Father was home! She wouldn't have to leave after all! She was saved! Throwing open the door, she saw her mother smoothing down her house frock and fluffing up her hair, the way she always did when visitors came calling. Behind her stood a scruffy man wearing a jaunty red stocking cap on his grizzled head and a stained leather jerkin over his short tunic. His hairy arms were ropy with muscle.

"This is Captain Rolc," said Milly demurely. "He's graciously agreed to escort you to his ship." She held up a handbag. "I've packed this bag with some food and a change of clothes. You'll also find a few gilders for buying more food when this runs out."

Numbly, Merryn took the bag, which felt much too light to sustain her on such a voyage. Rolc showed a mouthful of broken and discolored teeth to match his weathered face.

"Time to go, girlie," he sneered, reaching for her.

Bile rose in Merryn's throat as she stepped back, clutching the handbag to her chest. "I'm not leaving," she said stoutly. Why of all people had Milly chosen this ill-favored, ill-mannered man?

"Too late fer that now," growled the captain, and he grabbed her wrist. Merryn bit and kicked him, but he tossed her over his shoulder like a sack of fish and carried her out the door. Looking back, Merryn saw her mother waving good-bye, and the truth struck her: As Emory had hinted, she was not coming back.

CHAPTER 3

The Forest of Fellglade

Mercifully, the jouncing trip to Rolc's small, stinking ship was a short one. Minus her handbag, Merryn was thrown over the rail onto some coiled ropes. Then a short, gaily-dressed riverman dragged her into the low-slung wheelhouse and chained her to an iron ring set in the deck. "Jest till we get underway," said "Shorty" gleefully. "Can't have ye jumpin' ship, can we?" Chortling, the deckhand left Merryn to her misery.

She slumped onto the filthy flooring. Why hadn't she run away when she'd had the chance? Her mother had never accepted her, but who would have guessed it would come to this? Evidently, as sailors throw their cargo overboard to lighten a sinking ship, Milly was lightening her load by casting away Merryn.

Men shouted and ropes rumbled. The ship shuddered and strained at her anchor as the sails bellied out. Up rattled the anchor chain, and the dock slid away. As Merryn's home and familiar haunts shrank behind her, Shorty returned to the wheelhouse with Rolc, who took the wheel, ignoring Merryn.

"Let's have these irons off now," said Shorty. With the twist of a key, Merryn was free. Weeping in despairing fury, she rushed at the captain and pushed him away from the wheel.

"Let me off this boat at once!" she screamed. Shorty and another hard-bitten deckhand grabbed her arms and dragged her away from Rolc, whose seamed face twisted with rage.

"It's a ship, guttersnipe, not a boat!" he fumed. "And here's how we punish mutiny aboard our *ship*! Give her nine, boys!"

"But captain, she's only a child!" protested Shorty.

"Give her nine or you'll have thirty from me!" Rolc roared.

Merryn was wondering what the captain had meant by "nine" and "thirty" when he tossed a bundle of weighted leather thongs to Shorty, who caught it and with a flick of his wrist, sent the thongs whistling and snapping through the air. Merryn nearly fainted. She was about to be flogged!

The three men took Merryn outside, where a fourth whipped the scarf off her head and ripped off her smock. Uncovered, clad only in her sleeveless shift, Merryn sobbed out her shame and terror. All at once, the four leering rivermen turned pale, and Shorty howled, "Lor' ha' mercy on us, captain, but she's got the plague. We're all dead men walking!" The two frightened sailors holding Merryn's arms released her and backed away. Only Rolc's stern gaze kept them from leaping into the river.

The captain was clearly shaken. "Yer mother didn't tell me ye had the pox!" he hissed. "No wonder she was so eager to sell."

Merryn blinked in confusion. "Sell?" Maybe she had misheard the captain. Her mother would never do such a thing.

Rolc snorted. "Do ye think she shipped ye out o' town fer yer health? She needed the money, and I've got me some customers in th' market fer able-bodied servants. Now what will I do wi' ye? Nobody in his right mind would buy a girl with th' pox."

"I'll have her," said a soft voice. Merryn turned to see a man climbing through a hatch in the deck. He wore a peasant's tunic draped with a gray cape. It was Timothy.

Never had Merryn been so happy to see another human being. Timothy winked at her and tossed Rolc a bag that clinked when the captain caught it. "That should cover your costs and then some. I've been looking for a female servant myself."

Relief and greed chased each other across Rolc's features. "What does a young feller like ye need with a servant? I, ah—very well, ye can take her. Only don't blame me if she gives ye th' plague! If ye ask me, ye're diggin' yer own grave."

Merryn anxiously gazed at her benefactor. Although he had seen her uncovered in the square, she hadn't told him about her mysterious affliction. For an agonized instant, she thought he would change his mind and demand his money back. Stooping, she recovered her torn smock and draped it over herself.

"You see to your grave, and I'll see to mine," Timothy coolly replied. "If your men ill-treat this wench again, though, I'll have your head for it, bargain or no." He casually threw back his cloak to reveal the short sword strapped about his waist.

Rolc's mouth twitched. "As you wish." Then he sullenly retreated to the privacy of his wheelhouse.

"What bargain?" Merryn asked.

Without answering, Timothy drew her to the ship's starboard side. In the distance, greening fields dotted with sheep and goats slowly passed by, as if parading themselves before the two passengers. Closer at hand, tall, swaying poplars stood down to the water's edge, their sticky, fluttering leaves sweetening the air with a spicy aroma. A long-legged heron strutted into the water and speared a fish with its beak. Fields and wolds gave way to scrub land and then to low forests of beeches and oaks.

At last Timothy spoke. "My father Garth is sending me upriver to deliver some wagon wheels to his cousin Brannol—in exchange for a couple of sheep," he began. "For a share of the mutton, Rolc agreed to ferry me there with the wheels and back with the sheep. We'll see whether he keeps his end of the bargain."

Tears ran down Merryn's cheeks. "But why?"

Timothy turned his nut-brown eyes on her. "Why what?"

"Why did you buy me from that horrid man? You've rescued me twice now." Merryn made a clumsy curtsy, shivering all the while. The lusty spring breeze cut keenly through her shift.

Timothy's face clouded with concern. "You're cold. Here, take this." Removing his cloak, he wrapped it around Merryn's shoulders. "That will have to do until we find something warmer."

"You don't like looking at me, either," she pouted. Why else would the man give up his cape for her?

With a wounded air, Timothy said, "Is that what you think—that I'm disgusted by your appearance? The truth is that you're a very lucky girl, and a pretty one, too."

"Lucky? Me?" Merryn thought she was the unluckiest girl alive—and the ugliest. She surely didn't know anyone else named "Scabby," and nobody had ever told her she was pretty.

"Yes, you." Timothy brushed his fair, windblown hair out of his eyes. "Those sores of yours are only skin deep. Other girls may appear fair outwardly, but they harbor hidden sores."

Merryn turned away. How could pink-skinned Timothy know the misery of scraping one's weeping boils with the shells of river clams? What did he know of loneliness and rejection?

"The bullies used to chase me, too," he said gently. "I understand what it's like to be different. All I'm saying is that you mustn't let this sickness poison your heart, Merryn, because a bitter spirit is harder to bear than any bodily affliction."

Startled, Merryn asked, "How did you know my name?"

Timothy smiled. "I asked around town about you. It wasn't easy, since few people know your real name."

Merryn stretched out her bare arms, which were covered with angry, bleeding cankers. "Did they tell you how I got these?"

"Most folks thought you had the pox and expected you to die within the year," Timothy replied with a grin. "I've seen the pox, though, and you don't have it. Personally, I think you're much too feisty to let a few sores get the best of you."

In spite of herself, Merryn laughed. "So, Timothy Garth's son, you're not afraid I'll infect you with some terrible scourge?"

"You didn't the first time I met you," Timothy pointed out.

"Even so, I'm bad luck. You shouldn't spend too much time with me. Something terrible still might happen to you."

"Nonsense," said Timothy. "Now that I've bought you, I can't very well send you away, can I? People would talk. 'That finicky Timothy. He's always letting his servants go,' they'd say."

Merryn's face fell. "You know I can't repay you—at least not now. I suppose that really does make me your maid."

"Don't worry. I prefer to tote my own water and cook my own meals. Tell me, if you don't have the pox, what *do* you have?"

Merryn squirmed. "I don't know what's wrong with me. Nobody does. I've been this way since I was little." Her first muddy memories began when she had awakened with throbbing head in a numbingly cold swamp. Somehow, she had found her way into a hop field, where men were training the vines onto poles. Then came shouting and dogs barking and darkness.

"When they found me," she went on, "I had a terrible fever. Then something sloughed off my skin, leaving these nasty sores. They have never healed, despite all the salves we've tried. Now Father's gone and he'll never know what became of me."

"What happened to him?" asked Timothy.

Through her tears, Merryn retold the tale of Hamlin's disappearance. "I see now why Mother wanted me out of the way. She couldn't remarry if I were around to scare off her suitors. I've never been anything but an embarrassment to her."

"We still might find your father somewhere along this river, if we keep our eyes—" Timothy broke off at the sight of silent giants sliding past the ship on both sides. "We've reached the Forest of Fellglade!" he said. "There are miles and miles here of nothing but trees, snakes and marshes." Great swamp oaks and heavy-limbed ashes stood shoulder to shoulder with giant sycamores and tulip trees, all dwarfing the alders in Merryn's secret vale.

Suddenly, a whistling *crack* split the air and a searing pain lanced Merryn's back. Flanked by two ax-wielding henchmen, Rolc was standing beside the wheelhouse snapping a braided leather bullwhip. The captain's eyes glittered venomously.

"I want ye both off my ship—now!" he spat. Cracking the lash, he flicked Timothy's arm with its tip, raising a raw, ragged welt. "That's just a taste of what's to come," he cackled. As Rolc's whip arm raised again, Timothy shielded Merryn with his body.

Before the lash could land, though, Rolc dropped it with a cry and crashed to the deck. Then his men also lost their footing. Clawing at the slippery planks, they were dragged backward by an unseen force. Shorty stuck his head out the wheelhouse door and was promptly yanked through it. Horrified, Merryn and Timothy watched as their tormenters flew over the ship's side and vanished with a splash. Silence swaddled the ship.

"We've stopped moving," Timothy whispered. Though the sails still billowed in the wind, the ship was making no headway. Something very powerful had locked the ship in its embrace.

Merryn saw them first. Green, leafy snakes were slithering out of the shadows on the ship's port side, feeling their way across the deck toward her and Timothy. Others were crawling over the top of the wheelhouse like grapevines smothering an arbor.

"Don't move," hissed Timothy as several wriggly whips rose circling into the air in front of the pair. Merryn drew back, but a flailing tip brushed her hair. Instantly, the green tendril coiled around her throat and pulled taut, choking her. Then the snake-like whip jerked her off her feet and hauled her headfirst across the deck. Timothy's sword flashed and the snake went slack.

Gasping, Merryn crawled back to Timothy's side. As more leafy tentacles lashed out, their ends fell squirming to the deck under Timothy's slashing sword strokes. For every tendril he hacked off, however, five more took its place, creating a writhing jungle.

"It's no use!" he panted. "I can't hold off so many. Quick—into the river!" Still gripping his sword, he threw himself backward over the ship's side. Holding her nose, Merryn followed.

Swollen with frigid snowmelt from the Tartellan Mountains, the Foamwater ran chill, swift and deep. As the murky water closed over Merryn's head, icy needles pricked her skin and stabbed her heart. Feebly flailing, she sank into darkness.

The next thing she knew, Timothy was dragging her onto the riverbank. Gagging, she coughed up foul water. Her eyes smarted and her back burned where Rolc's lash had left its mark. She and Timothy huddled shivering under some overhanging brambles on the sandy shore. By now, the leafy whips had overrun Rolc's ship and were pulling it upstream the way brewery workers pass sacks of dried hops man to man down a queue.

"I wonder what they're going to do with that ship," Timothy mused. "It's obvious that's what they were after."

"If it's only the ship they care about, why did they try to pull my head off?" Merryn retorted. Still dripping wet, she wrung the water out of her hair and hugged herself to stay warm. Much to her chagrin, she had lost Timothy's cape in the river.

Timothy grunted, "I have a feeling we're about to find out."

Rolc's ship inched its way up a tributary stream and stopped under some low-hanging tree branches. Darting over the deck, the whips flung open hatches and doors. In a trice, boxes, crates, bags and wagon wheels were being dragged out of the hold.

Next, more green vines sprang up from both sides of the Foamwater. Rising over the treetops, the snakelike whips arched toward one other across the water until their tips touched.

"What are they doing now?" Merryn whispered.

Timothy put a finger to his lips as a bundle bobbed above the trees, bound in green coils. The bundle bellowed all the while it was being handed from whip to whip across the river. Three other bundles followed, each singing a new note on the scale of terror. Merryn's ears burned with their furious cursing.

Timothy clucked his tongue. "Those must be our shipmates. I wonder what's to become of them!"

"I guess they'll be squeezed to a pulp, the way mice are by snakes," said Merryn. She fingered the welts on her throat.

After Rolc and his men had been conveyed to Merryn and Timothy's side of the river, the ship's cargo came next. The whole leafy procession then moved deeper into the woods. A half-hour later, only crows cawing among the trees disturbed the sleepy forest. Timothy poked his head out of the brambles.

"The coast is clear," he announced. "Let's get going."

"But which way?" Merryn asked him.

"Since the rivermen were taken northeast, we should be safe heading south," Timothy replied. "If we don't stop too often to rest, we might reach the end of these woods before nightfall."

"We're going in *there*?" Merryn squealed. "Why can't we just float down the river on a log or something?"

"We'd be too easily spotted," Timothy replied. "Besides, we wouldn't last long in that freezing water. Now come on!" Shivering with dread, Merryn clambered up the brushy riverbank and followed Timothy into the murky forest.

Before Beechtown, before the bitter ax and the biting saw, a magnificent wood had filled the valley of the Foamwater. In those bygone days, a squirrel could travel from the river's highland source in the north to the salt marshes of the south without ever touching earth. Then came men to douse the woods' leafy light, leaving only brambles where monarchs had once stood.

Fellglade was the largest remnant of that vast and ancient forest. It, too, would have been razed long ago were it not for its mosquito-infested swamps and treacherous quicksands.

Merryn knew none of this. She only saw mighty trees reaching high overhead, their muscular trunks and limbs festooned with lush mosses and lichens. Filtering through the high-headed canopy, a wan, greenish light bathed the fern-rich forest floor.

"Brrr!" she said. "What a gloomy place!"

"Actually, I rather like it," Timothy said. "Look—here's a deer trail we can follow. Watch out for roots. You never know—"

Timothy left his sentence hanging. He had simply vanished where he stood. "Timothy!" Merryn called out. "Timothy! Where are you? If this is a prank, it's not very funny!"

All at once, a vice gripped her ankle, and her feet flew out from under her. "Help!" she cried. Then mud filled her mouth.

CHAPTER 4

The Greenies

Merryn bumped along the ground until the vice on her ankle relaxed. Quick as a flash, green tentacles encircled her torso and jerked her upright. She clawed at her bonds, but they only tightened further. Timothy lay beside her, his legs bound with other whips, which sported lush leaves except on their smooth ends.

"Aw, Molt," said a husky voice. "She ain't but a lil' tyke. Better we should let her go. We've got plenty without her."

Merryn scanned the surrounding forest, seeing only a couple of bushy trees resembling mulberries. The supple, running vines all appeared to lead back to them. One bush had slack leaves, while the other's foliage was crisp but sparse.

"That ain't our call to make, Droopy," growled a second voice. "Ye're new, ain't ye! Like it or not, we got to bring 'em both in. Can't have anyone goin' back to town and blabbin' about us, can we? Besides, the boss would toss us in the Hole if we let someone slip through. Now let's have a closer look at these two."

The vining whips tugged Merryn and Timothy closer to the two mulberries. Then the runners binding Timothy's legs loosened and refastened under his arms, allowing him to stand. Two more whips slithered along Merryn's arms. She shuddered.

"Eh! She's got the pox!" said Droopy of the lackluster leaves.

"Don't worry," said Molt. "Th' boss says only Smoothies can catch the pox, not Greenies. She can't hurt us."

Peering through Droopy's foliage, Merryn found two brown eyes glaring back at her. Then a leaf shifted, covering them.

"For a little sprout, she's sure a nosy weed," Droopy said.

Men were hiding in those bushes! Somehow, they could use these long, leafy tendrils as extra fingers and hands. But what could they possibly want with her and Timothy?

"This fellow might make a decent Greenie if he survives the outbreak," said Molt. "If he don't—well, there's always the Hole, ain't there?" The two mulberry-men shivered with laughter that quivered all the way down their vines, tickling Merryn.

Droopy and Molt were too busy enjoying their joke to notice Timothy's arm straying to his side. Before they knew it, his sword was slicing through the vines that bound him and Merryn.

"Run, Merryn!" he cried. Even as Merryn willed her feet to move, however, the howling mulberry-men flung out other whips and trussed up both their captives like chickens for market. Timothy's sword went flying and stuck in a tree trunk.

Now there was no question of gentle treatment as the two were towed through nettle-infested thickets and swamps. More than once, Merryn thought she would drown. However, Droopy always yanked her out of the mud or water just in time. When the harrowing ride ended, Merryn was sure all her skin must have been stripped off. Timothy lay wallowing in the mud beside her.

"Up!" commanded the bushes, hauling Merryn and her companion to their feet. The vine-whips fell away from their bodies. Exhausted, Merryn leaned against a tree for support.

"Through here, and no more tricks!" growled Molt. Ahead lay a reedy swamp that looked positively impassable. Beyond it rose a dark, tree-covered hill. Droopy's vines lifted Merryn into the swamp and deposited her on a rounded green hummock.

Under Droopy's prodding, Merryn jumped to the next hump, where she teetered and tottered, arms flailing. Timothy followed, swatting away a cloud of pesky mosquitoes. As the two hummock-hopped their way toward the marsh's middle, the tapering hillocks grew larger, making the going easier. In passing, Merryn saw frogs hunkered on lily pads and lace-winged dragonflies flitting about in search of prey. Red-winged blackbirds warbled from reeds and bulrushes, while a furry-faced muskrat munched on a snail before vanishing into his lodge. Animal burrows of another sort pockmarked the marsh, their low mud cones standing above the water like the craters of spent volcanoes.

Making landfall at the foot of the hill, Merryn and Timothy found more mulberry-men waiting to surround them. Some were tall and slender, while others were short and squat.

Merryn stamped her foot. "Cowards! Why don't you take off those silly disguises and show yourselves? I know you're in there!" The creatures answered her not a word.

"Hush!" Timothy said. "We have nothing to gain by offending these fellows, whoever they are. Let's play along and see what they want. Maybe this has all been a mistake on their part."

"Oh, we've made no mistake," said a deep voice. The mulberry bushes stood aside, revealing a dark cave in the hillside. In its mouth stood a throne-like chair of plaited willow branches. Spilling over it was a tangle of wriggling, twitching greenery.

"Who are you?" asked Merryn.

"I am the King of the Marsh," the greenery replied. "You have trespassed on my territory and have even attacked some of my people. What are your names, intruders?"

Timothy introduced himself and Merryn. "We were merely passing through, minding our own business, when our ship was set upon. If it is a crime to defend ourselves, then we stand condemned. Otherwise, the fault lies with you, not with us."

A ropelike whip shot out and knocked Timothy down. "Impertinent! I should have you torn limb from limb for your effrontery. Like it or not, you are in my kingdom now, and you will obey my words as law or suffer death as the penalty."

"No!" Merryn yelled. "You had no right to kidnap us. You're nothing but a fraud behind that bush, and I'm going to prove it." Before anyone could stop her, she jumped into the mass of foliage and began tearing off leaves. Then she tried pulling away some of the vines, but they didn't come free. Instead, she heard a groan. "Am I hurting you?" she asked timidly.

"Yes," came the soft reply. The vines untangled, revealing an unkempt man clothed in rags, his eyes clouded with a white film. From his body grew the green whips like limbs on a tree.

Merryn put her hand to her mouth. "I'm so sorry!" she gasped. "I didn't know they were *attached* to you!"

The vines cloaked their owner again in a green shroud. "Indeed they are. All of us here look this way underneath."

Timothy's eyes ballooned. "What happened to you?"

The king laughed bitterly. "Do you mean, how did we grow these vines? Now there's a tale to curl your leaves. Once, we were Smoothies like you. I'm surprised you didn't recognize me. Not so long ago, the streets of Beechtown knew me well."

Timothy turned to Merryn, who could only shrug and shake her head. She had never seen this man who styled himself "King of the Marsh." Apparently, neither had Timothy.

The bush trembled. "While begging in Beechtown, I was known as 'Bartholomew the Blind.' Men used to kick me and spit upon me as if I were a mangy cur. They would even steal my cane and beat me with it. If it weren't for the vicar, who kept me in clothing, and the baker, who gave me scraps of bread, I would have perished long ago. Fools! One day soon, every mother's son in Beechtown will bow trembling before King Bart!"

"I do remember you," said Timothy, his face ashen beneath its mud mask. "I'm sorry you were so badly mistreated, but how did you come to live in the Forest of Fellglade looking like this? What terrible disease has afflicted you and your men?"

Three of the king's coiling vines knitted themselves into a knot, much as a man might twine his fingers in thought. "Long years I wandered Beechtown's lanes and alleys, with little to show for my begging except bruises and curses. Little by little, from snippets of overheard conversations, I gleaned the town's secrets. I discovered where the cobbler's wife keeps her gold rings; how the mayor bilks merchants with his market tax; where the fishmonger hoards his gilders. No one ever suspected me of eavesdropping, since the fools assumed the blind man was deaf, as they suppose the deaf are blind. How wrong they were!

"Picking through the idle chatter, I also learned when the weaver's finest cloth leaves Beechtown for the hinterlands; when the barman sends his bagful of coins to the bank; when the travel-ing merchants arrive and depart during the spring and fall mar-kets. By keeping my ears open, I even pieced together the comings and goings of the richest caravans on River Road.

"All this and more I garnered from my years of scraping and scrabbling for a bit of bread crust or pork rind to gnaw. In time, I tried my hand at pickpocketing. No one ever suspected a blind man could snitch a purse from under its owner's nose, guided only by the jingle of coins. Ha! I fooled them again!

"Emboldened, I gathered other misfits around me, training them in the fine art of pilfering. We were doing a brisk business when it occurred to me that pickings would be sweeter on River Road, before wayfarers had the chance to spend their gilders in town. That is how Bartholomew the *Blind* became Bartholomew the *Bold*, to Beechtown's everlasting regret."

"You're Bartholomew the Bold?" said Merryn. How could this leafy man possibly be the notorious outlaw? She couldn't picture him sitting astride a horse, let alone riding one. Besides, a blind highwayman might easily be captured or robbed himself.

"So I once was called. Men lived in terror of my name back then, with good reason. Following the sound of the Foamwater, I would quietly lead my men along the road until hoofbeats sig-naled the approach of unsuspecting traders. Then we would fall upon them like famished wolves on a wounded stag."

"But how could you fight, being blind?" Timothy asked.

The marsh king harshly laughed. "Do not underestimate me! Those who make that mistake rarely live to make another. Riding a black stallion, dressed all in black with an eyeless hangman's hood over my head, I would terrify travelers into submission, speak-ing to them *seeingly* through my hood as if possessing supernatu-ral powers of sight. No one noticed the holes cut in the *sides* of my disguise, allowing me to use my ears as eyes."

Timothy frowned. "Still you prey upon the innocent, hiding behind your green disguises, you and these other, ah—"

"Greenies; we're the Greenies!" chorused the mulberry-men.

When you're riding on the river,
Passing field and fallow fen,
In the forest, shadows shiver,
Groping in the gloomy glen.

If you're wishing to be waylaid,
Where the skink and muskrat roam,
Tarry long beside the fellglade,
Where the Greenies have their home.

We will find you, we will bind you,
As our greenery entwines;
We will take you, we will make you
One of us with vagrant vines!

First the itching and the scratching,
Then the outbreak will begin;
Feel the horror at the hatching
Of the scabies from your skin!

We're the Greenies! We're the meanies!
Tremble at our tendrils' touches;
Captured by us crawly-creepies,
None escapes our clammy clutches!

Bearing out the men's words, a cool, dry finger caressed Merryn's cheek. "Get away from me!" she screamed, batting at the tendril that had crept up from behind her.

"Keep your hands to yourself, you scurvy weed!" roared the king. He shot out a whip, knocking away the offending vine.

"Aw, Boss," whined the owner. "Her cheek's got the smoothest skin ye ever saw, aside from them cankers. Reminds me of my wife. It's a shame that such a pretty young 'un has to—"

"Shut up and mind your manners, Scudder," snapped Bart. "You're a Greenie and she's a Smoothie, leastwise for now. 'Once a Greenie, always a Greenie.' Don't think about the life you left behind, or you'll go mad. There's punishment enough and to spare without dwelling on what we've lost."

"Punishment?" asked Merryn.

"Aye, punishment and torment, torment and punishment. In our smooth-skinned days, we took to living among the trees beside the river road, robbing the fat caravans that passed through the forest. When the sheriff's posses started hunting us down, we retreated deeper into the woods until the day we found the reward for our misdeeds." The marsh king's vines went limp. "We were all sitting around a roaring fire one evening, enjoying a highwayman's spoils, when it began."

"What began?" Timothy asked.

"You'll find out soon enough," Bart curtly replied. "That is when we became what we are, and there's no cure for it. We've tried to remove these green growths, but always they sprout right back. Cut or burn them all off, and we die. Now we've grown rather accustomed to our condition, and I for one like it."

"You like being this way?" Merryn said. "Why?" In spite of herself, she was warming to this viney highwayman. Beneath his leaves beat a bitter heart, but a human heart, nonetheless.

"I will show you," said the king. "Blind though I may be, I can still find you by the sound of your voice." A thin green whip flicked out to brush Merryn's face. She steeled herself against its touch as ever so lightly, the tendril traced the contours of her forehead, her nose and eyes, her cheeks, jaw and chin.

"Stop that!" she giggled. "You're tickling me."

"I apologize for the discomfort," said the marsh king in a surprising display of courtesy. "I wanted to know what you look like. These vines are more sensitive than my fingertips, you see. Instead of using my hands to 'read' a person's face, I now have at my disposal a hundred fingers that can feel any object's features. With 'eyes' like these, I prefer to remain as I am."

Timothy dryly remarked, "From what I've seen, those vines also come in handy when you're robbing the river traffic."

"That's right," said the king. "Now that riding horses is awkward for us, we can't keep up with wagons and carriages. Slow-moving boats and barges make easier prey—and the rivermen aren't as apt to carry swords or other weapons."

"Why don't you just stop stealing from people and give your-selves up?" said Merryn. At this, the mulberry-men roared with laughter, their whips flopping about like wounded snakes.

"Give ourselves up?" chuckled King Bart. "Maybe we should have when we could have, but that day has long since passed. If we showed up in town now, we'd be hacked to pieces as freaks and monsters. No, we'll be robbing the rivermen till we root or the sheriff's men catch up to us, and we're far too clever to be caught. Besides, we take only what we need. We can't eat gold or silver, and we can't sell our loot in town looking like this."

"Robbery is robbery, and I think you're horrid people," said Merryn. In her mind, stealing for any reason whatsoever was wrong, for so her father had taught her and so he lived himself.

Timothy asked, "If you steal only out of necessity, why did you strip our ship of its goods and then conceal it in that stream?"

"Since you'll never leave this marsh smooth-skinned, I sup-pose it won't hurt to tell you," said the king coolly.

Timothy and Merryn traded frightened glances. Had they al-ready caught some dreadful infection from the Greenies that would leave them looking like their captors?

"Some of the cargo was needed to replenish our scant sup-plies," Bart explained. "We've been on short rations lately. Baked muskrat three meals a day is three meals too many for me. The rest of the freight was removed to free up the hold."

"What do you want with the ship's hold?" Timothy puzzled.

"I will be filling it with my men when we sail down the river to bring Beechtown to her knees," the marsh king replied.

CHAPTER 5

The Green Mist

Y ou're mad!" Timothy exclaimed. "Why, the sheriff's bowmen would mow you down before you could reach town! Those fellows can hit a hawk's eye at a thousand paces."

"We won't have to leave the ship or lift a leaf to take over the town," said the king smugly. "And if those bowmen want archery practice, we'll offer them some of our hostages as targets."

"Hostages? Do you mean us?" Timothy demanded. "What have you done with the others? If they've come to any harm . . ."

The king of the marsh made a noise like rocks grinding together. "What I do with trespassers is my affair, not yours! Let their fate serve as an example to you, Garth's son."

One by one, four leaf-bound figures stumbled out of the cave behind the throne, tethered on viney leashes. The last man to emerge wore a red stocking cap and a furious expression.

"This is all your fault!" fumed Rolc, stabbing his finger at Merryn. "Ye're in cahoots with these—these *things*! When I get my hands on ye and yer friend, ye'll be sorry ye ever set foot on my ship! I'll flay th' living skin off ye; I'll have ye keel-hauled; I'll hang ye from the yardarm; I'll—" Rolc's threats ended in a gurgle as one of the vines cinched around his neck.

"I'd worry about my own skin, if I were you," hissed the marsh king. "Boys, I do believe it's time for some entertainment!"

Rolc's men were passed from bush to bush until they stood in a green-shackled line. Then more vines lifted them over the reeking swamp and set them on the three largest hillocks. "Stay put or die!" the Greenies shouted to them. Wild-eyed, the sailors held on as if the humps were the masts of a sinking ship.

Last of all, King Bart's sturdy whips hoisted a cursing, struggling Rolc out into the marsh—and dropped him. *Sploosh!* The captain sank up to his waist in the watery black muck.

"It's into the Hole for you, for you!" yelled the Greenies. They waved their leafy whips excitedly, as though some great spectacle were about to unfold. All the birds and four-footed creatures appeared to have fled, leaving the area uncannily quiet.

Rolc's face contorted with fear. "Don't leave me out here alone!" he cried. Merryn felt a twinge of sympathy for the man. Whatever the Greenies' swamp held in store for him, it couldn't be good. Still, the captain seemed in no immediate danger as he struggled to free himself from the clinging ooze.

"That's it! Now we'll see some real action! Run for it!" jeered the Greenies. All at once, a thick, gray trunk sprouted from the mud-volcano nearest Rolc. The "trunk" opened into a writhing nest of tentacles that reached for the hapless captain.

Seeing his peril, Rolc redoubled his efforts to free himself, but it was no use. With a 'pop,' he was yanked shrieking out of the mud and passed along to other waving tentacles. Carried across the marsh, Rolc was still hollering when—*slurp!*—he disappeared. Then the tentacles withdrew back into their burrows.

"Where did he go?" cried Merryn. "What happened to him?"

"The strogarns took him into the Hole," said the Greenies.

"Hole? What hole?" Timothy asked.

By way of answer, the mulberry-men chanted,

> Into the Hole you go, you go,
> Into the Hole you go;
> Over the brink, down you sink;
> Into the Hole you go!

Into the deep where strogarns sleep,
Into the Hole, into the Hole;
Wriggle and squirm; beware the worm,
As into the Hole you go!

Into the Hole you go, you go,
Into the Hole you go;
Over the brink, down you sink;
Into the Hole you go!

O! What a ride; slither and slide,
Into the Hole, into the Hole;
Struggle and stall, but down you'll fall;
It's into the Hole for you!

Into the Hole you go, you go,
Into the Hole you go;
Over the brink, down you sink;
Into the Hole you go!

Stuck in the slime, you'll never climb
Out of the Hole, out of the Hole;
Scream till you're hoarse; we'll show no remorse
As into the Hole you go!

Into the Hole you go, you go,
Into the Hole you go;
Over the brink, down you sink;
Into the depths of the Hole!

"Now the real show is about to begin," said King Bart.

"Here it comes! Here it comes!" cried the other Greenies.

The forest was dissolving into the drab tones of dusk when a greenish fog appeared in the swamp. The fog thickened and spread with fluttering fingers, reminding Merryn of the night Emory had dropped her precious stone into the quince sauce.

Slowly the mist flowed toward the stranded sailors. First it lapped at the hillocks with long green tongues. Then it began rising. Terrified, the men climbed higher on the humps until there was no higher to climb. They were screaming as the fog engulfed them, their cries soon subsiding into moans. At last the mist wrapped the marsh in a muffled, menacing silence.

"That's all for tonight!" said the king briskly.

"But what about those three men?" asked Merryn, the words catching in her throat. "Are they . . . dead?"

"Not yet!" the Greenies said.

"With any luck, they'll all survive the night," said Bart. "In the meantime, there's work to be done. When the swamp gas is up, it cloaks our movements. Hey, boys! Mugger! Tugger! Rank, Shank, Muddle and Tag! It's your turn to fish tonight."

Into the tall trees across the swamp flew garlands of graceful Greenie vines. Then their owners swung into the treetops. More whips shot out, fastening to yet other trees, and the mulberry-men rapidly swung out of sight into the whispering forest.

A grudging admiration grew in Merryn's heart for these viney robbers who had managed to make a life for themselves in the trackless wood. She envied their ability to travel swiftly through the forest without touching the ground. What other clever uses might they have found for their vines?

"How do they fish without hooks and such?" she asked Bart.

The marsh king twirled a vine. "That's easy! We dangle the tip of a whip in the water, and the fish think it's a wriggling worm. On good days, we can catch a supper's worth in no time."

"Why didn't you put us out there with the others?" asked Timothy. "After all, we're your captives as much as they."

"Let's just say I didn't like the way those rivermen roughed you up," Bart said gruffly. "As long as you both behave and don't try to escape, I will spare you the Initiation—for the time being. Besides, you may be more useful to me as you are."

By now, the swamp gas had reached the hill. Merryn backed away from the billowing fog, fearing its very touch. She wasn't sure what it would do to her and didn't want to find out, either.

King Bart flung a whip toward the cave. "You'll be safe in the Grotto tonight. As you value your skins, don't come out until after dawn! At night, fell creatures prowl these woods. Also, the mist has a mind of its own; sometimes it even flows uphill." Merryn eyed the green blanket that hung over the marsh, pooling in shadowy hollows and dells beneath the trees.

At Bart's insistence, Timothy and Merryn ducked into the cave, where a muddy darkness enfolded them. Merryn squealed when long, webbed fingers caught in her hair, but it was only tree roots dangling from the Grotto's dirt roof. She hoped that no snakes or bugs or other nasties were living among them.

Together, she and Timothy groped their way up through the cave until a tangle of roots stopped them. "This is far enough," said Timothy. "Now let's see about finding a spot to sleep."

Unfortunately, most of the level ground was full of roots and rocks. Feeling their way about, the two nevertheless managed to clear a space on the cave's floor. Merryn lay down and immediately regretted it. Plenty of sharp stones and gnarled roots still remained to jab her in the back and ribs. While she tossed and turned, Timothy murmured softly from across the cave.

"What are you doing?" she asked. Sleep would come slowly enough in that miserable hole without Timothy's babbling.

"Praying," came the reply.

"Praying?" Merryn repeated, thinking she must have misheard him. Prayer was for vicars, not for common people like her and Timothy. Besides, what good would it do them now?

"I'm talking with Gaelathane. He's gotten me out of worse fixes than this before, and He can do the same for us now."

Merryn sat up. "Who's Gaelathane?"

"He's the King of the Trees, and He looks after folk like us. Most people in Beechtown don't know Him, but He knows *them*."

Timothy spoke as if this "Gaelathane" were a real Person. The few times Merryn's parents had taken her to chapel, she hadn't understood a word the vicar had said. Oh, he was a kindhearted and honest man, all right, but when he prayed, he used lots of "thees" and "thous" and other high-sounding words. Merryn wondered whether Gaelathane was a "thee" or a "thou."

"Would He terribly mind my sores and cankers?" she asked. People were often friendly enough when they first met her, but one glimpse of her uncovered sores would drive them away.

"You needn't worry about that. From what I've learned, Gaelathane doesn't care all that much about a person's looks. He sees right past your outward appearance and into your heart."

"He can see my heart?" Merryn exclaimed. Instinctively, she crossed her arms over her chest.

Timothy's laughter echoed through the Grotto. "Yes, but He won't condemn you for what He finds there. In fact, He knows you inside and out and still loves you just the way you are."

A thrill of hope surged through Merryn. "Would He listen to me if I talked to Him?" she asked.

"Of course. He always listens, whether you know it or not. You can't always predict how He'll answer, though."

Merryn hesitated. Deep inside this dank, dark cave hardly seemed the place to pray. Still, what could it hurt? "Gaelathane," she began and then stopped, feeling foolish. She took a breath and blurted out, "I want to see my father again!"

A soothing warmth spread through her body, as if she had just eaten a bowl of hot potato soup. The Grotto no longer seemed as dark and threatening. For a blissful moment, she was back in her own bed, hearing her father's reassuring footsteps outside the door and his cheery "Good-night." Clinging to those comforting memories, she lay back on some roots and fell asleep.

CHAPTER 6

Marshquake

M erryn awoke as a greenish light crept into the cave, bringing with it the sweet smell of a dew-freshened world. Peering outside, she found the marsh and forest swaddled in a green haze. An early morning breeze stirred the fog, ruffling its surface and sending wisps curling into the trees. Merryn blinked. She distinctively remembered seeing a swamp oak standing at the water's edge the night before. Now it stood about thirty feet away on higher ground. Several other trees looked out of place, too.

Then the sun's first red rays lanced through the treetops to fall upon the green blanket. With startling speed, the fog burned away, revealing a marshy landscape of skunk cabbage and reeds. Frogs began to croak and birds tuned up their voices.

"It's safe to come out now, little girl."

Merryn stifled a scream. She hadn't noticed the mulberry-man hanging by his vines from a tree above the cave's entrance. Evidently, the marsh king had stationed him there to prevent Merryn and Timothy from attempting an escape.

The Greenie waved a whip at the vanishing fog. "Burns off like that every morning, it does," he remarked. "When I'm up early, I like the quiet of the dawn and th' mist lying over everything like the breath o' God. It hides the ugliness of the world, ye know."

"What happened to those trees?" Merryn asked him.

"Oh, that's jest th' mist at work," replied the Greenie. "It makes the trees grow bigger, and they can move, too. It's a funny thing, though—even dead wood will resprout in th' fog."

Just then, Timothy staggered up, bent nearly double. Holding his head and back, he wore a pained expression on his face.

"Between the roots and the rocks, I've never had a worse night's sleep," he groaned. "I doubt I'll ever straighten out this kink in my back. Say, what happened to that swamp gas?"

Before Merryn could explain, green tendrils snaked into the cave and whisked the two outside, where they found the other Greenies facing the sun, their vines stretched out and waving like the water weeds in Merryn's secret stream.

"What are you doing?" she asked them.

"Why, we're having us a spot o' breakfast," said one of the men cheerfully. "Beautiful day for it, don't ye think?"

At the mention of breakfast, Merryn's stomach churned. She hadn't eaten a blessed thing since a bowl of quince sauce the day before. How long ago it seemed when Rolc had come to take her away! She couldn't even recall the taste of quinces now.

"Breakfast?" Timothy repeated with a puzzled look.

King Bart sidled up, vines fluttering. "Aye, breakfast. When the sun is shining, we feed on its light. It's not as satisfying as mouth-food, but it's just as nourishing." He aimed a whip at the marsh. "Now it's time to meet our new initiates. Bring 'em in, boys!"

Out in the swamp, seaweed stirred on some of the odd hummocks. Throwing out their long whips, the marsh king's men plucked up three bunches of the weed and swung them back toward the hill like fishermen reeling in their catches.

"Why, they're Greenies!" Merryn cried. Recalling the sailors who had been marooned on those tall hillocks, she shuddered. The green mist must have made them all mulberry-men.

"Hey, Boss, there's a Smoothie!" shouted one of Bart's men. A white-cloaked figure was strolling among the hummocks. Before anyone could move, he had disappeared into the woods.

"Who was that, and why didn't the strogarns grab him?" the Greenies asked one another.

"You who have eyes to see would know that better than I!" snapped the marsh king. "I'll tell you this: If he comes around here again, it's into the Hole for him!" With that, he set one of Rolc's men upright, but the fellow collapsed. Merryn caught a glimpse of Shorty's terrified face behind the vines.

"Stand up!" ordered the king. "You're a Greenie now, and I am your new captain. Forget who and what you were; from now on, you're one of us. You'll have a new life and a new name. Now it's time you took your first vining lessons."

After speaking in similar fashion to the other two initiates, the king ordered them all led away. Merryn's bones went weak.

"They'll be all right," Bart told her and Timothy. "Once they've learned the vining arts, they'll gladly throw in their lot with us. I saved their lives; left to themselves, they would have come to a bad end on the river or in some drinking den."

"What about Rolc?" said Merryn. She couldn't help herself; memories of the wretched riverman's fate still haunted her.

"What about him?" the king retorted. "You and your friend are better off without that rogue, aren't you? As I recall, he was about to strip the skin right off you two when we commandeered your ship. You should thank me for doing you a favor."

"Please spare us any more of your favors," said Timothy.

King Bart's whips twitched. "I've decided what to do with you, Garth's son," he said. "On such fine mornings as this, we love to work the river traffic, and you're going to help us. You'll have a share of the booty—if you survive. I'm a fair man."

Through clenched teeth, Timothy said, "Keep your ill-gotten spoils for yourself. I will not profit from your plunder!"

The marsh king gave a viney shrug. "As you wish," he said coldly. *Snap!* His tendrils whipped out, binding Timothy. Then Bart and several of his men swung across the marsh, taking Timothy with them. Merryn was left standing alone at the foot of the hill. All the Greenies had now either left for the river or were playing nursemaids to their new comrades-in-thievery.

Wading into the water, Merryn climbed onto the nearest green hump and hopscotched her way across the marsh. The strogarns slept. Pausing to rest, she noticed how the hummocks traced a slinky "S" through the swamp. At both ends of the "S," the hillocks tapered off. Jumping onto dry ground, she followed a meandering stream for a short mile until it spilled into the river. She had just hidden behind a bush (a real one, not a Greenie) when she heard laughter. A freight-laden barge was floating down the Foamwater, poled by colorfully dressed raftsmen. One of them gave a shout and pointed toward the riverbank.

"Are you hurt?" he bellowed.

"No, I'm all right," Timothy's voice returned.

Then Merryn spotted her friend. He was standing with his back to a thick ash, his body pinned to the tree with vines.

"Hold on; we're coming for you!" called another bargeman as he and his companions guided their craft toward shore. Now Merryn understood the marsh king's clever plan: Bound by the unwritten code that obliged rivermen to help other wayfarers in need, the barge handlers were coming to Timothy's rescue. Meanwhile, the Greenies were concealed behind the tree, ready to fall upon this rich, undefended prize. Merryn felt sick.

"No! Go back!" Timothy shouted to the men. "Danger! Get away from here! Robbers are lying in wait behind me to seize your vessel. You must leave at once before it's too late!"

Frantically poling for all they were worth, the bargemen steered their craft back into the river's main channel. Vines whistled through the air, only to fall short of the barge or slide off its sloping deck. Others fell wiggling under savage ax-blows. Finally, the lumbering barge broke free and disappeared downriver.

Howling with rage, the Greenies vine-dunked Timothy in the Foamwater to the point of drowning. Next, they dashed him against the ground until he revived. Then it was back into the river. Their fury spent, the mulberry-men dragged their reluctant decoy back through the woods. Merryn waited until their racket had died away before emerging from her hiding place.

How smoothly and swiftly the sun-dappled river flowed beside her! Running along the bank, she could easily catch up to the barge and swim out to it. The rivermen would take her with them to Beechtown, where she could persuade the sheriff to send his men upriver to capture the Greenies and punish them for their crimes. She would be a hero! No more insults and indignities in the streets, no more wearing scarves and shawls, no more—

Merryn's visions of glory collapsed around her. Even if she did reach Beechtown safely, who would believe her? The bargemen hadn't actually *seen* the Greenies, and without solid evidence to back up her tale, Merryn could not hope to convince anyone of the peril lurking in the Forest of Fellglade. Meanwhile, the Greenies were doubtless leading Timothy into further torment.

Merryn ran, not downriver to follow the fleeing barge, but back toward the Greenies' swamp. Sweat stung her sores, but she paid them no mind. She had to stop the marsh king from doing to Timothy what he had already done to Rolc and his men.

An uneasy wind had sprung up when Merryn reached the marsh and hopped onto the nearest hump. She was promptly shaken off. Wrapping her arms around the green knob, she hung on until the shaking stopped, though the mucky swamp continued to quiver like her mother's cold chicken soup.

Seeing no signs of Greenies, she climbed onto the next hummock. The swamp lay undisturbed. *It must have been an earthquake.* Such tremors had been known to occur near Beechtown, although Merryn had never felt one before.

A-SHOOP! Merryn froze. Mud and water had spouted yards to her left, just beyond the last hump at the tip of the "S."

"Hoppy, if you don't stop sticking that scabby nose of yours where it doesn't belong," her mother had once told her, "you'll have more than scabs to scratch!"

Hoppy couldn't help herself. Retracing her steps, she followed the "S" curve until it ended in a wide, rounded hummock swimming in marsh weeds. The hump bore a snuffling hole in its top that gave off a steaming, pungent stench. Merryn gagged.

Just beyond that hummock yawned a much larger hole—*the* Hole. Strogarn burrows marched right up to its sulfur-crusted rim, which measured some twenty feet around.

Maybe it's just a geyser, she told herself. Her father had once taken her and Emory east of town to a hot springs where clusters of steaming geysers spat mud at the sky. "Mud pots," Hamlin had called them, and they stank worse than dead fish.

However, this was no mud pot, for a giant red worm wriggled in its depths. Greenish fumes boiled from within, only to evaporate in the afternoon sunlight. *Swamp gas!* Rooting around in the marsh, Merryn dug out a stone and flung it into the hole. *Squish.* Instantly, the stone shot out again, propelled by a roaring blast of hot, fetid air. The worm crawled out of the hole toward her.

Merryn's heart beat wildly. Just as the worm reached her, a green whip dropped down and snatched her away, gently setting her on another hump beside her leafy rescuer. Wordlessly, the Greenie escorted her back to Bart's throne under the hill.

"You fool!" snarled the king of the marsh. "If one of my men hadn't spotted you standing out there and grabbed you, you'd be dead by now. What were you doing, trying to escape?"

Merryn flinched as the marsh king's vines whipcracked mere inches from her face. She hung her head. "I—I didn't mean any harm," she said miserably. "I only wanted to see the geyser."

The king's whips relaxed. "You're lucky to be alive. I've sent many a man into the Hole and none has returned to the light of day. One false step out there and you'll never take another."

"I say we initiate her," said a mulberry-man Merryn had nicknamed "Ramble" for his rampant vines. "We could use a young whip around here. She looks plenty spry for the job."

"Not this time," said Bart. "Maybe she'll take her friend's fate to heart. If not . . ." He left the threat hanging in the air like a strogarn waiting in its burrow to snare its prey.

"What have you done with Timothy?" Merryn demanded. She hadn't seen him yet among the mulberry-men.

The blind king flicked out a vine, and two other Greenies glided up with Timothy. The tinker's son looked half-dead. His face was battered and bruised, and one eye was completely black. With the other, he managed a wink at Merryn.

"Let him go! Let him go!" Merryn cried. She tried to reach Timothy, but a thick wall of leaves hedged her in.

"Timothy son of Garth," said the marsh king solemnly. "Since you refuse to help us as a Smoothie, you will do so as a Greenie. Bid farewell to the life and the loved ones you once knew!"

"Once a Greenie, always a Greenie," murmured the mulberry-men. Then they lifted Timothy into the marsh and set him on a hummock. Snapping their whips with glee, they chanted:

> The fog, it comes, the fog it goes,
> And round about the forest flows;
> When evening falls and nighthawk calls,
> Then foggy fingers start to close!
>
> Flooding feet and then the legs,
> It drains your courage to the dregs!
> You can't escape; accept your fate!
> Breathe the mist and take its plagues!

All at once, Timothy sprang up and leapt into the swamp. Merryn covered her mouth, but a scream broke through.

"Pity the poor fool!" groaned Bart. "He was in no danger from the fog yet. If only he knew what he was throwing away! He would have made a fine Greenie, once he saw things my way."

Timothy had made scant headway when a strogarn popped up in his path. Its tentacles seized and passed him along to other strogarns that blossomed above the mud like giant sea anemones. Their fleshy fingers rippled in gruesome waves, carrying Timothy toward the Hole, where he disappeared with a shriek. Closing their deadly petals, the strogarns sank back into their burrows.

"Timothy! Timothy! Come back!" cried Merryn, wringing her hands. "You can't go away now. I need you!" Sobbing, she let the marsh king's vines envelop her with unexpected gentleness.

"I'm sorry you had to see that," he said. "I never intended to send Timothy into the Hole, stubborn though he was. He's past help now. Let's see about finding you something to eat. I tend to forget that Smoothies can't feed on sunlight."

Bart took her around the hill to an ancient ash tree. Nestled among its ropy roots lay a stone slab, which he pulled up. From the hole underneath, his vines removed a basket of brown eggs, a side of fat bacon, a whole ham and a sack of red potatoes.

Carrying the food in his whips, the king led Merryn back to the cave. "Gather me some dry moss and twigs," he ordered. Using her shift as a collecting-apron, Merryn dutifully filled it with handfuls of tinder, weeping all the while. Then she dumped her gleanings where Bart could find them. Next, the king produced a piece of flint and struck it a glancing blow with an iron bar. Sparks flew, and a tiny flame flared in the pile of twigs and moss.

"We don't often build fires out here," said the king. "The smoke might attract attention. I reckon no one will notice a wisp or two so late in the day, though. Now fetch us some wood."

Merryn obeyed, quickly returning with sticks and branches culled from a dead tree at the swamp's edge. These she expertly arranged on the smoldering tinder, and in seconds, bright yellow and blue tongues were spurting through the kindling.

"Can you cook eggs?" asked Bart. "I've tried, but I can't see when they're ready, and I usually break the yolks. My boys don't like their yolks fried hard as shoe leather." He chuckled. "They can't cook, either. Someone always singes a leaf or a whip."

No sooner had Merryn admitted to her cooking talents than Bart's men appeared, waving various kitchen utensils they had no doubt pilfered from passing ships. Before you could say, "Pass the salt and pepper," frying pans heaped with eggs, ham and bacon were sizzling over the fire. Using a fork, Merryn flipped the eggs and tended the ham and bacon. When those were done, she cut up some of the spuds and cooked them in the bacon grease. Molt juggled the remaining potatoes with his vines.

"Thirty-five at once!" he crowed. "That's me new record!"

Supper was scarcely ready when greedy tendrils stripped the pans right down to their bare, black iron. As the Greenies noisily gobbled up all the food, Merryn wondered if they ever accidentally bit down on their whips while eating.

"Leave some for me next time!" she grumbled. Quicker than thought, more eggs, bacon, ham and potatoes appeared. These also Merryn cooked, but this time, the Greenies respectfully kept their distance while she ate. Food had never tasted so delicious.

When Merryn had finished, King Bart waved a vine at his followers and growled, "You're forgetting your manners, boys."

"Thank you, Miss Merryn!" they all shouted.

"Boss, let's keep her on as our cook," declared "Curly," a high-voiced Greenie with wavy, light-green leaves. The other mulberry-men heartily chorused their agreement.

"What say you, Miss Merryn?" asked the king of the marsh.

Merryn scratched her arms. Her sores always itched when she was flustered. However, she preferred cooking for these funny, frightening creatures to becoming one of them, which would certainly happen if she refused their request. Besides, they seemed to accept her as she was, sores and all. "All right," she said.

"Hooray!" whooped the Greenies. With their whips they scooped up stones and flung them into the air. Even the marsh king forgot himself and flipped a stick or two into the swamp.

As the evening sky purpled into dusk, the green mist crept out of the marsh and into the woods. Listening to her bushy captors swap tales around the fire, Merryn realized that beneath their leaves beat the hearts of ordinary, rough-hewn men.

Presently, the raucous laughter and good-natured ribbing gave way to a fog-swirling silence. The marsh mist had risen to the Greenies' waists, driving Merryn to higher ground. "Let's hear from the short-vines," someone suggested, and Rolc's men were pushed to the front near the leaping green fire.

Under prodding from the "long-vines," the newcomers haltingly spoke of their former lives. The others greedily hung on their words, chiming in with remarks of their own.

"I spent some time in the Beechtown jail, too," one said.

"Is the food still as bad?" said another. It was.

"If I could git within vine-reach o' that jailer, I'd throttle the scoundrel!" declared a third.

"Don't fergit th' mayor," grunted Ramble. "I hear he's up to his old tricks again. I'd like to see 'im swing!"

"There ain't no rope thick or strong enough to hold his weight!" offered "Stumpy," a dour oldster with stubby vines.

"We'll be making plenty of changes downriver when the weather warms, won't we, boys?" said the marsh king darkly.

"That we will!" they all agreed.

"Say, who was that feller in the marsh with ye?" Droopy asked the short-vines, a question none of the three could answer. They recalled only that a man had sat unspeaking with them through the night, comforting them during their agonies. Apparently, neither strogarn nor marsh mist had affected him.

"My daughter Lara's turnin' twelve next week, and I won't be home to see her," said Shorty sadly. An uneasy hush stole over the scene. Molt brought out a jug of ale and passed it around. Merryn's nose wrinkled. The stuff smelled as if it had been brewed in a pig's sty. A pull or two from such a jug could turn a man into a mouse—or a louse. She edged up to the cave.

Befuddled with drink, the Greenies grew weepy, each retreating into his own huddled knot of leafy misery. All but one, that is. Long after the others had collapsed snoring under their green blanket of swamp gas, one remained erect and alert at his post beside the Grotto's entrance. As Merryn brushed by the guard, a stifled sob—or was it a groan?—escaped him.

That night, the darkness pressed in upon Merryn with its hot, humid breath. Alone with her thoughts, she wept out her regrets. She had just lost the only true friend she had ever known, and without him, she was defenseless against the Greenies. Overcome with weariness and grief, Merryn fell into a restless sleep.

After that, it was "Miss Merryn" this and "Miss Merryn" that. *Cooking* became *Cooking; Cleaning; Dressing Out Game* (disgusting!); *Hair and Toenail Trimming* (very awkward with a knife); *Fire-Building; Wood-Gathering; Mushroom-Picking; Wound-Bandaging* and a host of other tedious chores that the Greenies foisted off on her. Few of them ever lifted a whip to help.

One drizzly spring morning, Merryn emerged from the Grotto to find the camp once again scoured clean of food scraps. She assumed the Greenies were sweeping up, although they thought nothing of flinging bones and other refuse about. Merryn was forever picking up after them, like a mother with small boys.

On rainy days, she built her fires inside the Grotto, where she kept a supply of dry tinder and sticks handy. However, on this particular morning, there was nothing left to burn, and Merryn was forced to forage in the wet for something that would.

"Bother these Greenies!" she said crossly, and not for the first time. "Why can't they gather their own firewood? They can reach higher than I with those whips of theirs." Indeed, most of the nearby trees had been stripped of their dead limbs. Feeling oddly weak and lightheaded, Merryn climbed the hill. At its top, she found a tree loaded with dead wood. Long of limb and thick of bark, the fire-scarred sentinel stood broken but unbowed.

Her hair dripping, Merryn climbed the tree's trunk to reach some promising branches. *Crack!* A leafless limb gave way, and Merryn plummeted to the ground. Tumbling over the brow of the hill, she crashed through bushes and bracken until she sailed into the air and landed bruisingly in front of the cave.

Groaning, she picked herself up, but the world spun and her ears roared when she stood. A fever heat pricked her face. Then came the cool touch of leafy vines—and darkness.

CHAPTER 7

Waking Dreams

So hot, so very hot. *Papa, Mama, where are you? Don't leave me in the fire. It's hurting me. My skin is burning. Help me!* Somber voices swimming in a sea of green shadows. ". . . swamp fever . . . bad . . . needs rest . . . nothing . . . do . . ." Soothing darkness, cool water, voices of the dead. *Timothy, where are you? The bullies are after me! Cover me, cover me!*

Merryn forced open her eyes. Her head throbbed and her throat hurt. Where was she? A green-tentacled cup poured water down her parched throat. She fell back into the darkness, where weedy fingers were dragging her into the strogarn-infested swamp. *Rolc? Rolc has me! Let me go! Somebody help me!*

Merryn shrieked herself awake. Something *was* grabbing her! She tried to squirm away, but iron bands held her. "Hush, Hoppy. Just lie still. You're having a nightmare. Everything is all right now. I'm here, and I'll stay with you till you're well again."

Father? Papa, is that you? I'm here, Papa; I'm here in the marsh, down in the Hole. Captain Rolc has me . . .

"Go back to sleep, Hoppy. Go to sleep. Rest . . ."

Rest. Sinking, sinking into darkness, into the bottomless Hole, where Rolc awaited her. Squirming red worms reached up. *So heavy, so heavy. Down I sink; into the Hole I go.*

Light. Light all around her, light above, strong arms beneath. The cave and hill were floating far, far away. *What a lovely tree shining in such a clear blue sky! I simply must climb it.*

Merryn stood beside a rainbow-shimmering lake whose waters overflowed with living light. The light filled her, too, making her strong and whole and bursting with life. *Peace, such peace.*

A white-robed Man came to her, and the Light poured from His being like rivers of diamonds. *Who are You?*

"I am your best Friend and Champion," He said. "I will never leave you or forsake you. You must return now and plant this special seed in the forest. Do not be afraid, for I will help you." Then the Man dropped a nut into her outstretched hand.

But I don't wish to leave! I want to stay here and gaze upon You forever. You are sending me away because I am ugly.

The Man smiled. "Look at yourself."

Arms and hands, smooth as kidskin. *What about my face?*

"The Lake does not lie."

A lovely stranger with clear, flawless skin looked back from the water. She even shone from within. *I must be dreaming.*

"You are not dreaming, Merryn. Gaelessa is your home, where one day you will live with Me. Now, let us walk together."

Merryn and the Man stepped onto the lake's placid surface. Merryn found herself walking on the water, which rang like crystal beneath her feet. She could see fish and other creatures swimming below, singing in their melodious water-language to the King. Who was this King? What realm did He rule?

I am the King of the Trees, the Man silently explained. *My realm lies wherever a willing heart invites Me in.*

The lake might have been a mile wide, or a hundred, or a thousand. While Merryn trod its ringing waters, she drank in the loving presence of her Friend. As soon as she could frame a question in thought, His answer would spring into her mind.

They reached the other side after and before they had left, before and after the world began. Without asking, Merryn knew exactly what to do. She walked on while the Man remained standing on the lake, smiling and waving. "Do not forget to plant the nut!" He called after her. She smiled and waved back.

As Merryn pushed through the shoreline trees, they bade her farewell in breathy voices. Beyond that forest fringe lay a swamp— *her* swamp. She walked across it to the hill and through the hill into the Grotto; she saw a crumpled, blotchy-skinned form lying limp on the floor. What poor creature was this?

So cold, so very cold. Where am I? Who am I? Where are You, Friend? Do not leave me like this! Merryn opened her eyes. Was she blind? Then she remembered the cave's close darkness. Her headache was gone, and she felt strangely airy and free. Her fist was clenched around a smooth, hard object, which she thrust into her pocket. Close beside her, someone was sobbing.

Nobody ever bothered to visit her in the Grotto. Timothy was gone; Father was gone, too. "Who's there?" she called out. Her voice sounded as hoarse and cracked as an old woman's.

The crying slid into a gasp. "Hoppy?" A warm voice, a comforting voice, like hot tea on a chilly day. Whose voice?

"Hoppy?"

Hoppy. The nickname resounded in Merryn's head like a drum, and her heart lurched with painful hope. Could it be—?

"Father?"

The weeping began again. "I thought you were dead! To find you after all this time and then lose you again was more than I could bear. Now that you're back, I'll never let you go."

"Father, I can't see you! Where are you?"

"I'm right here, Hoppy. I can't see you, either, but that doesn't matter as long as I can hear your voice. I have been so worried about you, dear child, but now you have returned to me."

Merryn reached into the darkness. "Where are you, Papa? Let me touch you! Hold me in your arms, the way you used to do every night before I went to sleep. Are you really there?"

Choking sounds. "Not now, Hoppy. I will see you again soon. I promise." With a flutter and a sigh, he was gone. Merryn felt his absence in the hollow of her heart. She wept for joy and for fear she was dreaming, and weeping, she slept again.

Light. Light around her, light inside her, light beneath her. She opened her eyes and snapped them shut again against the burning brightness. Warmth. She blinked. The sun was shining gloriously upon her face. She crawled toward the light until rock and root fell away, and the green world embraced her.

"Merryn! She's here! She's coming out!"

Rough voices stung her ears while gentle leaves lifted and set her beside a fire. After the stale cave air, the marsh smelled as sweet as lilacs. "Get her something to drink! Yes, you! Flip a whip and bring her some water. Bern, fetch that mince pie!"

Water. Merryn greedily drank it down, feeling it soothe her cracked lips. "More." The cup returned, brimming with cool liquid that flowed into her limbs and cleared her mind.

Food. She gobbled up the pie in gulping bites, full too soon.

Weeping. *Where is Papa?* The Greenies gathered around her, their vines caressing her matted hair. "We saved the pie for you," they said. "Bern went all the way to Beechtown for it, snatched it right out of the bakery window, so hot it scalded his leaves."

Words. She drank them in like the light, the water, the food. The Greenies wept and laughed and held her in their vines.

Love. Love in word, love in touch, love in deed. These crusty, quirky mulberry-men loved her, and she loved them, too. That was enough, and contented, she slept again.

As she regained her strength over the following weeks, Merryn realized she was different. Oh, her body hadn't changed; she still wore the same pockmarks and scars, but *inside* she was different. Her marred skin no longer mattered, for she had a Champion Whose love filled and surrounded her wherever she went.

The Light remained, too. It crowned the sun, shining out of the trees and sky, a glory lying lightly over the world like a bright mist to shame the green, whiter than any Foamwater fog. The Light recalled her waking dreams in the Grotto, and she yearned for the Lake and walking hand-in-hand with the Man across the glassy waters, a lifetime lived in one beat of a moth's wings. And she wondered whether her father's voice was but a dream also, for when she asked among the Greenies for Hamlin son of Harmon, nobody had ever seen or heard of him. Besides, how could he have tracked her to the Greenies' swamp?

Then there was work again, but the Light touched it, too, so that Merryn's fingers flew with knife and needle and stone, for she was no longer alone. Always she tried to remember what the Man had told her, but most was forgotten.

On a glorious June morning, Merryn found her Greenies sunning themselves outside the cave. "Picnic!" they cried when they saw her. Then they whisked her away on willowy vines beneath the roundheaded, sky-singing clouds. Near the river, they dropped into a meadow sprinkled with wild roses and irises. Out came baskets and bags of food, more food than Merryn had ever seen outside a shop. There were apples, winter pears, strawberries, meats, cheeses, cakes, pies and breads of every sort. The river had been generous of late, the Greenies told her.

Merryn ate until she could hold no more, and after resting, she ate again. Afterwards, the mulberry-men stretched out on the grass, unfurled their vines in the sun, and slept.

Merryn clucked her tongue. "You know you're not supposed to eat and sleep at the same time!" she teased her friends. The Greenies only snored. Leaving them, Merryn picked wildflowers until the broiling sun chased her into the woods, where woodpeckers drummed and furry creatures scurried through the undergrowth. Green light filtered through the trees' lazy leaves.

Merryn sat on a log, watching butterflies flit around her. How her life had changed since the Greenies had captured her! She had suffered much, but she had gained much more. If only she could find her father. She wondered whether Gaelathane had heard her prayer that night in the Grotto. Her lower lip trembled.

The world went dark. Merryn squealed and reached for her eyes, but just as quickly, they were uncovered again.

"Guess who!"

This time there was no mistaking that voice. Leaping up from the log, Merryn whirled to face her father. She found only some white-flowering currant bushes. "Who's there?" she cried.

"Hoppy, it's me," returned the voice. "I told you I would see you again. You look so much better now that you've recovered from the swamp fever. I've heard you can't catch it twice."

Still Merryn saw nothing but leaves and branches. She began to cry. "If you're really my father, show yourself! If you're not, then go away and leave me alone. I don't like mean tricks."

The bushes groaned. "I can't, Hoppy. You're not ready—"

"Show yourself!" Merryn screamed. "Show yourself to me, or I'll hold my breath until I faint!" The threat was one she had used in her younger years to get her way, and it usually worked.

It worked this time, too. "Very well," said the father-voice.

The shrubs stirred again, but now the snaky whips and leafy garb of a mulberry-man emerged from the woodsy shadows. Seeing the veiled face within, Merryn really did faint.

She groggily awoke under a leafy tent. Where was she? Grotto images flooded back. *I must be delirious again.*

"I didn't want you to sunburn," said the gentle father-voice. The tent broke apart into long, leafy vines; among them knelt the father-bush. Greenies rarely sat, Merryn knew, since they couldn't get up again without falling all over themselves.

"Who *are* you?" she asked, already suspecting the truth.

Leaves parted and Merryn caught a glimpse of those familiar hazel eyes that could so warm her with a glance. As that warmth again rekindled in her heart, she sprang up and threw herself at the father-bush. Deep inside those leafy vines, she found real arms and hands to hold her and real lips to kiss her.

"Papa! Papa! Papa!" she cried. "It really is you! I've found you at last." With great heaving sobs, she wept for all the pain and sorrow and fear she'd known since leaving Beechtown.

Hamlin's bearded cheeks were wet, too.

The storm passed, leaving Merryn as drained as a new kitten. She leaned back against her father's chest, content with his closeness, entwined in his vines, basking in his presence.

"How did you—when did you—?" she asked.

The brewmaster sighed. "The Greenies set upon our ship as we were heading upriver. I was one of the few to survive. Bart sent the captain and many of the crew into the Hole."

"What *is* the Hole, anyway? I looked into it once—" Merryn shuddered at the memory.

Hamlin shuddered with her. "What's down there is a mystery. None of us is allowed near the spot, especially with strong drink. It seems Bart lost several good men that way. We do know the swamp gas comes out of the Hole. The stuff burns off in sunlight, but at night, it spreads for miles. When the wind is right, it can even catch people on the river. Bart likes that."

"What about the strogarns? Are they Bart's pets?"

"You might say that. We don't know what they are or where they came from, but they're loathsome, horrid creatures. Still, they're harmless if left to themselves. Mostly they feed on frogs, turtles and other small animals that live in the swamp."

Merryn was perplexed. "Then why don't they eat people, too, instead of passing them down to the Hole?"

The brewmaster scratched his shaggy head with a vine tip. "That's also a mystery. Maybe we're too big for them to swallow." His eyes flooded with tears again. "I was so afraid when I saw you by the Hole! I've never been more thankful for my vines than I was then. Without them, I could not have saved you in time."

"It was you who rescued me?" said Merryn wonderingly. "I should have known. The others wouldn't have bothered."

"Now, Merryn," said Hamlin with reproach in his tone. "They're really not such a bad bunch. I think they actually dote on you more than I do, if that's possible!"

Merryn drew back. "Then you help them rob people?"

Hamlin's eyes slid away. "The others call me 'Stickler,' because they know how I detest stealing, but Bart lets me help in other ways. When I can, I try to return valuables to their rightful owners by dropping the stolen goods onto boats as they pass by."

Playfully tugging on her father's beard, Merryn said, "You should have let me shave this off or at least trim it, as I do for the others. You look just like the Old Man of the Mountain."

"Hmph!" grunted the father-bush. "From the day you first joined us, I wanted to reveal myself to you, but I was afraid to let you see me like this. I'd rather go to the Hole than to be rejected by you, Hoppy. When you fainted, I came near to leaving, since I couldn't be sure what you would do when you awoke."

"This is what I would do!" said Merryn, and she kissed her father on the cheek. He grinned.

"I offered to guard the Grotto after dark, just to be near you," Hamlin went on. "Often, I tried to make your work lighter, too. When you fell ill, I sat by your side day and night till you—"

"Until I what, Father?"

Hamlin looked away. "I lost you. You quit breathing and grew as cold and stiff as an old stone. You died, Hoppy; you died."

Merryn rocked back on her heels. *Died?* How could that be, when she had felt so alive? She had climbed a tall, shining Tree; talked to a Man; walked with Him across a crystal lake. She shook her head. What she had experienced was life, not death.

"While you were . . . gone, a Man in white visited me," said Hamlin. "He seemed to know everything about me, and yet I felt He loved me all the same. I begged Him to spare your life, and when He granted my request, I vowed to serve Him the rest of my days. I'm a different man now, Hoppy; He's changed me."

"He's changed me, too," said Merryn softly, and she told her father of the same Man she had met beside the lake.

Hamlin rattled his leaves. "I only wish our Friend had found us before Bart did. Still, I bless the boat that brought you to me, for now I won't be so lonely." A cloud passed over his face. "What were you doing on that dilapidated old scow, anyway?"

Merryn couldn't help it. Her face screwed up the way it always did before the dam burst. "M-m-mo-*hic!*-ther s-s-s-sold me to C-captain Rolc," she sobbed out. "As a s-s-slave!" The last word ended in a wail that brought down the last of the dam.

"Sold you? As a slave?" Hamlin repeated dazedly. "Oh, my poor, dear child, I never thought it would come to this. Your mother loved you, Hoppy, but her fear of poverty got the best of her, it seems. She married me to escape the poorhouse, where she lived with her mother. I was nothing more to her than a stepping-stone to respectability. She's a conniving woman, that one."

Merryn kissed him. "I'm so sorry, Papa, but can we talk about this later? It's time for introductions!" When Hamlin balked, she tugged on his vines. "Come along, Mr. Greenie!"

Hamlin laughed. "All right, then; lead on, Miss Smoothie." His voice lowered. "I haven't told the others that you're my daughter for fear Bart might use you against me. He'd do it, too."

"I won't let him!" Merryn declared. "If he tries, I'll hold my breath again. He won't want me turning purple and fainting!"

"You're a sly one, aren't you, Miss Merryn!" Hamlin said. "Keep this up, and we'll be calling you 'Queen of the Greenies'!"

Thinking Merryn was lost, Bart's men had been searching for her. When she and her father emerged from the forest to announce their news, the gleeful Greenies gathered around to pepper the pair with questions. Out came the food and drink again, including bottles of ale and mead—some of Hamlin's best.

"It's a sad day when I must grow leaves to taste my own brew!" he said with mock disgust. The Greenies all guffawed at that, and even Merryn had to laugh.

CHAPTER 8

A Faithful Staff

After the picnic, Merryn and her father were inseparable—save when the swamp gas was gathering. Often the two would sleep in the Grotto for companionship. Serving the Greenies became a joy, and Merryn often hummed and sang her way through her chores, something she'd never done while living by the brewery.

On a steamy summer afternoon, she really did become lost. Shouldering a bag woven of cattails, she set off for the woods to gather mushrooms, fiddlehead ferns and watercress, which would add variety to the Greenies' woefully bland diet.

Merryn was wading through a patch of lacy bracken when she walked right into a mulberry-man. "Oh!" she gasped. "I'm terribly sorry. I wasn't watching where I was going. Are you all right?" There was no answer. Merryn repeated her apology.

Was she addressing a real bush? The long, vining tendrils did resemble a Greenie's, though they weren't moving. Perhaps the fellow was playing possum. "You can't fool me, Mr. Greenie!" she said loudly, and she pulled the whips aside.

Behind thick masses of leaves, she found an old mulberry-man sleeping, his chest rhythmically rising and falling. However, it was his feet that captured Merryn's attention. They had sprouted thick roots that firmly anchored their owner to the ground.

"Oh, dear," Merryn said. The marsh king had once mentioned something about "rooting." Apparently, when the Greenies stood in one spot too long, they rooted in place like this oldster. No wonder they preferred to sleep hanging from trees!

Merryn was patting the sleeping Greenie's leaves back into place when the sky darkened and fat, heavy raindrops spattered on her head. *Not again!* She vividly recalled the last time she had been caught out in the rain. Hoping to avoid another bout with the swamp fever, she turned back—only to find that she had completely lost her way. Using her bag as an umbrella, she took shelter under the spreading limbs of a ragged yew tree.

"It won't last long. These early summer storms rarely do."

Merryn shrieked and the bag went flying. A little old man was sharing her tree. Shrouded in a hooded white cloak, he bore a glassy staff that shone with an inner light. "Who are you and where did you come from?" Merryn asked the stranger.

"People in these parts know me as 'Andil of the Wood,'" he softly replied. "This is my forest, you see, and I enjoy visiting it in all seasons. The trees and flowers are lovely at this time of year, don't you agree?" He waved his staff toward the woods, and the curtains of rain appeared to part for an instant.

Merryn nodded woodenly. She didn't like to think she and the Greenies were squatting on someone else's territory. To her mind, the Forest of Fellglade belonged to no one but those who lived there. She would have to weigh her words carefully.

Andil of the Wood chuckled. "You needn't worry about your friends. I have their lives well in hand—and yours, too."

Merryn blinked and stepped back. "You do?"

"Oh, yes. Your Greenies have strayed far from me, but they will soon come full circle. As for you, my dear Merryn, you have already tasted my love and are ready for better things."

By now, Merryn was shaking too badly to scratch herself. How could Andil of the Wood know her name? She felt certain she'd met him before—but where? Edging away from the funny little man, she found that rain was still pouring down all around the yew. Under the tree, however, it was warm and dry.

She swallowed. "I—I think you've mistaken me for someone else. And they're not 'my' Greenies, either."

"Ah, but don't they think of you as their 'Miss Merryn'?" said Andil with a smile that lit up the gloomy yew tree.

Merryn wilted. "What do you want with me?"

"What is that in your pocket?"

My pocket? As far as Merryn knew, her pockets were empty. Maybe if she humored the old man, he would go away. Turning the left pocket of her shift inside out, she found only dirt and a few mummified berries. When she pulled the right one out, however, a dark brown, flattened seed fell to the ground.

"Don't you recall what I told you?" said Andil gently. "You should have planted that nut weeks ago. Now there is not a moment to lose." He threw back his hood, and light flashed forth from his face. A veil fell from Merryn's eyes as she recognized Andil as the Champion. She knelt before Him in awe and terror.

"I'm sorry!" she gasped. "Please tell me what I must do."

"First, you must learn to accept yourself as I accept you. Look at Me." Merryn raised her eyes. Red welts and ropy scars veined the Man's hands and arms. When He bent down, she could see the ghastly marks running down His back as well.

"You see, Merryn, I know what it is to live with disfigurement," He said. "I will ever wear these scars as a reminder of My love for you, since I suffered them in your place. Henceforth, when you look at yourself, remember Me and the price I paid for you."

What does He mean? "Then I will never be whole again?" She thought back to the perfect reflection she'd seen in the lake. *That* was how she wanted to look, not like "Scabby."

"You shall be whole again, inside and out," He promised. "Now you must plant the seed and watch over it until dawn. Do not leave before then, or you will be in grave danger."

"But—the swamp gas!" Merryn protested.

"As long as you obey Me, you need fear nothing the night will bring. Remember, I will be with you always, even in your darkest hour. My rod, My staff will comfort and protect you."

Merryn quailed at the prospect of spending the night alone in the Forest of Fellglade. "You'll stay here with me, won't You?" she asked, but her Champion had vanished. Only His staff remained, bravely glowing in the lengthening shadows. Taking it up, Merryn set off to find a suitable spot for planting her little brown nut.

Outside the yew, the rain had stopped and the sun was shining. Wispy steam rose from the warming earth, dancing fairylike in the cool air. In a nearby glade, Merryn pressed the nut into a patch of loose loam. Then she sat down to watch and wait.

Lulled by the bees droning in the tops of the murmuring trees, Merryn dozed. Dreaming, she saw the swamp gas rising out of the marsh, engulfing her. Green whips poked through her pocked skin. She snapped awake to find the sun still shining and no sign of the green fog. If she hurried, she could reach the Grotto before dark! Wishing to obey Andil, though, she remained at her post.

As the sun's last golden spears slanted through the forest, Merryn shivered with fear. Never had she stayed out so late before. Surely she must have been missed by now; surely her father and the other Greenies would come looking for her!

No one came. Instead, out of the frog-croaking quiet rose the babbling thunder of the "fog-flight." Each day at dusk, birds and beasts fleeing the swamp gas stampeded to the forest's fringes. It began with flocks of ducks and geese, followed by troops of four-legged animals. A family of skunks bustled by, their tails held high. Squirrels leapt from one bearded swamp oak to the next. A pointy-eared lynx slunk past, paying Merryn no mind.

Then deep darkness fell over Merryn's patch of earth as a gigantic beast shambled by, its shaggy coat stained green with swamp slime. A marsh bear! Some years back, a hop-field worker had vanished while hunting. Weeks later, his body was found torn to pieces in a swamp. When word reached the brewery, the old-timers sagely nodded and declared, "Marsh bear." Like all the other forest creatures, though, the bear ignored Merryn.

The commotion died away, leaving a deathly stillness in its wake. Merryn felt terribly alone without the Greenies. For good or ill, they were the only friends she had left. She missed their rough ways—their coarse jesting, good-natured pranks and awkward courtesies. Most of all, she missed her father.

As dusk thickened under the trees, the first ribbons of marsh mist floated into the glade. Dry-mouthed, Merryn raised Andil's staff, which enclosed her in a dome of light. She held her breath as mist-fingers tested the dome, feeling around it for a way in. Like swirling green seawater, the fog rose until it completely covered the dome. Then Merryn discovered she was not alone.

The mist-creatures had come out of their caves and hollow trees to haunt the green-foggy night woods. Using their long claws and sharp teeth, they scratched and bit at the light but could not break through. With lidless, long-stalked eyes, they glared at Merryn from flabby, fishbelly faces. Muffled by the mist, Merryn's screams came out sounding like hiccups.

A hundred lifetimes passed before the beasts gave up to go in search of other prey, leaving Merryn to weep out her relief. Falling to earth, her tears watered the seed, and a green tendril wormed out of the dirt. The sprout rapidly grew into a sapling, sending out sprightly leaves that hung from slender limbs.

Birds twittered. Dawn came swiftly to pierce the green fog. Caught betwixt the light above and the light beneath, the mist vanished in a thought. Merryn's tree quivered, and bright pink blossoms burst from its branches. The air sang with a heady sweetness like linden flowers mingled with hyacinths. Exhausted from her ordeal, Merryn let the ground catch and enfold her.

She awoke in the Grotto, lying on the pile of rags that served as her mattress. The staff lay beside her. Its light played over a welter of Greenie vines hovering protectively over her body.

"How do you feel?" asked the mulberry-men anxiously.

She yawned. "Much better, thank you. How long have I slept?"

"All day! We feared you had the fever again. What happened? Were you lost? What's this shiny stick we found with you?"

Oh, so many questions! Merryn had to explain everything she had seen and done since leaving the marsh at least five times, and still the Greenies were not satisfied with her answers.

"But how did you escape the swamp gas?" asked Bart.

Merryn sighed. "I already told you. Andil's staff kept it away. And you fellows are keeping me from my breakfast, or whatever you call it at this time of day. What's that I smell cooking?"

"Did this Wendil character hurt you?" asked Hamlin. He it was who had found Merryn lying under the pink-bloomed tree, still clutching her staff. Fearful she had fallen under a spell or enchantment, he had dragged her away from the spot.

"It's 'Andil'—and of course not!" Merryn replied. "He's much too kind to do anything of the sort. Now about breakfast . . ."

Breakfast had to wait while the Greenies puzzled over Merryn's tale. "An old man?" they said. "In these parts? You don't suppose he was the same Smoothie we saw in the marsh before, do you?" Nobody knew for sure, and Merryn was too hungry to care.

From that day on, Merryn always kept the staff at her side. She took it with her to greet the dawn at the Grotto's mouth; when she ate, it lay on her lap; when she crossed the marsh, it kept her from stumbling; when evening fell, it lit her homeward steps, and at night, the rod shone the way to her bed, where she slept with it under her head. No nightmares of Rolc troubled her then.

Most importantly, Merryn no longer feared the swamp gas, for the staff's light kept it at bay, behind and before. Now she could freely walk the woods after dusk, enjoying flaming sunsets and fireflies blinking their way among the trees. Instead of retreating into the Grotto at the first hint of green fog, she could even join her father and the other mulberry-men around the campfire.

One stifling July evening, brooding clouds gathered over the forest, blotting out the light. With peals of thunder, they loosed a downpour that swept across the marsh, thrashing the water to foam. Everyone took cover in the Grotto, where the Greenies crowded the cave from wall to wall with their dripping vines.

When three days had passed with no letup in the deluge, patience wore thin. Unaccustomed to living in such close quarters, the mulberry-men were stepping on vines not their own and getting in each other's way. Tempers flared. Merryn could only huddle at the back of the cave and pray for the rain to stop.

On the fourth day, it did. Whooping and cheering, Merryn and her companions rushed out of the Grotto. They found water lapping at its mouth and tattered clouds streaming across a washed sky. In the marsh, the flood had inundated all but a few of the higher hummocks. The treed hill alone stood tall above the torrent, an island in a surging brown sea.

Vining into the trees, some of the men went in search of food; others made for the river to rescue Rolc's ship, in case it had broken free of its moorings. Hamlin was the last to leave.

"Won't you come along with us?" he asked his daughter. A stray vine playfully encircled her waist, ready to sling her like a sack of potatoes into the waiting trees across the marsh.

"No, thank you," she told him. "I think I'll stay here." She never did like being "vine-handled," even by her father. After he had left, though, she feared the rising floodwaters might trap her in the Grotto, and she set off across the swamp to find him. Unfortunately, the slick, submerged hillocks made poor footholds, and she kept slipping off into the water. To make matters worse, black clouds had appeared on the horizon and before long, a wind-driven rain was lashing her with stinging whips.

Drenched to the skin and utterly miserable, she reached the end of the slimy humps—but not of the swamp, which stretched like a muddy lake through the trees. Flummoxed, Merryn was debating whether to wait for the Greenies to rescue her or to turn back when she heard a low rumbling noise. *Not another earthquake!* she thought. Faint warning cries rang out ahead.

"Run, Merryn, run!" Greenies were yelling from the forest.

"Go back, Hoppy!" shouted Hamlin, swinging through the trees toward her. "Make for the hill!" All at once, the wind snapped his anchor vine in twain and hurled him into the dripping sky. "Goodbye, Hoppy! I love you!" he cried as he sailed away.

Before Merryn could fully grasp what had happened, her perch bucked violently, heaving her head-over-heels into the marsh. Into the deep she sank, into a cold world of clinging water weeds and swirling silt. Strogarn tentacles floated and flailed around her like the hair of drowned women. *Rolc is here. He's waiting for me.* Gasping for air, she took in foul water that stung her aching lungs with nettle-fire. *Father, where are you?*

A star rose out of the darkness. *The Light is coming for me. I am here, Champion!* Grasping the light, she found it was solid. The staff had come to her aid! Floating, it pulled her toward the speckled, silvery underside of the rain-spattered marsh.

Sputtering and coughing, Merryn broke through into the sweet, blessed air. She was furiously treading water when a roaring filled her ears. A green mountain was rushing toward the marsh, snapping off trees in its path like toothpicks.

Merryn barely had time to scream before a watery fist flung her across the swamp and drove her to the mucky bottom. Like a waveworn seashell, she tumbled blindly along. When she tried to rise, the marsh wrapped its slimy fingers about her body and held on until Rolc-of-the-Hole came to claim her as his prize.

Yet, prizes can be lost as well as won. Merryn awoke to find herself entangled in tree roots, as if Rolc and his swamp had spat out their scabby victim in disgust. Beside her shone the staff; beyond all hope it had stayed with her during the wild ride.

She groaned. Her head was splitting and her chest ached. By staff-light, she could see a humpy, reddish monster floating in the waters below. Her rag-mattress! Incredibly, the floodwaters had carried her into the Grotto. The rain-swollen river must have overflowed its banks and sent out the mountainous wave surge that had nearly drowned her. Merryn sneezed, and the jumbled roots gave way. *Sploosh!* She and the staff fell onto the floating rags. Paddling with her hands, she reached a spit of dry ground, safe for the moment. Still, the air was growing thick and foul, and black specks swam before her eyes. Then she passed out.

A numbing chill awoke her. She couldn't feel her legs. The spit had shrunk and water was creeping up her body. Shivering, she scooted backward, but a thick maze of roots blocked the way.

Merryn wept. Had she escaped so many perils only to drown like a swamp rat? "No!" she screamed. Clawing furiously at the roots, she tore a hole large enough to crawl through. The water followed. More dangling roots blocked the passage, but with desperate strength, she ripped them away. Squeezing through the opening brought her close to a root-walled space that was already filling with water. Beyond that, the Grotto simply ended.

Merryn sagged. She was finished. After the floodwaters had subsided, the Greenies would come searching for her. She hoped her father wouldn't be the one to find her sodden body.

Forcing her way past the last curtain of roots, she stumbled and fell. Water covered her face. Sweet violin music rang in her ears as the Grotto turned topsy-turvy, and she tumbled backwards down a long, dark passage into Rolc's waiting clutches.

CHAPTER 9

Out of Flood, Into Fire

Merryn blinked at the puffy white animals chasing each other across a roofless sky. Fresh air flooded her starving lungs; mellow sunshine warmed her bruised limbs; fiddle notes still echoed across the marsh. The Grotto apparently ran all the way through the hill, though Merryn had never seen a second entrance. Perhaps Bart had hidden the tunnel mouth from her prying eyes.

A larger hill stood a half-mile off, joined to hers by a land bridge from which a rocky dike snaked away. Parts of the dike had sloughed off, as if it hadn't been kept up in many years.

She blinked again. Here was another mystery: A treeless swampland spread for miles around both hills. Perhaps the floodwaters had washed away the forest, leaving only this uninviting marsh, featureless but for the familiar humps that broke its surface. Among the hillocks jutted conical strogarn burrows.

Hoping the dike might hold some answers, Merryn plotted the shortest course to it through the swamp and charged ahead. As the first strogarn popped up and unfolded, she ducked under its fleshy feelers and slogged on, dodging burrows even as their occupants emerged. Now a forest of writhing tentacles was reaching for her. Diving, she belly-flopped onto the slippery muck and slid the last few feet to the dike, her staff beneath her.

As she was getting up, a tentacle knocked her down again, pinning her to the mud. If only she had a knife! Pounding the feeler with her staff until its grip loosened, she squirmed out of its slimy embrace and clawed her way up the crumbly slope.

On reaching the top, she discovered that the dike was actually a rutted causeway wide enough for two wagons to pass abreast. So much the better! While she caught her breath, Merryn leaned on the staff and surveyed the swamp spread out below her.

Like blind, grotesque sea creatures, the strogarns were waving their arms to and fro, as if still seeking their quarry. Without warning—*Slap! Clap!*—the beasts began snapping their tentacles together like grisly gray flowers opening and closing.

Abruptly, the strogarns folded up and withdrew into their burrows. An uneasy silence settled over the swamp. Merryn was about to set off when she noticed some of the matted water weeds stirring. Their edges curled and began to flutter. Dripping green heads on shaggy necks heaved out of the muck and shook themselves, followed by long-tailed, hump-backed bodies. With a *whoosh*, the dragons (for so they were) took flight.

"Use your staff! Point it at them!" shouted a reedy voice.

Running, Merryn looked back but saw no one, save several of the horrible creatures bearing down on her from the air. Fire spewed from the closest one, scorching the grass behind her and singeing her hair. She tripped on a rock and fell on the staff.

The dragons overshot her. Banking on their green, ribbed wings, they came at her again. Realizing she could not outrun the swift beasts, Merryn took her stand on the causeway.

"You can't have me!" she cried, shaking the staff at her flying foes. "Begone and leave me alone! You have no right to—" She nearly dropped the rod as a brilliant light beam shot out of it and struck the nearest dragon, turning it from green to gray.

No longer flapping its wings, the beast glided over her head so low that she could see the webbing between its clawed toes. Then it veered away from the causeway and headed for her hill.

Kerr-oom! A cloud of dust and dragon parts exploded on the hillside. Merryn hadn't time to gawk, because the creature's companions were still looking for an easy meal. Pointing her staff, she brought them down as she had the first. One after another, they plunged into the swamp or smashed onto the land bridge.

Merryn shook like a wobbly wagon wheel and stars danced before her eyes as she sank onto the causeway. How many more of these dragons were hiding in the Greenies' ruined swamp?

Rocks rattled, drawing Merryn's attention back to her hill. Tiny figures were leaping down the side, weaving among the trees and bushes until they reached the land bridge. Halfway across the bridge, the strangers turned and pounded down the causeway. All at once, the frontrunners stopped dead and pointed above Merryn's head, their mouths agape. Merryn whirled to face a monstrous dragon diving on her. She aimed her staff at the beast, and it crashed onto the causeway, showering her with stony shards. *What are these dragons made of, anyway?*

Moments later, a man whose chestnut hair fell to his shoulders clambered over the shattered dragon. Carrying a wooden staff and a wicker basket full of mushrooms, he was dressed in a green tunic and cloak and wore a gold pendant around his neck. He grinned and winked at Merryn, as if he were out for a stroll and dragon-slaying was quite commonplace where he lived.

"Hullo, there!" he said cheerfully. "That was pretty fair shooting, young lady. Where did you get the staff, anyway?"

Before Merryn could answer, six more green-cloaked men trooped up with two golden-haired women, all carrying mushroom-filled baskets. One of the younger men looked vaguely familiar. He was wearing the filthiest tunic, jerkin and trousers Merryn had ever seen. To her surprise, he gaily waved at her.

"So here you are!" he said. "I'd nearly given you up for lost."

Merryn gasped. The stranger spoke with Timothy's voice. She pinched herself. *Now I know I'm dreaming!* The pinch hurt. She was awake and to all appearances, still in her right mind. "Timothy? You're alive? I thought you were gone for good! How did you escape the Hole? Where have you been all this time?"

The young man smiled, cracking the caked-on mud around his mouth and eyes. "Keeping an eye on you, Merryn! I'll explain the rest later. Do you know where this road leads, by any chance?"

Still stunned by Timothy's return from the grave, Merryn shook her head. "Who are all these people with you? Are they friends of yours? They look like Greencloaks to me."

Living next to the town brewery, Merryn had heard many fanciful tales about these green-garbed strangers. Some folk said they were elves or wood sprites; others held they were sorcerers. Nobody knew where they lived. Whenever anyone tried to follow a Greencloak, he ended up wandering the woods in circles. Was Merryn the first to discover the Greencloaks' country?

"That's what we are, all right," said the auburn-haired man with a bow. "I am Rolin son of Gannon, 'King of the Greencloaks,' if you please." His wife, Queen Marlis, greeted Merryn with a smile that lit up her snapping, long-lashed green eyes. Beside her stood a younger version of herself, Gwynneth, who released Timothy's hand only long enough to curtsy. Gwynneth's brother Elwyn was a serious-looking youth with flaming red hair.

The sons of Nolan, Gemmio and Opio, offered a study in contrasts. Aside from their long faces and curly brown hair flecked with gray, they were as unalike as brothers could be. Opio's cloak barely concealed his ample girth, while Gemmio swam in his. Still, their kindly green eyes told Merryn, *Welcome, friend.*

That left Bembor son of Brenthor, a snowy-maned old man with emerald, ageless eyes, and Marlis's brother, Scanlon, a head shorter than Rolin with large ears, dark hair and a mischievous grin. At the moment, however, he wore a solemn expression.

"We've got to keep moving," he announced. "There's no telling how many more of these brutes are about."

As the Greencloaks broke into a brisk trot, Timothy grabbed Merryn's arm and pulled her along. "Come on!" he said. The two had run only a few paces when more dragons lumbered out of the marsh and took flight. Sulfurous fire rained down.

"Your staff, Merryn!" panted Timothy.

Merryn raised the rod, and white light stabbed the evening sky. One by one, the diving dragons plowed into the causeway, pelting Merryn and Timothy with bits of wings, teeth and claws. When the sky was clear, the two caught up to their companions by following a trail of broken mushrooms and discarded baskets.

"Well done!" Bembor boomed, patting Merryn's shoulder. "Since none of us had the foresight to bring our own lightstaffs, we'll be depending on you to keep those beasts off our backs!"

"Lightstaffs?" The word was new to Merryn, though it made perfect sense. "What do they *do* to dragons, anyway?"

Elwyn eyed her quizzically. "They turn them to stone."

Merryn had assumed all the dragons were dead when a black cloud overshadowed the company. "They're attacking in force!" King Rolin cried. "Make for that mountain up ahead!"

It wasn't really a mountain, not by comparison with the Tartellans, but this craggy hump rising out of the marshes did dwarf Merryn's hill. The causeway rose to meet it and wound around its flanks to the top, where a great grim castle brooded with frowning stone towers and dark, slitted lancet windows.

The whirring cloud descended in fire and smoke, engulfing the ten travelers and slowing their headway to a crawl. Merryn fell into a deadly "dragondrop" dance: *Run-turn-point-dragondrop-run-turn-point-dragondrop*, performed to the drumming din of screams, whooshing wings, belching fire and shattering stone.

Only a few hundred yards from the mount, Merryn collapsed. Her near drowning, lack of food and sleep, and the strain of fighting off dragons had taken their toll.

"The staff-bearer is down!" Timothy cried. Strong hands seized and carried Merryn, relieving her of the rod. Bumping along on a bony shoulder, she thought, *This is worse than fighting dragons!* Then thunder struck the causeway, and she felt no more.

Merryn rejoined the world with a raging headache. Someone was rubbing her hand and patting her cheek. She opened her eyes to find a face framed in golden hair hovering over her.

"Are you feeling better?" Gwynneth asked.

Merryn nodded weakly. She lay in a natural alcove at the base of a beetling cliff where the causeway joined the castle-mountain. Muted voices anxiously muttered against the rumble of smashing stone and the bellowing of flying beasts.

Though she didn't catch every word, Merryn heard enough to know she was slowing up her companions. Setting her jaw, she sat up and held her head to keep it from spinning off her shoulders. With the rock face as a prop, she pushed herself upright.

"Merryn!" Gwynneth clucked her tongue. "You shouldn't try to stand yet. A stone dragon fell beside you and a piece of its jaw struck you in the head. You're fortunate to be alive."

Fingering the lump on her forehead, Merryn said, "I'll manage, thank you very kindly. Now, where's my lightstaff?"

Scanlon was pointing the bright stick at a dragon looming overhead. With a thunderous roar, the petrified beast smashed into the cliff and exploded in a cascading spray of stony rubble. Fortunately, the overhang protected Merryn and her companions from the worst of the avalanche.

Brushing herself off, Merryn held out her hand to Scanlon. "May I have my staff back now, please? If you want those dragons turned to stone, I've got as good an aim as any man." While Marlis and Gwynneth hid delighted smiles and the men chuckled, a rueful Scanlon bowed and handed over the lightstaff.

"My pardon, fair Merryn," he said, his eyes twinkling. "You shall soon have your chance to drop some more dragons."

"Where did you get that staff, if I may ask?" said Opio.

"I didn't steal it, if that's what you are thinking," said Merryn defiantly. "Andil of the Wood gave it to me."

Timothy staggered violently to one side. "Andil of the Wood? I haven't heard that name in ages! Where did you meet him?"

Merryn described her woodland encounter with the white-robed old man. "Do you know him, too?" she asked.

Timothy's eyes danced. "Of course! Andil of the Wood is Gaelathane, and Gaelathane is Andil of the Wood."

"Hmph," grumped Opio. "I must say, I've never known Gaelathane to hand out lightstaffs freely like candy to children."

Gemmio pulled Opio's hood over his face. "Don't listen to my sourpuss brother! I don't know why Gaelathane gave you this lightstaff, but I'm certainly glad He did. It saved our lives!"

Scanlon groaned. "What does it matter where she got the staff when we're all sitting ducks out here? Let's keep moving."

Lightstaff held high, Merryn led the way up the winding causeway road. High above, the turreted fortress glowed orange in the setting sun; below, a rising darkness had devoured the marsh and was gnawing at the mountain's rocky base.

At eventide, dragons glide. The words sprang unbidden to Merryn's mind. How could she know anything about dragons? Just in case, she glanced up, but the blue-black sky was a blank. Still giddy from the blow to her head, she steadied herself with the staff and hastened onward while the sinking sun burned above the distant horizon like a great, flaming dragon's eye.

"This is as bad as climbing the stairs in the Hallowfast," Opio grumbled, and he kicked a loose rock off the road. Its clattering passage down the mountainside jangled in Merryn's head like a gong. Could dragons hear? She didn't think so.

"Quiet!" Bembor scolded the heavyset Greencloak.

When darkness finally overtook Merryn and her companions, they were still toiling up the mountain, having seen no further sign of dragons. Once or twice, though, Merryn heard a soughing sound in the night, as of reeds rustling in the marsh.

Hugging the mountainside to avoid the black gulf on her right, Merryn was rounding another bend when rocks rattled onto the road. Knowing that nothing falls by itself, she motioned to her friends to fall back. Then she stole forward and looked up.

Twin red coals glowed at her from the mountain. They blazed up, and fire spilled down the slope. Merryn jumped back.

"Going somewhere?" rumbled a voice that stank of things long dead and rotten. "You can't sneak past me! My fires melt iron and burn brass; my tail topples trees; my teeth grind stones to powder." Scant feet above Merryn, a dragon's jaws opened with waves of blistering heat. "Give it back!" the beast growled. "Give it back, or I'll scorch you to soot and cinders!"

"G-give what back?" Merryn stuttered, her teeth chattering. She was cornered. Under cover of darkness, her fiery foe had glided up to the heights and latched onto the mountainside with his sharp wing-claws. There he had hung over the road like a giant green bat, waiting to pounce on unwary passers-by.

"The thing!" hissed the dragon. "Give me the green thing!"

Cold fury doused the fear in Merryn's heart as she raised her lightstaff. "No!" she shouted. "You can't have it! It's mine!"

"Ah, I wouldn't use that if I were you," said the serpent.

"Why not?" Merryn asked. "If I don't, you'll eat me!"

More rocks tumbled onto the road as the dragon inched closer. "True," he admitted. "But if you turn me to stone, I'll fall on you and crush you like a miserable leech." His eyes burned with a greedy fire that left Merryn feeling weak about the knees.

"I'll just have to take that chance," she said and brought the staff to bear on the great domed head. Light met flame, and the light won. Scrambling backward, Merryn narrowly escaped being flattened as the petrified dragon slid down and crumbled into stony ruin on the road. Oh, how her sores itched then!

"Very crafty, these dragons," Bembor observed as he and the others came up to observe the creature's remains.

"And very persistent," added Gemmio.

"There are bound to be more of them, too," said Rolin. "We must keep our wits about us, as Merryn has." However, Merryn's wits were badly addled by her encounter with the talking dragon.

Clambering over dragon debris, the ten were trudging on when the road behind them collapsed. "That beast must have weakened the hillside when it fell," said Rolin. "There's no going back now!" After that, four more green shadows turned gray and sloughed off the cliffs before Merryn's lightstaff could rest.

As the road crested the last rise, up loomed the mammoth castle. Forbidding guard towers flanked its massive front gates with their iron portcullis that was poised to devour the puny prey at its feet. Higher still rose a moon-tipped, tapering inner tower.

Drop-jawed, Bembor gazed at the castle. "This is some of the finest masonry work I've ever seen. The stone alone must have taken an army of laborers years to quarry and haul up here."

"The place looks deserted to me," Elwyn offered.

"Maybe we should spend the night out here," said Gemmio. "If the people in that castle keep dragons as pets, they won't be happy to learn we've been making statuary of them."

"Nonsense," said King Rolin. "From the looks of it, whoever built this fortress wanted to keep the dragons out, not in."

"Maybe not just the dragons," said Scanlon uneasily.

Dwarfed before those mighty gates, Merryn and her friends searched in vain for a bell-pull or a brass knocker or a speaking-tube with which to announce their presence. When rattling the sooty portcullis brought no response, they threw rocks at the gates. The citadel remained as silent and aloof as ever.

"I see they took in the welcome mat," observed Opio dryly.

"Hey! Hi! Is anybody home?" shouted Elwyn.

"Shush!" his sister scolded him. "That won't do us any good, you silly goose. You'll only bring more dragons down on us."

"I suppose you have a better plan?" Elwyn said archly. The two began to squabble as only brothers and sisters can.

"Oh, stop your bickering," said Merryn. "I think I can get into that castle, but you'd all better take cover first!"

Once the others had grumbled their way out of sight, Merryn hiked back down the road a short distance. She stopped at the mountain's edge, where she could look down over the moonlit marshes. Then she began to wave her staff in wide circles.

Soon, her efforts were rewarded as a winged form blotted out the moon and stars. Merryn dropped to the ground just as the beast passed over her with a *Whup! Whup!* Then she ran for the castle. The dragon came for her again, its taloned feet poised to rip and snatch. At the last second, she threw herself to one side and hugged the earth. Claws gouged the ground beside her. Up she jumped again, this time to face her foe. Fear squeezed the air out of her chest as the dragon flew at her, jaws spitting fire.

Lower, lower. Not yet . . . wait . . . now! Merryn threw up her staff arm, catching the oncoming beast with a burst of searing white light. The dragon flew blindly on, gliding heavily on outspread stone wings, straight for the castle gates.

CHAPTER 10

The Castell Mawr

WHOOM! The petrified dragon plowed into the portcullis and gates with an earth-shaking roar. Under its onslaught, the portcullis flew to pieces. A jagged instant later, the gates burst asunder. Still the stone beast ground on through the breach, shattering a set of inner gates. With nowhere else to go, the inferno brewing in its belly exploded in a fireball that melted everything in its path. Long seconds later, unrecognizable fragments of the pulverized dragon were still raining down on the mountaintop.

After the dust had settled, Merryn collected her scattered wits and her lightstaff and picked her way through the dragon's wreckage to the smoking citadel. Covered from head to toe with gray dust, Timothy and the Greencloaks were just creeping out of hiding. Coughing, they stared at the gaping hole in the castle wall and then at Merryn. No one spoke for a stunned minute.

Bembor cleared his throat, and the other Greencloaks looked to him expectantly. Bembor always knew the right thing to say. "Never have I seen a more courageous—or foolhardy—act," he declared. "You might have lost your life and killed us in the bargain! Whatever possessed you to do such a thing?"

Merryn stared at the ground. She was exhausted, and her head felt as if the dragon had driven it through the portcullis. "I don't know," she replied tonelessly. Then she burst into tears.

Queen Marlis wrapped a consoling arm about her shoulders. "There, there, you poor dear," she murmured. "What's done is done. You were only trying to help. You're a very brave girl to risk your life for us, and we're all immensely proud of you."

"Hear, hear!" chorused Gwynneth and Elwyn.

"Do you think they'll make us fix the hole?" asked Opio. Gemmio snorted and yanked down his brother's hood again.

"Quiet!" Scanlon hissed. "Someone's coming!"

Out of the dust and smoke swirling in the breach emerged a tall man in a heavy black cloak. He gawked at the ruin of the castle's defenses and muttered something unintelligible. Then he noticed Merryn and her friends. Gesturing at the shattered gates, he spoke angrily in a musical language. To her utmost astonishment, Merryn found she could understand him.

"Couldn't you have used the servants' entrance?"

Bembor haltingly replied in the same language. "I apologize for the damage to your castle. Dead dragons oft land in the most awkward of places. We'll find a way to make this up to you."

The man appeared not to hear him. Looking dazed, he kicked at the dragon's remains. Then he picked up a piece of petrified tail. "'When the gates shall fall from a stony foe . . .'" he murmured. "Could it be? But what could turn a *draig* to stone?"

"Only the power of Gaelathane," said Bembor, and Merryn held up her lightstaff. Blinded by its radiance, the startled stranger dropped the tail fragment and covered his eyes.

"Who are you, and what are you doing outside the walls at this perilous hour of the night?" he growled.

Bembor bowed. "I am Bembor son of Brenthor. My companions and I have been knocking on your gates, hoping to be let in. We have come from a far country through the swamps and are in desperate need of food and lodging. Please—may we enter?"

The man snorted. "We don't hold with tramps and beggars up here. The queen would have my head if I let you in. She probably will anyway once she sees this breach, and that will be the end of Dewi son of Dylan, bailiff of Castell Mawr."

Dewi's eyes took in Merryn, and he frowned. "I am sorry. I'd like to help you, but the choice is not mine to make. These are hard times for us all. You may stay the night outside if you wish, but you must leave at first light. Dear me! To think that I should have lived to see Galdur's Gate thrown down and burned."

"Please, sir!" Merryn cried in Common Speech. "Don't blame my friends. We couldn't get into your castle, so I used my staff—" She raised her rod again, and its light fell on Marlis's face.

Dewi gasped and staggered as if struck. "A *croen-esmwyth!*" he croaked in a strangled voice. Rushing forward, he tore off Scanlon's cloak, then Rolin's. Merryn thought his eyes would fall out of their sockets. "You are all . . . all—" he sputtered.

"What's gotten into this fellow? Has he lost his senses?" the Greencloaks asked Bembor. The old man shook his head. "This is incredible. Our friend here is speaking 'Low Llwcymraeg,' an ancient Lucambrian dialect that until now existed only in written form on some parchments that survived the Dark Years. However, his actions are as puzzling to me as they are to you."

Dewi son of Dylan stood by impatiently. "You must come with me at once," he said. "Except for her." He pointed at Merryn.

"She is our friend and we will not leave without her," said Bembor firmly. "Either all of us go or we all stay right here."

Dewi waved his hand imperiously. "*Ffrind* or not, she is a *gwas* girl, and I cannot allow her to enter the queen's presence."

Merryn opened her mouth, and strange words tumbled out. "I . . . am not a *gwas*," she said. "I am freeborn, not a servant."

Bembor wheeled on her. "You speak the same dialect! You know Low Llwcymraeg, too! I must be dreaming. Timothy, where did you find this girl? Did you teach her our language?"

"I first met her in Beechtown, and no, I didn't teach her Lucambrian. I don't know that language myself!"

Dewi tugged on Bembor's cloak. "Hurry! Bring along the girl if you must, but do not keep the queen waiting. We have stayed out here too long already. Other *dreigiau* will follow this one."

Climbing over heaps of petrified dragon parts, Merryn and company followed Dewi through the archways of the inner and outer curtain walls. Becloaked men hurried past the visitors carrying wooden beams and sheets of iron. Merryn supposed these were to be used for blocking up the breached walls.

The bailiff started across a shadowy courtyard where more men were milling about. In the dark, Merryn ran into a wooden pole standing in the hard-packed earth. Similar poles were set in the ground at intervals, creating a forest of tall spears.

"What are these for?" she asked, rubbing her shins.

Dewi smiled grimly. "Those shafts are sharpened to impale any *draig* foolish enough to fly over our walls and attack us."

"It seems you've thought of everything," said Bembor.

"Not everything," said Dewi darkly. He led the visitors past some thatched huts parting a river of milky moonbeams. "That's the Hall of Meeting," he said, pointing at a low building slouching in the shadows. Farther along, he stopped before the base of the inner tower. "And this is the Carreg Keep," he whispered, as if fearing to wake the spire's sleeping stones. Opening a narrow door at the bottom, he led his guests inside.

With her lightstaff, Merryn illuminated a cavernous, cellar-like space. Crates and sacks, wooden casks and barrels were piled high against the walls, as if to buttress them against the dragons.

"In case of a siege, the Keep is stocked with enough provisions and water to last us a year," Dewi proudly explained.

"How many souls live within the castle walls?" asked Opio.

"Over five thousand," Dewi replied. "However, the stores are reserved for the royal family, nobles and the *Aberth*."

Merryn was about to ask what an "aberth" was when she noticed a colossal iron cage standing in the chamber's center. Resembling a dragon's skeleton set on end, the vast scaffolding rose through a hole in the ceiling and vanished into the darkness.

Merryn felt drawn to the tapering cage like a magnet to metal. Heedless of the Greencloaks' warning cries, she ran to the ribbed structure and passed through one of the four iron-rimmed, arched openings that were cut into its base.

Impelled by some ancient instinct, she raised her arms, not knowing what to expect. When nothing happened, she dropped them again, disappointed. A hand fell upon her shoulder.

"Those days are long gone, wench," said Dewi. "Now we must do everything the hard way. Let's see you put your hands to the *sgaffaldwaith*." Leading Merryn back through the arch, he began climbing the scaffolding ladderlike from the outside. Merryn followed. She found the going easy, since the rough iron rungs were closely set. She glanced down and her head spun.

"Look out!" "Be careful!" shouted the others from below.

"I'm all right," she cheerfully called back. "It's perfectly safe up here. You'd better hurry, or you'll be left behind!"

While her companions crept up the scaffolding, Merryn flew along behind Dewi, her hands and feet guided by some sixth sense. "Twenty-five, twenty-six . . . thirty . . .," she counted as she passed through the Carreg Keep's floors. At each landing, oval holes in the framework allowed climbers access into or out of the cage, although Merryn couldn't see why anyone would want to climb the scaffolding on the inside.

"Thirty-nine, forty," she gasped, and then the dragon's ribcage ended in an open ring that was level with the last landing. Merryn climbed out onto the floor to find Dewi waiting for her.

"Not bad, for a gwas," he allowed. Merryn could see he was pleased, though he tried to hide it behind a scowl.

"I told you before that I'm not—" She stopped mid-sentence as a hand grabbed her ankle.

"Oh! I'm so sorry," said Queen Marlis. She released her grip on Merryn and pulled herself panting onto the landing. "Dear me, what a climb that was! I must be out of shape."

In quick order, Rolin, Scanlon, Elwyn, Timothy, Gwynneth and Gemmio followed. Then Bembor crawled out and flopped down on the floor. "I'm too old for this sort of thing," he groaned.

"At least you beat Opio," Rolin said, helping him up.

"Is this all of you?" asked Dewi. Merryn translated, since Bembor hadn't quite recovered from the climb.

"I'm afraid not," said Gemmio. "My brother is still down there. He doesn't like climbing or heights. He'll be along soon."

"Soon" had stretched into five minutes when at last the sound of wheezing echoed up the scaffolding, and a sweat-soaked Opio heaved into sight. Gemmio pulled him onto the landing.

"Why must we always climb to the top floor?" Opio grumbled. "Couldn't we have stayed on the first floor instead?"

Merryn translated, and Dewi laughed. "As *crwyn-esmwyth* and draig-slayers," he said, "you will have the high honor of sharing the top of the Carreg Keep with the queen and her son."

"We're sleeping . . . up . . . here?" Opio gasped. "What about food? What about drink? What about the dragons?"

"What about them?" said Dewi. "Not even dragons can break through three feet of solid stone. As for your meals, we have a well-stocked larder and kitchen on this floor."

"In the meantime," King Rolin muttered, "please try to behave as if you hadn't just fallen off the potato wagon!"

While the grownups talked, Merryn slipped off to explore. She discovered that the landing served as a circular corridor connecting a ring of rooms. Oddly enough, covering the stone ceiling was an iron grid whose purpose Merryn couldn't guess.

Cutting short her investigations, she joined the others outside a door carved with leafy designs. Dewi knocked and then entered, closing the door behind him. Presently, the door opened again, and Dewi ushered his charges into a dingy chamber filled with racks of glass beakers, bottles and tubes. A sharp, unpleasant smell reminiscent of dragon's breath hung in the air.

Amidst the shelving sat a hooded figure at a desk. Long, gray braids spilled out of the hood, which hid the face within. Slender fingers beckoned. "*Croeso, ffrindiau.* Welcome, friends."

"May I introduce to you Queen Rowena," Dewi announced in a resounding voice. "Your Highness, here are the crwyn-esmwyth— and this." He pointed at Merryn and grimaced.

While Bembor interpreted, Merryn cringed. Would the queen order her to be scourged with whips or thrown out of the castle?

Bembor asked, "Queen Rowena, do you understand Common Speech, and if so, may we use it in your presence?"

"Certainly," the queen replied, speaking in that language. "Tell me, now: Who are you and whence have you come? We have not seen any crwyn-esmwyth here in many a year. Indeed, according to Dewi, your coming may have been prophesied from long ago:

When the gates shall fall from a stony foe,
And the green is gone that once did flow;
Then the smooth ones come from a far kingdom,
With a loved one sold for a servant's sum.

Rolin answered, "Most of us hail from a country known as 'Lucambra,' where I am king and my wife Marlis here is queen. These are our children, Elwyn and Gwynneth; my chief deputy, Scanlon son of Emmer; Lucambra's high chancellor, Bembor son of Brenthor; and Gemmio and Opio, my trusted advisors."

"It is a pleasure to make your acquaintance," Rowena said. "I apologize for the cramped quarters. Rarely do I entertain guests in my study. As you may imagine, the *cors dreigiau*—the marsh dragons, that is—discourage visitors. We are most grateful to you for slaying one of the beasts, although Dewi tells me it cost us our front gates." As she spoke, the bailiff brought in enough stools and chairs for everyone to sit.

Merryn squirmed while Rolin apologized for the ruined gates and promised to pay handsomely for their repair. Borrowing Merryn's lightstaff, he explained how its miraculous powers had brought down dozens of the marauding marsh dragons.

"How marvelous!" said Rowena. "Where might we obtain another such wand? In all our years of battling these accursed creatures, we have never found an easy way to destroy them."

"Alas, fair queen," said Bembor, "neither mortal hand nor sorcerer's spell fashioned this staff. Rather, it was cut from the Tree of Life by King Gaelathane, Creator of man and woman, bird and beast, mountain and hill, marsh and sea—and of love itself."

"Your King is unknown in my realm, I fear," said the queen. "That reminds me: You have neglected to introduce the last two members of your party. May I know their names?"

"My pardon, good lady," said King Rolin. "These are Timothy son of Garth and Merryn daughter of—?"

"Just Merryn," she mumbled. She no longer had a mother.

"Very well," the king said. "They both hail from Thalmos."

"I have not heard of it," said Rowena. "However, we may know that land by another name. Vast are the uncharted territories that lie to the south and west of our marshes, and strangely woven are the tales that travelers bring with them thence."

"Queen Rowena, what is *your* country called?" asked Marlis.

"*Gwinwydden*—'Vineland,' in your tongue. Tell me more about Merryn. The girl intrigues me; how did she come here?"

The Greencloaks pointedly stared at Merryn. "How *did* you end up in this place, anyway?" they asked her.

"The same way you did. I came from the hill!" she said. "You were lucky enough to be sitting at the top of it, but I was swept into a cave underneath it when the floodwaters caught me."

The Lucambrians exchanged perplexed glances. Then Timothy cleared his throat and beginning with the seizure of Rolc's ship, described his and Merryn's encounter with the Greenies and their deadly swamp. His friends looked askance at him.

"That's the most absurd story I've ever heard," said Gemmio. "Vines that can move ships? Green men? Green mist?"

"Please let him finish," said Queen Rowena.

"After I escaped," Timothy went on, "I stuck around to keep watch over you, Merryn. I spent some long, hungry weeks spying on you and the Greenies from that hill. I've got the mosquito bites to prove it, too. Most mornings after the green swamp gas burned off—but before anyone was stirring—I scavenged scraps from your campground." He grinned. "You're not a bad cook!"

Merryn blushed. So that explained the camp's tidiness! She began to weep. "Why didn't you tell me you were still alive? And how did you get out of the Hole in the first place?"

Timothy looked pleased with himself. "When the Greenies were using me as 'bait' for that river barge and I warned it off instead, I retrieved one of the vines the bargemen had hacked off. I wrapped it around my body beneath my tunic and waited until King Bart had dropped me into the 'death swamp.' Then I purposely let the strogarns carry me toward the Hole, where I unwound the chopped-off vine and flung one end into the trees. As I had hoped, the vine-tip curled around a branch. Then I swung across the swamp onto dry ground, just as the Greenies do." He thumped Merryn's shoulder. "I didn't reveal myself to you for fear of endangering your life. Then as time went on and I saw you weren't able to escape, I decided to call for help."

Merryn's head ached. "But—where would you find help in the middle of the marsh with the Greenies so close at hand?"

"That was easy," said Timothy with a smile. Unbuttoning his tunic partway down, he pulled out a silver pipe hanging on a gold chain. "This whistle was a gift from a friend of mine named Keeneye," he said. "Blowing on it produces a pitch far beyond the reach of human hearing, but easily heard by griffins."

"Griffins!" Merryn said. "I thought they existed only in fairy tales." Though her mother disapproved of reading ("A perfect waste of time and a shortcut to the poorhouse, if you ask me!"), Merryn often borrowed books from the vicar and read them in her secret streamside hideaway. Her favorite was *Dragons and Their Ilk*, although her encounter with the real thing had already dampened her enthusiasm for studying the creatures.

"Sometimes *we* wish griffins were purely mythical," said Scanlon with a sigh. "Especially when they're hungry."

"Our ancient legends speak of such beasts, although I have never heard of any living in Vineland," Rowena remarked. She shot a glance at Dewi, who shook his head and shrugged.

"At any rate," Timothy continued, "the griffins not only showed up, but they brought my friends with them."

"Interrupting a delightful mushroom-gathering expedition in the Beechtown hills, I might add," said Gemmio wistfully.

"And forcing us to leave Meghan at her Grandfather Gannon's," added Marlis. "I just hope she can manage without us."

"And stranding us on that mosquito-ridden hill for three days in the driving rain," said Scanlon crossly. "You wouldn't let us climb the torsil, either, though I never understood why."

"I couldn't desert Merryn!" Timothy shot back. "If it hadn't been for the flood, we could have rushed the Greenies' camp and rescued the poor girl. As it was, I was about to go down when our torsil shivered and I guessed that Merryn had made passage."

"Torsil? Made passage?" Merryn said, bewildered.

"She really doesn't know what's happened to her," murmured Marlis. "You see, dear, torsil trees don't behave the way ordinary trees do. If you climb one to the very top and then down again, you'll end up in another world, in this case, Vineland."

"'Touch the top, then drop,'" chorused the Greencloaks.

The queen wore a thoughtful look. "We know of these 'torsyls.' We call them *hudo* trees, and few of us dare climb them."

"But I didn't climb any trees today!" Merryn protested.

"Was your cave full of tree roots, then?" Rolin asked.

"Lots!" Merryn replied, and she shuddered at the thought.

"The mystery's solved!" cried Marlis. "'Roots and shoots!' Isn't that what you always say about the torsils, Grandpop?"

"Yes, that's right," Bembor gruffly replied. "Passing under a torsil's roots will send you to the tree's 'other side' just as readily as climbing it will. And don't call me 'Grandpop'!"

Icy water. Gasping for air. Panic. Curtains of clinging roots. The dead end. Merryn trembled. The Grotto hadn't extended completely through the hill at all. Those strangling roots had actually sent her into another world! "I want to go home—now!"

"Look at yourself, child," said Queen Rowena. "You *are* home at last, and like it or not, home is Gwinwydden."

Again the words of Low Llwcymraeg sprang to Merryn's lips. "*Na!*" she cried, balling up her fists. "Beechtown is my home, or at least it was." Surely this was all just a dream!

A low chuckle stirred in Rowena's throat. "Nay," she replied in the same language. "You are one of us." She drew back her hood. The queen's face was pockmarked, a mirror of Merryn's own.

CHAPTER 11

The Greenstone

W hat happened to you?" gasped Gwynneth.

"Hush, daughter!" Marlis scolded her. "You mustn't ask such questions of your elders, much less of a queen. It's impertinent."

Queen Rowena laughed. "It's no more impertinent than my calling you 'croen-esmwyth,' meaning 'smooth-skin' in Common Speech." Timothy and Merryn traded knowing looks as the queen removed her long cloak. Beneath it, she wore a sleeveless golden gown. Like her face, her exposed arms were covered with sores.

"Now let us see your skin, Merryn, if we may," she said.

Gazing into the queen's kindly eyes, Merryn couldn't help but obey. She rolled up her smock sleeves and held out her arms.

"Oh, my," said Rowena sympathetically. "Your pocks have become infected. We have a special ointment that will ease the pain and swelling. It's made of *lafant*—lavender—and comfrey."

"Will it make my skin whole again?" asked Merryn.

Rowena hung her head. "How I wish we could find such a cure!" She gestured at the rows of shelves. "Do you see all this? I have spent years searching in vain for a salve that would restore our skin to what it was before the dreigiau arrived."

"You used to be smooth skinned?" Elwyn asked.

"Many generations ago, yes," Rowena replied. "Then came the dreigiau—the dragons—and the swamp mist."

"What color was the mist?" asked Timothy sharply.

"Green—as it was in your world," said Rowena. "It had the same effect here as it did on your robbers. You see, all of us in Vineland once resembled the Greenies as you described them."

"You were a Greenie?" Merryn gasped.

The queen laughed. "We call ourselves 'the People of the Mist,' or 'mist-people.' In our vining days, we practiced the leafy arts, creating works of beauty and building stone fortresses. The Castell Mawr—the 'Great Castle'—is one of the last and largest of its kind; the dreigiau destroyed most of the others. Now we live in the shadow of those glory days, as one of our bards has sung,

> How glad were our days when our hearts knew no wrong;
> How bright were our ways when our runners grew long;
> For upon hilly crest we did build castles grand,
> And east unto west our brave kingdom spanned.
>
> Alas, came the night when the fickle mist failed,
> And a long, bitter blight left us leafless and frail;
> Now shriveled and shorn in our smoke-darkened halls,
> We still languish forlorn behind four stony walls.
>
> Please green us again, O Marsh Mist of the Mount;
> Do come out of your den, and flow from the Fount
> That hides in the Hill, with the split 'cross its top;
> We're still dying to know just what made you stop!

"Then you have the green mist here, too!" said Timothy.

"Although we call it the *niwl gwyrdd*, it means the same thing," said the queen. "What I do not yet understand is how this fog—and Merryn, too—found their way into your world. Perhaps you should finish telling us about yourself, Merryn."

The words leapt from Merryn's mouth, so relieved was she to recount the sorry story of her life. Opio seemed to take special interest in the way she had earned her nickname, "Hoppy."

"Your father's the brewmaster?" he said. "Now there's a man worth knowing! Perhaps he could teach us the finer points of brewing our own drink. Lucambrian ale tastes like swamp water. Next time I'm in Beechtown, I may look him up."

"You can't," said Merryn miserably. "He's a Greenie, too—or was." How she missed him! Not for the first time she wondered where the storm had blown him and whether he had survived the ordeal. "King Bart says, 'Once a Greenie, always a Greenie.'"

"Not necessarily," said Queen Rowena. "Look at me. My vines withered on me long ago, as they must have also on you."

Merryn was horrified. "Me—a Greenie?" She had learned to accept others who had sprouted leaves—even her own father—but it was quite another matter to see herself as a mulberry-girl. "No!" she cried. "You're wrong! I never was a Greenie and I never will be! Leave me alone; I just want to go back home!" Bursting into tears, she rushed out the door and into the hallway.

"Wait, Merryn!" Marlis called after her.

I don't belong here! thought Merryn as she raced down the corridor. *The sooner I leave this place, the better.* She had passed the queen's study three times before realizing she was running in circles. Where was she to go? Even with her lightstaff, she would be hard pressed to fend off all the dragons—and the castle road was now impassable. She needed somewhere to hide and think.

She tried some of the doors opposite the queen's study, but all were locked. Slumping to the floor with her back to the wall, Merryn began to weep again. A sob died in her throat as her weeping was echoed—but from behind the nearest door. Putting her ear to it, she heard muffled crying. She rattled the doorknob, and the crying stopped. "Are you all right?" she called out.

"Get away from there."

Startled, Merryn looked up. A torch-bearing figure was advancing upon her. At first Merryn thought it was a ghost, but then she saw the apparition was a lithe mist-girl clad in a sleeveless shift. Her comely face shone through waves of jet-black hair that fell about her shoulders like ravens' feathers.

"My name is Cari," the torchbearer said. "You must be the gwas girl that arrived tonight with the crwyn-esmwyth."

Merryn felt the heat rising in her cheeks. Would these people never listen? "I'm not a gwas girl!" she protested.

Cari brushed the hair out of her eyes. "Of course you are. No Hood would leave herself so shamefully uncovered."

Falling back on old habits, Merryn adjusted her ragged smock, but her pocked skin still showed through, and without her scarf, she couldn't hide her neck and face. "What of it?" she snapped.

Cari rolled her green eyes. "Only the Hoods—royalty, nobles, yeomen—have the Right of Coverage. The rest of us must show our arms, faces and necks, at least while indoors."

Merryn recalled that almost everyone she'd seen in the court-yard and the castle was wearing a hooded cape or cloak, usually black. "Why can't servants cover themselves, too?" she asked.

Cari was aghast. "Why, then nobody would know who was a peasant or a servant and who wasn't! I could lose my position as the queen's maid for going cloaked. At least the Hoods let us girls wear our hair long. That way, we don't feel so naked."

Merryn patted down her own hair. She must look a fright after being dragged through water, muck and mire. Longing to sink into the floor, she tried the doorknob again.

"Don't," Cari said and drew her away from the door.

"Can't we have a peek? I heard someone crying inside!"

"No!" Cari's face went fury-white, and she brushed a quick tear from her eye. "No one, but no one except Dewi son of Dylan may enter the chamber of the *Aberth*—the Protector."

"The Protector?" Merryn said. She took another look at the door and was surprised to see words and phrases in Low Llwcymraeg and Common Speech carved in its scarred wood. Most of the messages were declarations of farewell, love or gratitude, such as, "Good-bye!" "I will never forget you!" "I'll miss you!" "I will always love you!" and "Thank you!" In the stone lintel above the door more words were written, but the shadows cast by Cari's torch blotted out all of them but the last one: DREIGIAU.

Cari tugged on Merryn's sleeve. "Come away from here. If the bailiff catches us near this door, we could both be punished."

Merryn let herself be led back to the queen's study, where her friends were enjoying a supper of duck eggs, fish, and cattail-pollen bread slathered with honey, all washed down with goat's milk.

While Cari attended to the queen, Merryn wolfed down five thick slabs of honey-smothered bread and a full flagon of milk. The bread tasted sweeter than Baker Wornick's finest cakes.

A knock came at the door. Dewi opened it, and a young man of Timothy's age and build swaggered in. Hooded and cloaked like the other mist-people, he was tall and rugged looking, and his eyes burned with a fierce green fire. "Hello, Mother," he said.

"This is my son, Huw," said the queen. "Huw, these are the crwyn-esmwyth who have come from afar to meet us. Then we have Merryn, who is one of us and yet not one of us."

Huw ignored the newcomers, but Merryn thought he and Cari locked eyes for a smoldering instant. "The work of repairing the breach is going apace," he said. "The patch should hold for now." He glared at the Greencloaks. "Let us hope the dreigiau don't put it to the test before we can rebuild the gates and portcullis." With that, he turned on his heel and stalked out the door.

"It was a pleasure to meet you, too," muttered Gemmio.

Scanlon stood and bowed to Rowena. "We wish to thank you, good queen, for your hospitality. We'd like to know, though, whether we are in any danger here of, ah, well, *sprouting*."

Rowena laughed. Then her haggard features turned somber. "You have nothing to fear," she said. "In our land, at least, the marsh mist is no more. The loss has been a bitter one for us to bear, seeing that we may have been the cause of it."

"I should think you'd be glad of the chance to become smooth skinned again," said Rolin. "Isn't that what you've wanted?"

"At first, that's what we thought as well," Rowena replied. "Once our leaves and vines had withered and dropped off, however, they left these weeping sores." She threw Merryn a keen glance. "They torment a body like bedbug bites, don't they?"

Nodding, Merryn risked a furtive scratch behind her knee. She wondered if the queen's salve would ease the itching as well.

Rowena continued, "You see, we lived so long with our leaves that life has become very difficult without them. When I realized our sores would never heal properly, I bent all my efforts toward bringing back the green mist—so far without success."

"But what makes the mist?" asked Elwyn.

From her desk drawer, Rowena took a plain wooden box about four inches wide by six inches long. Opening it, she removed an oblong, deep-green stone, the twin of Merryn's own.

"You are looking at my dearest possession and the source of the marsh mist," said the queen reverently. "A greenstone."

Merryn gasped and backed into a shelf, knocking it over with a tinkling crash. Shattered glassware flew everywhere.

"Is she always so clumsy?" Opio asked Timothy.

"Only around castles," Timothy replied with a wink.

"Whatever is the matter with you, girl?" Rowena demanded.

"Nothing," Merryn replied. She tugged on the pouch-string that hung around her neck. Thankfully, her stone was still hidden under her shift. Like the lightstaff, it had stayed with her through mud, flood and dragonfire. However, if she revealed her green treasure, would the queen take it from her by force?

While Gwynneth and Marlis helped Merryn clean up the broken glassware, Bembor examined Rowena's greenstone. "I've never seen the like," he said. "It looks similar to a piece of polished jade or emerald. How does it produce the mist, anyway?"

"I wish I knew," said the queen. "Marsh water makes it slimy; vinegar makes it shiny; ale makes it froth; my lotions, potions and powders make it stink, but nothing makes it mist."

"Have you tried boiling it in quince sauce?" Merryn asked. She shrank back as the others stared at her in frank disbelief.

"Quince sauce!?" they said. "Where did you get that notion?"

"What is a quince?" Rowena asked.

As matters stood, there were no quinces in the castle (or anywhere else in Vineland, for that matter), but Cari scrounged up a few moldy apples from the kitchen. "Will these do?" she asked.

"I suppose so," Merryn said, feeling nervous. She didn't want to admit that she wasn't certain what had first set off her own stone. Perhaps it was the iron in Milly's pot, or the cooking water, or the temperature of the sauce, or even the sugar and spices.

Right or wrong, Merryn helped the queen peel and cut up the apples, which they dumped into a pot. Cari fetched water to cover the fruit and set the pan over a flame to simmer.

No one spoke as the applesauce started to *glop-glop*, filling the room with a delicious, tangy odor. With trembling hands, Rowena dropped her greenstone into the pot. Breathless moments passed, but only white steam roiled off the sauce's surface. Then big, green bubbles began forming. Popping, they released clouds of bilious green gas that drifted toward the onlookers.

CHAPTER 12

Singing in the Washroom

Though Merryn might have been a Greenie once, she wasn't anxious to become one again. As soon as the green fog began floating toward her, she bolted for the door. A green-cloaked stampede followed her into the corridor. Dewi and Rowena emerged at a more leisurely pace, after the queen had doused the flame and retrieved her greenstone from the applesauce.

"This is wonderful!" Rowena exclaimed. "Boiling the stone! Why didn't I think of it before? Now if only we had more of these things, we could make enough mist to do some real good!"

"It looked like plenty of mist to me," said Merryn.

Dewi shook his head. "One greenstone probably won't produce enough niwl gwyrdd for a complete *blaguryn*—a 'budding out.' We can't risk that, especially where the queen is concerned. I have seen those who had only a taste of the mist instead of a full dose." He shuddered. "It was horrible. They always died."

Bembor took Merryn aside and quietly asked her, "How did you know that boiled fruit would cause the stone to mist?"

Merryn hitched up her shoulders in imitation of a casual shrug. "I don't know," she hedged. "I've seen my mother use quince sauce for lots of things. It's good for burns and bee-stings, for sore throats and stomachaches. We even make beer out of it."

Bembor gave her a hard look but said nothing. Feeling itchy, Merryn clawed at her weeping sores. Her half-baked answer would have to do until she could think of something better.

"I bid you good-night, dear guests," Rowena said. "Dewi will show you to your quarters. 'May your vines grow long!'"

Dewi unlocked five rooms, two on one side of the queen's study and three on the other. Each had a lancet window and was furnished with thin mats and thinner blankets. Merryn shivered. Even in summer, the Castell Mawr was drafty and cold. She wondered if the mist-people ever built fires. Oddly, none of the rooms had beds, chairs, stools or benches. Perhaps her hosts hadn't needed such things before they had lost their leaves.

Rolin and Marlis shared one room; Gemmio and Opio another; Bembor and Scanlon a third; Timothy and Elwyn a fourth; and Gwynneth and Merryn, the last. Dewi had a room to himself. The queen slept in her study rather than retiring to her bedroom.

While Gwynneth and Timothy talked in the hall, Merryn stole into her room and lay down. Tears flooded her eyes. Would she ever see home, brewery and Beechtown again, or was Vineland to be her new home? And could the prophesied "loved one sold for a servant's sum" refer to her? Lulled by fiddle music floating through the window, she dreamt of Rolc-faced dragons.

When she awoke, hale summer sunshine was streaming through the window, casting a bright bar on the opposite wall. Banded with light and shadow, Cari was squatting on the floor.

"You're awake, are you?" she said. "You've nearly slept the day away. I brought you breakfast." On Merryn's mat, she placed a tray filled with dishes of broiled frogs' legs, steamed marsh marigold roots and wild currants. Accustomed as she was to marsh fare, Merryn set to her meal with relish. When she had finished, Cari removed the tray of empty dishes and made for the door.

"Now come along," she said, beckoning to Merryn. "We've got to get you properly cleaned up, and then we'll have some fun."

Merryn followed the gwas to a room beside the Protector's. Inside sat a tub of steaming water flanked by closets and cupboards. Opposite the tub stood another door, bound with iron bands. A mirror, soap and towels lay at the ready, along with a clean, white tunic. Tears of gratitude filled Merryn's eyes. She hadn't taken a real bath with hot water in months. Mostly she'd made do by scrubbing herself with scratchy horsetails.

"We collect rainwater in cisterns," Cari was saying. "Nobody likes to bathe in swamp scum! Just knock when you're done and I'll let you out. Oh, the queen sent along some of her special salve for you." She tossed Merryn a jar full of white cream. "Once you've bathed, rub it into your skin, and you'll feel better." Then the gwas girl backed out the door and locked it.

A gaunt, hollow-eyed waif with filthy, matted hair stared back at Merryn from the mirror. She spent the next hour scrubbing the grime out of her skin, and even then, a marshy odor still clung to her. After bathing, she toweled dry and applied the queen's soothing salve to her sores and bruises. Then she threw on the clean tunic and studied her image in the mirror again. She appeared much more like her old self, except for the haunted look in her eyes.

"Cheer up!" she said aloud. "You've had a rough time of it, but now things are about to change for the better."

Going to the outer door, Merryn found it had no knob or lock on the inside! She was about to knock for Cari to open it when she heard a girl's voice singing mournfully through the inner door. Merryn pressed her ear to the door and listened:

I sit alone, a bird in barren cage,
My only wish, to stretch my wounded wings;
My life shall pass upon an empty page,
With none to mark the melodies I sing.

How soon I must embrace the dreaded stake,
That stands between the heavens and the earth;
Though men might say there must be some mistake,
For this, I know, my mother gave me birth.

Oh, how I yearn to kiss the rising sun,
To feel its warmth upon my feathered breast;
To ride the wind before my race is run,
To find true love before my final breath.

Alas, to ride the cart my destiny,
In satin white to stand before the king;
A broken heart my only dowry,
The circled stars my ransomed wedding ring.

Merryn cupped her hands around her mouth and whispered into the door, "Who are you? Please answer me!" However, she heard only weeping, followed by a heart-hammering silence.

Knock! Knock! Startled, Merryn realized she had forgotten about Cari. She hurried to the outer door and knocked back. Cari flung open the door and looked Merryn up and down.

"Goodness!" she said. "That bath made a new girl of you. Now let's go up on the roof and you can dry your hair in the sun."

Cari led Merryn down the hall to a roof support pillar, which was enmeshed in the same metal latticework that hung suspended from all the ceilings. With a cat's agility, Cari climbed the ladderlike grid to reach a hole covered with an iron cap. Sliding aside the cover, she pulled herself up and through.

Following her example, Merryn squirreled up the post and through the hatch to find herself on the Keep's roof, which was enclosed by a low, slotted wall. "Don't look down!" Cari was saying, but Merryn was already gazing through the ramparts. A dizzying drop of five hundred feet forced her eyes from their sockets and the breath from her lungs. She sat down suddenly.

Cari was laughing. "You'll get used to it. Everyone feels dizzy the first time. It's not so bad in the dark, though, since you can't see the ground. I often come up here of a summer's eve to see the stars. Sometimes I even spend the night, though the queen thinks it's too dangerous with all the dreigiau about. I'm not afraid. I've dealt with dragons before." From the folds of her shift Cari produced a blue shawl, which she pulled around her shoulders.

"But what about your parents? Don't they mind?"

Cari shrugged. "My parents were both killed when I was eight. After that, Queen Rowena took me in, though she hasn't adopted me because I'm a gwas. She's been like a mother to me."

"Do you have brothers and sisters?" Merryn asked.

"I have—I *had* a younger sister," said Cari lamely. "She . . . died, too. What about you? Are your parents still alive?"

"I don't know," Merryn replied. She was telling Cari of her lonely life as the brewmaster's adopted daughter when Prince Huw's hooded head appeared at the roof hatch.

"Cariad, are you up here?" he whispered.

"I am here, Huw," she said and helped him up. The two embraced. Then Huw noticed Merryn sitting by the ramparts, and he smiled sheepishly. "Sorry—I thought Cari was alone."

"That's all right," Merryn said. "Don't mind me." She was used to people ignoring her, as if the world were a great glass globe filled with life and she was always on the outside looking in.

Cari blushed. "Huw and I are . . . friends, but we can't talk when others are about. Huw's mother wouldn't approve of her son speaking with a lowly gwas. Up here, Huw can uncover and I can wear a shawl. You can, too, if you wish."

A wind gust whipped off Huw's hood and made a flapping sail of his cloak. "You won't tell anyone, will you?" he asked Merryn anxiously. "If Mother found out, Cariad would be banished."

"No, of course I won't," Merryn replied. All the same, she wished a boy would look at her the way Huw had gazed at Cari. The only looks she'd ever known were ones full of loathing.

"'Cariad' is my full name," Cari put in. "It means 'Sweetheart.' Huw likes to call me that." She threw him an affectionate smile.

Huw cleared his throat. "The queen asked me to thank you, Merryn, for helping her make the greenstone work. She says that boiling it in water also produces the niwl gwyrdd, and it's not so messy as applesauce. Now then, I promised some of our other guests a look-round. You won't mind, will you, Cariad?"

Cariad didn't, and after Huw had left, Merryn risked another peek at the ground. This time, she didn't feel faint. The marshes bunched like green quilts around sleepy hills that straggled up to distant blue mountains. Following the causeway's pale ribbon, she found "her" hill, a brown bump crowned with trees. Then with a start, she realized the swamp was looking back at her!

"The marsh—it has many eyes!" she cried.

"Eyes?" said Cari. "Oh, you're looking at the dragons' breathing holes on the tops of their heads. They have nostrils, too, but those are only for flying. Most of the time, a draig will lie just under the swamp's surface with only his back-humps and head-hump showing. That's when he uses his breathing hole."

Merryn shuddered. In the Greenies' marsh, she had actually walked upon a submerged dragon's humpy back and head! But why hadn't the beast reared up and grabbed her at the time?

All at once, a flurry of mud and water disturbed the marsh below. "What was that?" Merryn exclaimed.

"Mealtime," Cari said offhandedly. "Some poor raccoon or duck strayed too near a draig. Marsh dragons have a green fringe of skin around their heads and necks that spreads out like swamp weeds when they're lying under the water. It's a kind of disguise. They also use their long, red tongues to lure in animals and catch them. If nothing else works, they rely on the hydras."

"What are hydras?"

Cari wiggled her fingers. "You know, those tentacled things that infest the swamps. You must have seen them already."

Merryn had. "Oh. Don't the dragons eat them?"

Scratching herself, Cari said, "Probably so, when there's no other food. Hydras grow back quickly, though. They start out as little grubby things that ride on the dragons' hides and feed on the scraps that fall from the dragons' mouths. When they're large enough, the grubs drop off and burrow into the mud. Whatever the hydras can't swallow, they share with the dreigiau—and the hydras get the leftovers. Dragons are terribly sloppy eaters, you know. They have absolutely no table manners."

Merryn felt positively ill. In escaping the Greenies and their swamp, she had landed in a far less hospitable place. "Can't you ever leave the castle, then?" she asked.

"Oh, we can," said Cari. "At the end of each month, we open the gates and go outside to hunt, fish and play games. We're due for another Opening soon." Her face darkened. "This will be a special occasion. On Opening Day in the month of *Awst* we also celebrate 'Protector's Day.' It's a solemn event but also a time of feasting and merrymaking. This year, I'd give anything if the queen would cancel the celebration—or find another Aberth."

"Anybody home?" Huw crawled through the roof hatch and faced the girls, followed by Elwyn, Gwynneth and Timothy.

"Hullo!" said Elwyn. "So this is the top of the Carreg Keep. Our Hallowfast isn't nearly so tall, but the sorcathel is roomier."

"Look!" Timothy said. "There's our torsil hill by the road, but what's that bigger hill beside it?"

Huw's mouth tightened. Evidently, he felt put out at playing host when he could be spending time alone with Cari, but he knew his duty. "The larger hill on the left is known as 'Split-top Mountain.' To the right of it is 'Ifan's Hill.'"

"Ifan's Hill? Why is it called that?" Gwynneth asked.

Huw scratched his sandy hair. "Legend has it that Ifan son of Ifor was the first to discover our land by climbing a hudo tree on that hill. He called this place 'Gwinwydden' for its lush greenery, and he named the hill after himself. Like you three, he was smooth of skin, as all our people were in the days when Vineland had forested hills and fewer swamps. Then the dreigiau came, burning up the trees and generally laying waste.

"One morning, Ifan had just begun exploring Split-top when a ragged figure carrying a fiddle stepped out from behind a cedar tree. 'Who are you?' Ifan asked, quite taken aback.

"'I am who I am,' replied the man. 'I come in friendship, but be warned, Ifan son of Ifor, that if anyone climbs this mountain and the leafy tree that stands upon it, the land will be cursed for many of your generations. You will do well to heed my words, lest you bring great sorrow upon yourself and your people.'

"When Ifan swore never again to set foot on Split-top, the stranger swiftly climbed down the mountain and disappeared into the swamp. From that day on, his music has echoed over the marshes at night, although he must be hundreds of years old by now. For lack of a better name, we call him 'the Fiddler.'"

"Why haven't the dragons eaten him?" Merryn asked.

"It's a mystery," Huw replied. "We also wish we knew why the swamp hydras don't seem to bother him, either."

"That's what strogarns are called here," Merryn told Timothy.

Elwyn squinted into the distance. "If Split-top is off-limits," he said, "why do I see a track leading up to its summit?"

Huw spat. "We have Ifan to thank for the Aberth Road. Four years after the Fiddler's warning, Ifan was chasing an unusually large, black boar around his hill. Before he knew it, the boar had led him up Split-top and across its forested summit. His quarry mysteriously vanished at the edge of a great chasm that clove the mountain cleanly across, hence the name, 'Split-top.'

"Among Split-top's gloomy cedars stood a lone, leafy tree—a hudo. Had Ifan left the mountain then, our lives would be much different today! Instead, he climbed the tree and had many adventures of the most disagreeable sort. During his journeys, he came across a precious, jade-colored stone. In bringing it back with him to our world, he lost an arm and nearly his life."

"And now it belongs to your mother?" Merryn guessed.

"No, that stone comes into another story," Huw replied. "When Ifan returned, he was so guilt-stricken that he hurled the greenstone into Split-top's ravine. Years later, a green haze began drifting down from the mount at night. Next came the dreigiau, and with them, the hydras. The mist thickened until nightly, it covered the highest hills. There was no escaping it then, though if that fog still flowed today, we would be safe from it up here."

"What made it stop?" asked Gwynneth.

Huw's face turned a brilliant scarlet. "That was my fault," he muttered. "I wanted to be the first to find the source of the green fog. While the world slept, I climbed Split-top Mountain."

CHAPTER 13

Lost Lucambrians

"I forbid you from leaving this castle until further notice!" King Rhynion roared, his whips all a-quiver. Through the greenery, his shaking finger pointed at young Huw.

"Father, please don't shout," Huw said. "Don't you want to know what makes the niwl gwyrdd? I'll only have a look and then I'll come right back. We can't cower in our castle forever."

"We're not cowering!" the king bellowed. His vines whiplashed about the room, knocking over vases of flowers and baskets of summer fruit. Huw had never seen his father so agitated.

"Why won't you let me go?" he asked. "I can vine more swiftly than anyone else in the land, and I've got my sword to stab any draig that gets in my way. I'm an expert swordsman, yet you allow me to fence only with wooden dummies and sacks of flour."

The king snorted. "No sword is long enough to reach one of those fire-breathing beasts. You wouldn't stand a chance."

"I've gone out in the marshes plenty of times before," Huw argued. "I know how to avoid the dreigiau and the hydras. I've even killed a couple of hydras with my spear. I'll be careful."

The king's vines stiffened. "Even the bravest of our yeomen is no match for the dreigiau, while you are but a callow youth whose whips are still untested. Mark my words, tampering with the niwl gwyrdd will only bring trouble. Remember the fate of Ifan son of Ifor! His overweening curiosity cost him an arm."

"But Father—"

"My answer stands, Prince Huw!" King Rhynion growled.

Huw's whips wilted. "Very well, Father. Perchance when I am older, you will change your mind." He dragged out the door, his vines trailing limply behind. His mother met him in the hall.

"You mustn't take this to heart," she told him. "Your father has good reason to fear for your well-being. Many a stalwart yeoman has come to grief on those marshy flats. Be thankful you are privileged to live within these walls, where the dreigiau cannot come. Off with you now; it's time for your music lessons."

Still simmering inside, Huw did not reply. How could mastering the harp compare with feats of daring-do? The very walls that shut out the dreigiau closed him in, too, and he chafed under their cold confinement. Maybe if he found the source of the niwl gwyrdd, Dewi son of Dylan could retire the black cart.

A vine tickled him behind the ear, but it wasn't his. Touching the whip with one of his own, he discovered it belonged to his impish sister. Just the other day, she had goaded him into an egg-hurling match. After raiding the kitchen for some duck eggs, the pair had climbed onto the Carreg Keep's roof and flung them at guards on the walls. Their contest ended when one of the eggs narrowly missed their father's bald head forty stories below.

"What do you want?" Huw said gruffly.

A small mound of bluish-green foliage sidled up to him. "What did he say? What did he say? Will he let you go? Will he?"

"What did *who* say?" said Huw, already knowing what she meant and wishing she would pester the servants for a change.

"You know who! Papa, that's who. Will he let you go to the mountain? Will he? Can you take me with you? Please?"

Huw sighed heavily. His sister was much too lively for her own good, a mist-girl constantly in motion, her vines snapping and popping with a life of their own. Wherever she went, others scattered, lest they be mowed down by the "blue terror."

"He didn't go along with it," Huw told her. "Maybe I can try again next year." He brushed a leafy vine across his teary eyes and twisted another into a hard knot of anger. He *did* know how to take care of himself outside, and he would prove it!

His sister's slack-vined mound melted into the floor like wax left in direct sunlight. "I never get to do anything fun any more," she muttered and slunk down another corridor.

That night, Huw couldn't sleep. It had been a fine, late-spring day, laden with the sweet-and-sour scents of warming moor and marsh. Frogs chorused through the barred window, each one singing lustily in defense of his tiny plot of mud and reeds.

Going to the window, Huw looked out upon his father's kingdom. Moonlight falling from a sharp-starred sky frosted the landscape in pale silver. A passing owl screeched. *Even the birds are freer than I,* Huw thought. How he envied them!

Spiky shadows fouled the moon's face as hunting dragons flew over the marshes. Their harsh cries split the still night air, sending shivers up Huw's spine. Undaunted, he yanked out the window bars, which he had already loosened. Then he strapped on his sword and emptied the pockets of his sash before fastening it under his vines. Finally, he hitched a whip around his doorknob and crawled through the window into the cool, windless night.

Below, a leafy guard patrolled the courtyard. Waiting until the man passed, Huw lowered himself down the wall until he reached another barred window. Wrapping his tendrils around the rungs, he continued his descent, a green spider dangling from strands of green silk. Once on the ground, he coiled his whips and scuttled across the courtyard to the inner curtain wall. As quietly as death, he began climbing, his whispering whips seeking out tiny cracks and crevices. Halfway up, he flung a couple of vines over the wall and pulled himself to the top. After leaping the gap between the two walls, he let himself down the outer wall.

His heart was thudding wildly when he touched earth. He was free! The gates were still closed and barred, yet here he was, standing outside the Castell Mawr, alone and unchallenged.

Disdaining the winding castle road, he vined straight down the mountainside, using trees and bushes as whip-holds. The marsh oozed up to meet him, its rank breath burbling through the moonlit mist that hung over all like green smoke. Ever so lightly, Huw skated across the swamp, his whips smoothing the way like skis. Slumbering in their slimy holes, the hydras did not stir.

At last, he reached Split-top Mountain. Like a dormant volcano that vomits sickly fumes instead of molten rock, the hill spouted clouds of green fog that rolled down its flanks. The *niwl* left a sharp taste in Huw's mouth and itchy bumps on his skin.

Whip over whip, he dragged himself up the hillside to the rutted Aberth Road, which led him at last to level ground. He was feeling his way through the swirling fog when a tall, charred post suddenly loomed up. Shuddering, he gave it a wide berth.

Hurrying on, Huw came to a void where the mountain had been riven as if by a giant ax. Searing green smoke billowed out of the fissure in shimmering waves. Crowding the chasm's throat were thousands of emerald-green stones clustered as thickly as frogs' eggs in a stagnant pond. Green streamers danced on each stone, twining with others to form twisting sheets that resembled the Winter Lights weaving through the northern night sky.

Snaring a stone with his vines, Huw reeled it in and dropped it on the ground, where it lay smoking like a green coal. *Father was wrong to forbid me from coming here,* he thought. *I have found the gateway to the world's heart, and yet I still live!*

He snagged more of the stones, letting them cool before filling his sash pockets with them. On his last attempt, the stone slipped out of its viney snare and bounded into the gorge, dislodging its neighbors as it went. The trickle of green rocks became an avalanche that rattled and rumbled its way into the mist. Huw heard a final, muffled *boom* and then an uneasy silence.

He was turning to leave when something *swooshed* out of the ravine like a flock of geese. The next moment, Huw was lying face down on the ground, a terrific weight crushing his back and cracking his ribs. Tiny, haloed lights danced before his eyes. Abruptly, the pressure ceased and he could breathe again.

He rolled over. Four sinewy legs with webbed claws enclosed him in a scaly cage, while a green, glistening stomach swayed inches above his head. A marsh dragon! It must have landed right on him. The beast was rumbling. His sword! Where was his sword? The *draig* was standing on it. Huw groaned in terror.

The dragon's horrible, high-domed head swung under its belly to fix a glaring red eye on Huw. Stinking smoke poured out of the beast's flared nostrils. A strangled scream clawed its way up Huw's throat as the draig nosed at him and tore away his vines with its fangs. Having nothing else at hand, Huw dug the stones out of his sash and flung them into the beast's pink maw.

The draig gave a wheezing gasp and its eyes bulged. For a moment, Huw thought the dragon was going to cough up the stones. Instead, it swallowed them with a convulsive gulp.

Closing his eyes, Huw braced himself for the end. Then the earth shook, accompanied by rending and crashing noises. Huw raised an eyelid. The beast was moving down the mountainside, flattening bushes and trees as it lumbered along. At last, its sinuous tail slithered out of sight like a gigantic snake.

Huw nearly fainted with relief. He was still alive! Thanking his good fortune, he ran to the brow of the hill and looked down. The moonlit draig was plodding across the spit of dry land linking Split-top and Ifan's Hill. Huw retreated in the opposite direction, not noticing that the green fog was already thinning.

Ruefully concluding his tale, Huw said, "I've had many close calls, but none like that one. After I arrived home and told my parents what I'd done, they restricted me to the Carreg Keep for months. Thanks to my little caper, the green mist dried up for good. Sometimes I wish that draig had eaten me after all!"

"Why do you suppose it didn't?" asked Gwynneth.

"Maybe it choked on the stones," Elwyn suggested.

Huw shook his head. "Only at first. Then it swallowed them. However, about a year later, someone found a draig skeleton on Ifan's Hill, so I'm sure the beast died of pure indigestion!"

Reeling from the visions Huw's account had called forth, Merryn was suffering from indigestion of a different sort. To hide her distress, she asked, "If Ifan threw his greenstone into Split-top's canyon, and you threw all yours into the dragon's mouth, where did your mother get the stone she showed us?"

"I gave it to her," Huw said. "After returning to the castle, I found one last greenstone tucked away in my sash pocket."

"I still don't understand all the fuss over this green fog," said Elwyn. "It seems to me you're better off without those leaves and vines, even if it means scratching a few sores now and then."

Cari's face shone pale beneath her dark hair. "If it were only a matter of 'a few sores,' we could endure our lot. However, the marsh mist has changed us. Without it, our race is dying."

Several days later, Merryn was in her room rubbing more salve on her skin when Cari burst inside. "I have a surprise to show you!" she announced, her eyes shining with excitement. She then took a brown-and-gray pincushion out of her pocket.

"This is Drelli, my pet *draenog*," she said proudly. "Huw gave her to me for my birthday. Draenogs make wonderful pets, you know." She placed the pincushion in Merryn's cupped hands.

"Ow!" yelped Merryn. "Those spines are sharp! As I recall, back where I come from, we call these animals 'hedgehogs.'"

"I can't imagine why," said Cari, frowning. "They don't look anything like pigs or hedges to me."

A pinched nose and two beady eyes poked out from under the ball. The nose twitched and the eyes blinked.

"Why, she's unrolling!" cried Cari, clapping her hands. "She never unrolls for anyone but me. That means she likes you."

Merryn wasn't sure whether to be flattered or not. "What does a pet 'draenog' *do*?" She couldn't picture the reclusive creature performing tricks or catching mice or warding off dragons.

"I'll keep your room free of cockroaches, bedbugs and potato-lice, that's what, *no-spiner*," said a squeaky voice.

"I beg your pardon?" Merryn said. She stared at Cari and then back at Drelli. The hedgehog's tiny mouth was moving.

"Isn't that cute?" Cari said. "She makes those funny noises when I'm talking with other people. It's almost as if she's trying to talk, too. When I want her to come to me, I do this."

Pursing her lips, Cari whistled shrilly. The draenog rolled up into a ball, its prickly spines sticking out in all directions.

"Must she do that?" said the ball. "It's most annoying!"

Just then, a bell sounded. "The queen is ringing for us!" Cari said. "I hope she's all right. We mustn't keep her waiting."

Merryn handed Drelli back and the two girls hurried to the queen's study, where Dewi, Timothy and the Greencloaks were waiting outside. "There you are!" the bailiff said, throwing open the door. "You're late. The queen wishes to see you." Merryn followed the others inside, where they found Rowena lying on a cot. Vineland's queen feebly raised a bony, bloodless hand.

"Forgive me for not rising to greet you," she said. "I have not been feeling well of late. It's my sores. I'll be right as rain in a day or two. Dewi, bring our guests something to eat, won't you?"

As Dewi disappeared out the door, Huw entered the room and took a seat beside his mother's cot. His eyes found Cari's in the crowd of visitors, though no one but Merryn noticed.

"Let me speak frankly," Rowena said. "I am sure you smooth-skins are anxious to return home. The damaged castle road has been repaired, so you are free to leave. Still, I am hoping you will stay on with us a bit longer. You see, one greenstone is not sufficient to restore our leaves. We must have more. South of here lies Split-top Mountain. It is full of the stones. If someone could bring back but a bushel or two of them, I would gladly give him up to half my kingdom and anything else he desires. You could set out on Opening Day, with Merryn's shiny stick to protect you."

Merryn's insides knotted up. She couldn't bear to see Queen Rowena weak and bedridden. Yet, neither could she bring herself to reveal her own greenstone for fear of losing it to the Vinelanders. Besides, there was no way of knowing whether the second stone would produce enough additional mist to help the queen.

Rowena's eyes glittered in the torchlight. "What say you, good guests; are you willing to undertake this perilous endeavor?"

Bembor bowed. "It would be an honor to help you however we can. We ask no reward but to see our people restored to health."

Confusion flitted across the queen's haggard face. "Your people? Surely it is we who have need of the marsh mist, not you."

Marlis pulled back her cloak hood and smoothed her hair. "With Dewi's consent," she said, "Grandfather Bembor and I have been poking about in your library. We found an old book written by Ifan son of Ifor that chronicles much of Vineland's history."

Bembor produced a tattered volume from under his cloak. "I took the liberty of borrowing this to read from it a certain intriguing riddle," he said. Squinting, he held it at arm's length. "This writing is too fine for my old eyes to make out."

"May I see it?" Merryn asked. With a shrug, Lucambra's chancellor handed her the book. It felt warm and heavy in her hands. "*Dyddiadur*," she read from the cover. "'Diary.' 'The Diary of Ifan the One-Armed.'" The room fell as still as the Grotto.

"Not only can she speak Low Llwcymraeg, but she can read it as well," said Bembor softly. "Here is the real riddle that begs solving." He pointed to the top of a page. "Go on, dear girl; tell us what this says, if you are able." Merryn read:

In olden days, we oft forgot to watch our ways;
Then shadow came, a blackness burnt with blazing flame;
The tower fell, and though we rang the silver bell,
We fought and died, for never *griffwn* came beside.

We fled his breath; the draig pursued us unto death;
We sought a tree to take us far from misery;
We found a home, a place where we could freely roam;
We built a realm, with only watchmen at the helm.

I climbed a hill and held the stone that haunts us still;
I gave my arm to take that green, unchanging charm;
I hurled it hence, into the greedy gulf and thence
There rose a wraith, a phantom fog to test our faith.

The Wand'rer wept, for all my promises unkept;
He gave me hope, beyond the years of mortal scope
An heir would come, who would with beat of deadly drum
Confound the king, and unto dust the dragons bring.

But on that day, another life the king will slay
Upon a stake; another arm will fall to make
Our people free, when death retreats behind a tree,
And all's restored, removing threat of hungry horde.

Reverse the curse—

"No!" cried Huw, snatching the book out of Merryn's hands. "You mustn't read further. The last two stanzas are sacred to the Aberth, and only she and the queen may read them."

"What—or who—is an 'Aberth'?" asked King Rolin.

"And what is the 'stake' in the last stanza?" Merryn asked. She recalled hearing that word sung through the washroom door.

Rowena waved her hand dismissively. "Of such things we may not speak just now. Every mist-child knows Ifan's prophetic riddle. Neither he nor any other king of Vineland has ever unraveled its meaning, although I still have hopes for my son Huw."

"Then who is the 'Wanderer'?" Opio asked as Dewi came in and set down a tray of steaming bowls.

"Oh—*him*," said the bailiff offhandedly. "He's just a shabby tramp who roams the marshes playing his battered violin. Nowadays we call him 'the Fiddler.' I suppose he must be very old."

"What you do not know," said Bembor, "is that long years ago, our first king erected a stone tower near the sea. He called it 'the Tower of the Tree,' or 'the Hallowfast.' Later, our defenses grew lax and we neglected to post lookouts. One black day, a dragon and his cohorts fell upon us and swept away our puny forces.

"We rang a silver bell to summon our griffin allies—Ifan calls them 'griffwns'—but the creatures were either too sick or too cowardly to join the battle. Consequently, our king Elgathel was lost and the kingdom fell into shambles. The survivors fled their homes to live in caves and hollow trees. Others left Lucambra altogether and passed into various torsil worlds as exiles."

Rowena propped herself up on her cot. "What are you saying?"

Bembor's eyes shone fiercely beneath his bushy eyebrows. "I am saying the People of the Mist are 'Lost Lucambrians'!"

CHAPTER 14

The Gwledd Mawr

P oppycock!" Dewi sniffed. "Forgive me, my queen, but we are neither lost nor Luc—whatever these people call themselves."

"Hear them out, Dewi, hear them out," Rowena replied.

"That would explain why they speak Low Llwcymraeg," said Rolin. "When they broke away, their language never changed."

"It also explains their eye color," Marlis put in. "I've been noticing they have green eyes, just as we do."

"And they wear cloaks remarkably like ours, except in color," said Gemmio. "In fact, I'd say theirs are a finer cut!"

"We haven't always worn cloaks," Dewi pointed out.

Queen Rowena lifted her head and said, "If you will recall, we only stopped wearing them when the marsh mist changed us."

"It's no wonder Rowena's people set 'only watchmen at the helm,'" Opio said. "We all paid a terrible price for letting our guard down. If it weren't for Gaelathane, Lucambra would have been completely overrun with dragons, yegs and ashtags."

Huw frowned. "Who is this 'Gaelathane'?"

"He is the King of the Trees and the Maker of all things, including this place you call 'Gwinwydden,'" Scanlon replied.

"Since He wears a different guise in every world," said Rolin, "I'm guessing that in Vineland, He's your wandering 'Fiddler' who gave Ifan his poetic prophecy. Gaelathane likes riddles."

"Hrumph!" Huw snorted. "Judging from the Fiddler's garments, he must be a poor king indeed. I've seen penniless beggars dressed in finer rags than what that fellow wears."

"You mustn't judge Him by His clothing," said Gwynneth. "He only appears in humble garb because that is His nature."

"And where is this mythical king's realm?" asked Dewi.

"Gaelathane's kingdom lives in every heart that owns Him as Lord," Marlis said. "His is a dominion of love and light that grows quietly, unseen and unfelt, not marked by fences or borders or castle fortresses but by deeds of faith and charity."

"He lives in a place called 'Gaelessa,'" Merryn broke in.

The Greencloaks stared at her. "How could you possibly know about Gaelessa?" Gemmio demanded. "Few Thalmosians have ever heard of it, and fewer still believe it truly exists."

Merryn paused to scratch a maddening itch that was crawling up her back and neck. "I didn't just hear about Gaelessa. I met Gaelathane there beside a crystal lake that rang like a bell when we walked across it. I wish I could go back, too."

"You've been there?!" the Lucambrians exclaimed as one.

Beginning with her bout with the swamp fever, Merryn described meeting her Friend and crossing the glassy lake with Him. "He wouldn't let me stay," she said sadly. "After I returned to the Greenies' marsh, He met me again as Andil and gave me my staff." She didn't mention the seed He had asked her to plant.

Bembor wore a perplexed look. "Incredible! Very few people have ever journeyed to Gaelessa and returned to tell the tale."

Marlis said, "Do you know, dear girl, how most people reach Gaelessa?" When Merryn shook her head, Marlis took her to the window and pointed at the star-strewn sky. "If you love Gaelathane," she said, "when you die, He takes you to live there with Him forever. His Tree is the only way to that place."

"How can you speak of 'living' after a person dies?" puzzled Huw. "All the dead bodies I've ever seen stayed put where they lay. They didn't go anywhere at all, much less climb trees."

"That's right," said Cari. "When you're dead, you're dead."

"But the real you isn't your body," Elwyn argued. "It's just a house for your spirit, that part of you that goes on living after you're dead. The body may decay, but the spirit never dies."

"Then . . . I really did die!" Merryn murmured. While her father had been weeping over her cold, still corpse, the real Merryn had been visiting Gaelathane's country! She wondered whether the King had already welcomed her father Hamlin to Gaelessa.

"How very touching," sneered Dewi. "However, we have no need of another king. Her Majesty Queen Rowena reigns over Vineland, and that is enough for her subjects." With a worried frown, he covered the queen with a blanket. Then he passed out the soup bowls, which held stewed meat and vegetables.

Opio grimaced suspiciously at his bowl. "What is this? I like to know what I'm eating before I put it in my mouth."

"Don't put it in your mouth, then," Rolin said. "After all, we're guests here, so we should eat whatever is offered us without turning up our noses at it. This certainly smells better than the jailhouse fare you and Gemmio enjoyed in Beechtown!"

"To answer Opio's question," said Queen Rowena, "Dewi is serving us one of Vineland's delicacies, young terrapins stewed in bulrush-seed oil with new arrowhead tubers on the side."

"Turtles?" Opio said faintly, his face blanching. "Ugh!"

Scanlon grinned. "I've seen Opio face down dragons and rout a pack of batwolves without flinching, but he can't look boiled turtle in the eye because it doesn't have fur or feathers!"

"You're picking on me because you miss Medwyn," said Opio. "Anyway, I don't see *you* digging into your dinner, Emmer's son!"

"Who is Medwyn?" asked the queen.

"My wife," Scanlon said with a sigh. "We're newlyweds."

Rowena smiled at him. "Then I must make your stay with us as brief as possible so that you may return to your bride!"

Bembor hoisted a spoonful of stew. "But not, good queen, until we have done our part to help fulfill Ifan's prophecy."

Huw faced his mother. "May I remind you and our honored guests that if anyone is to fulfill Ifan's riddle, it is Ifan's heir! How much longer must we live like cornered rats within this prison of our own making? Let me wield the staff of light to rid Vineland of its vermin and reclaim the stones on Split-top Mountain!"

"Ever the rash one you are, Prince Huw," Rowena sighed.

"Don't be too sure of yourself, young man," said Bembor. "These lightstaffs have a mind of their own. They may do what you wish them to, and then again, they may not. Gaelathane has His own purposes for them, since they belong to Him."

"We'll see about that," snarled Huw. Hurling his empty bowl across the room, he stormed out the door.

"You must forgive my hot-blooded son," said the queen. "Since his father died, he has been impatient to restore the kingdom to what it was before the dreigiau came. I fear his ambitions will bring him to a bad end, and all Vineland with him."

That night, Merryn walked the Lake again in her dreams.

A week later found her at the windy top of the Carreg Keep, petrifying troublesome dragons while the mist-men finished their repairs on the gates and portcullis. She had just sent her thirtieth draig to a muddy grave when Cari appeared at the roof hatch.

"We're having a *Gwledd Mawr*—a 'Great Feast'—this evening in the Meeting Hall to celebrate the raising of the gates," she said. "You and your friends are invited to join us. Will you come?"

"I'd love to!" Merryn said, glad for any excuse to leave the exposed rooftop and her lonely, boring stint on "dragon duty." She and Cari dropped through the hatch and climbed down the sgaffaldwaith. When they stepped outside, Merryn was struck by the pungent aromas of burning peat, roasting meat and a sharp, sour smell as of ale gone bad. This last odor was wafting from a rambling structure that dwarfed the Hall of Meeting.

"What's that shed over there?" Merryn asked, pointing to it.

"Oh, that's the brewery," said Cari. "Would you like to have a look inside? I'm sure the brewmaster wouldn't mind."

Merryn could think of nothing finer. "Of course I would!"

Working their way through the crowds of people gawking at the newly raised gates, the girls reached the high-walled brewery. Cari opened the massive door and motioned Merryn inside.

Merryn gasped. Hundreds of hulking vats stood shoulder-to-shoulder in stolid rows, putting her father's brewery to shame. Workmen on ladders were pouring buckets of boiling water into some of the tanks. Others were stirring the fermenting contents with wooden paddles. As they stirred, the brewers sang:

Crush up the malt and mix with the oats;
Pour on the water and make sure it soaks;
Drain off the wort and chase off the rats;
Can't have them falling into the vats!

That's how we make the mist-men's ale!
Drink it up quick before it grows stale!
Only the best for the Hoods, so they say,
Saving the dregs for Opening Day!

Once it's all cooled, stir in the yeast;
Better be ready for the Opening feast!
Let it ferment, and when it's quite stout,
Serve it up fresh from an ample spout!

That's how we make the mist-men's ale!
Drink it up quick before it grows stale!
Only the best for the Hoods, so they say,
Saving the dregs for Opening Day!

Just then, a plump little man in a leather apron appeared and shouted at one of the workmen, "You there! Dribble! Keep your cup out of the vat! And put an arm into that paddle. You stir like a lazy washerwoman at her tub. Opening's three days away, and you fellows would rather swill ale than stir. Oops! Who are—?"

So engrossed was the man in his lecture that he had walked into Merryn, nearly bowling her over. Cari burst out laughing. "You should watch where you're going, Brewmaster Brynnor!" she said. "If I didn't know better, I'd say you'd been dipping into one of those vats yourself. How brews your ale this week?"

Brynnor broke into a grin that stretched from ear to ear. "It brews well! What errand brings the queen's comely maid into my humble shop? Has her majesty a hankering for a keg or two?"

"This is my new friend, Merryn," Cari explained. "She wanted to visit your brewery. Her father is a brewmaster, too, you see."

"Indeed?" said Brynnor. "Then I am doubly honored to make your acquaintance. I apologize for bumping into you. My name is

Brynnor of the Brew. My father was brewmaster, and his father before him. We take great pride in the quality of our ale." Wiping his hands on his apron, Brynnor bowed, showing the top of his head, which was as wrinkled and red as a newborn baby's.

"Oh!" he said, clapping a hand over his naked pate. "I suppose Cari didn't forewarn you. In my youth, a cantankerous draig burned all my hair off. I was lucky to escape with the rest of me intact. It's one of those hazards that comes with the job."

Merryn searched for the right words. "I am pleased to meet you, Brewmaster Brynnor. May your vines grow long!"

Brynnor cocked a hairless eyebrow at her. "Though my vines aren't likely to grow again, short or long, I do thank you. Since I presume you hail from another hill, what is your castle's name?"

"Ah, the Castell *Beech*," Merryn replied, flushing. Changing the subject, she remarked, "You must brew a lot of ale here."

Brynnor beamed. "That we do! For Openings, our busiest time of the month, we produce at least twenty thousand gallons."

"Twenty thousand gallons!" Merryn gasped. "How can you possibly drink so much in one day? In Beech-, I mean, in our castle, that much ale would supply us for an entire year!"

The brewmaster was about to answer when Cari cut him off. "Opening Day festivities last a whole week. Besides, we don't drink all that ale ourselves. We have lots of . . . *visitors* to help us." She tugged at Merryn's arm. "Now we really must be going. I'm sure the others are waiting for us in the Hall of Meeting."

Brynnor's pocked hand flew up in protest. "But you haven't—"

"We'll sample your brew another time," said Cari. "Thank you for your hospitality! Mind you don't fall into a vat, now."

"But—"

"We'll see you at Opening!" Cari called over her shoulder as she herded Merryn out the door.

The girls found the meeting hall filled with chattering mist-people. Most were already seated at long tables that sagged under their burdens of fruits, nuts, meats, soups and breads. Musicians wove among the tables playing flutes and stringed instruments. In one corner, sweating cooks tended cauldrons bubbling over a roaring fire. In another, more cooks were roasting a spitted haunch of meat. Smoke rose lazily through a hole in the roof.

Huw, Timothy, Elwyn and Gwynneth beckoned to the girls from a table by the wall. "Come join us! There's plenty of food," Huw called out. After the two were seated, the prince shoved a plate of meat toward Merryn. "Here, try some of this. It's juicy and tender. We're not supposed to eat until Mother arrives, but I'm sure she won't mind. She's always late for celebrations."

Merryn chewed on a piece. The meat had a muddy flavor, but it was better than muskrat. "Not bad," she said. "What is it?"

"Roast dragon," Huw replied with his mouth full of meat. Gwynneth turned pale, while Elwyn and Timothy sniggered.

"Roast dragon?" said Merryn faintly. "You actually eat—?"

Huw smirked. "Why not? How else could we feed all the hungry mouths in the Castell Mawr? Draig must be stewed before roasting, or it's as tough as—well, it's as tough as draig."

Merryn had eaten many unusual dishes during her stay in Vineland, but she drew the line at dragon. The bile rose in her throat and she gagged. Then she needed to scratch.

"It's not so bad, once you get used to it," said Cari sympathetically. "If you don't care for draig, maybe you should try the eel stew. It's very sweet." Merryn chose fish chowder. Looking famished and out of sorts, Gwynneth nibbled on a hazelnut while her brother and Timothy helped themselves to more draig.

Cari playfully ran her fingers through Huw's hair, and he lightly kissed her on the cheek. She giggled and blushed.

"Aren't you afraid of being seen together?" Merryn asked.

Flashing a smile, Cari pulled her shawl around her shoulders. "On feasts and other special occasions, we can wear whatever we like and keep whatever company we wish." As if to prove her point, she leaned over and hugged Huw. Then they kissed.

All at once, a commotion broke out at the doorway, and the Hall of Meeting fell silent. Huw and Cari froze in mid-kiss with stricken looks. Queen Rowena stood at the door, leaning on Dewi's arm. "You!" she cried, stabbing her staff at Cari. "How dare you!" Shaking off the bailiff, she hobbled over to the table, grabbed a handful of Cari's hair and yanked her to her feet.

"Is this how you repay my kindness to you, gwas?" she screeched at her. "I have treated you like a daughter, and in return, you have betrayed my trust! Speak, child, but consider your words carefully, for they may well be your last."

Knotting her fingers, Cari turned whiter than birch bark. "I— I do not understand, my lady. What have I done?"

Rowena laughed scornfully. "Do you take me for a fool? Your trysts with Prince Huw are well known to me. Heretofore I have kept silent, not wishing to embarrass my son. This time, though, you have gone too far. Not only have you stolen away his affections, but you dare embrace and kiss him in public!"

The queen nodded, and Dewi escorted her to the front of the hall, where she seated herself upon a stark, wrought iron throne. Then a burly yeoman dragged Cari before her, tore off the girl's wrap and flung it on the floor. The hall held its breath.

"Gwas," said Rowena, "I hereby sentence you to confinement in the dungeons of the Carreg Keep. At sunset on Opening Day, you will be banished outside the gates. Guards, see to it."

With a shriek, Cari fell to the floor and seized the queen's feet. "Please, please do not send me away," she wailed. "I will do whatever you wish, only let me remain here. Forgive me!"

"You will never see my face again!" Rowena replied as she rose unsteadily from her throne. "Henceforth, alone you must wander the marshes. You will live outside these walls and you will perish outside them." Kicking Cari away, the queen took four black stones from her robes and dropped them in a line between her and the huddled, sobbing girl. "A stone for every wall, a wall for every stone. Our walls have turned their faces against you."

"Our walls have turned their faces against you," echoed the other Vinelanders, and they drew their hoods over their heads.

An anguished cry wrung itself from Huw's throat. "No, Mother! For the love of my father, please don't do this! Blame me if you will, banish me if you will, but have mercy on your faithful gwas girl! She has done nothing worthy of this punishment."

Queen Rowena fixed him with a stony stare. "You are as guilty as she! Carrying on this—this illicit *romance* with my maidservant under my very nose is conduct hardly befitting a prince, let alone a son of mine. What have you to say for yourself?"

Huw clenched his fists. Then he knelt before the queen. "Love needs no defense, Mother. I apologize for deceiving you, but it was only for Cari's sake. I did not wish to see her banished. Is it so wrong to care for another of a different station than my own? Besides, who of the royal line is left for me to marry?"

Color rose in the queen's wan cheeks. "We will discuss that matter later in private. I have made my decision, and it is final."

As the guards led Cari away, Rowena beckoned to Merryn, and she timidly approached the throne. "Now that I have banished Cari, I will need a new maidservant," said the queen. "For the time being, you will take her place. Come with me, please."

CHAPTER 15

A Feisty Draenog

Merryn's first task as the queen's gwas was to take dinner down to Cari and the other prisoners. Stopping by the kitchen, she picked up the sacks of bread and meat Dewi had left inside the door. She was lugging them toward the scaffolding when several Greencloaks climbed down through the roof hatch.

"Where are you going with the bags?" King Rolin asked her.

Merryn tried to contain the raw emotions boiling up within her. "I'm bringing supper to the prisoners in the dungeon."

"I didn't know they had a dungeon here!" said Scanlon.

"Why doesn't Cari help you?" Queen Marlis asked.

Merryn burst into tears. When she found her voice again, out came the grim tale of Cari's public humiliation and banishment.

"How dreadful!" said Rolin. "Once outside the gates, she won't last long against all those dragons and hydras. The queen holds us in high esteem; perhaps one of us could talk her into releasing Cari or at least reconsidering her sentence."

"You'd better wait until she cools off a bit," Merryn sniffled. "She seemed awfully upset this afternoon. That's when she ordered me to take Cari's place. Oh, what will happen to Cari now?" Merryn covered her face and let the tears flow again.

"She'll be all right," said Marlis, patting Merryn's arm. "After all, she is not yet banished beyond the gates, and we will pray that Gaelathane changes the queen's heart before then."

"In the meantime," said Rolin, "we can't let poor Merryn drag those bags down to the dungeon all by herself."

Opio stepped forward. "I'll help her," he said gruffly. The Greencloaks all looked at one another and burst out laughing.

"Have you already forgotten how you hate climbing?" Gemmio said. "Remember, what goes down must come up again."

"I need to stretch my legs!" said Opio indignantly. "There's nothing to do up here except look out the windows, eat and sleep— and I can't sleep with those blasted dragons flapping and thumping around the Keep at night. Besides, there's bound to be some leftovers with my name on them in that assembly hall. Dewi serves good food, but I have yet to see a cake or a pie."

Chuckling, Rolin slapped Opio on the back. "At least we know where your loyalties lie—in the kitchen! I'll go with Merryn. Maybe that way I can learn something more about Cari's predicament. Then I'll see about bringing a pie back for you."

After the king had divided up the bags, leaving Merryn with the lightest, the two began climbing. Merryn nimbly scampered down the scaffolding, meeting several Vinelanders on the way. Following Dewi's directions, she found the dungeon trapdoor in a corner, but it was too heavy for her to lift. She waved her lightstaff, and Rolin quickly came to her rescue.

"Here, let me help you with that," he said, and he pulled up the heavy wooden door. Shining her lightstaff into the hole, Merryn saw a set of steps spiraling down into the dank darkness.

"Ugh!" she exclaimed. "What a gloomy, smelly place. Poor Cari!" Shouldering her bag, she followed Rolin down the stairwell. After three or four turns, the stairs ended in a low passage that led to a long bank of barred cells lit by a single torch. A cloaked figure stood before the third cell. Merryn lifted her staff.

"Who's there?" cried the visitor, whirling to face her. It was Huw, his eyes hollow in the shadows. Behind him, Cari peered through the cell's rusty iron bars, despair etched on her ashen face. Her hair was matted and disheveled, as if she had been languishing in the dungeon for months instead of only hours.

"It's just King Rolin and I," said Merryn in the bravest voice she could muster. She thrust the staff into her tunic belt.

Huw threw back his hood and spat. "Come to gloat, have you, traitor?" he growled. "I should never have trusted you. You've been spying for my mother—telling her about our secret meetings in the Keep so you could betray Cari and take her place."

"No! That's not true!" Merryn protested.

"Hey! Pipe down, will you?" grumbled a voice from the second cell. "We're trying to get some sleep in here, if you don't mind."

"I was just leaving," Huw said. Throwing Merryn a frosty stare, he pushed past her and stalked out of the dungeon.

"Let him go," said Cari wearily. "My misfortunes are not your fault, and he knows it. It was only a matter of time until his mother confronted us. He's just upset over my banishment and the queen's choice of you to replace me as her maidservant."

"Who are your neighbors?" Rolin asked as he and Merryn opened the bags of meat and bread. Merryn gave Cari a portion.

Sticking her hand through the bars, Cari pointed left. "Meet Lemmy and Welt. Lemmy made the mistake of stealing bread from the queen's kitchen, and Welt drained off a vat of Brynnor's ale for his personal use." She sighed. "I'm in fine company."

"After Opening, we're to be impaled," announced Lemmy as he and Welt reached through the bars for their share of the victuals, which they wolfed down without ceremony. Ragged and filthy, the men blended in with their equally squalid cell. Merryn covered her nose and mouth against the awful stench.

"Impaled?" she said. The word had a chilling ring to it.

Cari said, "That means they're to be thrown from the top of the Carreg Keep onto the dragon poles below. It sounds horrible, but impaling is a quicker death than being banished." She pressed her pleading face against the cell bars. "Now, please tell me: Does the queen really mean to let my sentence stand?"

Collecting the empty food bags, Rolin said, "I'd better be going. If I don't bring Opio that pie, I'll never hear the end of it."

After Rolin had left, Merryn said to Cari, "My guess is the queen doesn't really wish to banish you. In a few days, she'll tire of me and call you back into her service. Leaving you down here may be just her way of keeping you and Huw apart for now."

Cari wiped away her tears, smudging her grimy face. "She can't separate us forever! Only she and Huw remain of the royal family, so he has no one to wed. I suppose he could marry a girl of noble birth, but most of that lot are uglier than a swamp hydra. Anyway, I'm glad you're here. I have a favor to ask."

Retreating to the back of her cell, Cari returned with a spiny ball. "I need someone to care for Drelli until I'm released—or banished," she said. "Just let her out of your pocket every so often so she can forage for bugs and such. She'll need water, of course. Beyond that, she's no bother at all." Cari's voice dropped. "If the queen does banish me, Drelli is yours for good."

"Thank you—I think," said Merryn. She'd never kept a pet before, except for a frog she'd found in the garden, and that didn't count. What if an accident befell Drelli while in her care?

As she cradled the hedgehog in her hands, its mouth and snout twitched. "Just give me a warm place to sleep and a tummy scratch every so often, and we'll get along fine. You'll see."

"A warm place to sleep and a tummy scratch?" Merryn repeated, scarcely believing her ears. Drelli really *could* talk!

Cari gave Merryn a queer look. "Why, yes, I forgot to tell you: Drelli does need a comfy nook for sleeping, and she loves to have her stomach rubbed or scratched. How did you know? Do people keep draenogs as pets where you live, too?"

"No—I mean, I suppose so," Merryn replied. How very odd! Apparently, Cari hadn't heard or understood what Drelli had said, although the creature had spoken quite clearly.

"There's one more thing," said Cari, handing her a folded scrap of parchment. "If I'm not out of here by Opening Day, I'd like you to find a way to give this to the Aberth."

"But I thought nobody could enter that chamber!"

Tears welled in Cari's eyes. "She'll be let out on Opening morning for all to see. You'll have to watch for a break in the crowds, because everybody will be clamoring to catch a glimpse of her."

I was right! thought Merryn. *There is a girl in that room.* "I'll do my best, dear friend. Is there anything else I can do for you?"

"Please look after Huw, won't you? I know he is angry and bitter now, but soon he will need a friend." When Merryn promised she would, Cari cast a last, longing look at her pet. "Good-bye, little Drelli," she said softly. "Behave yourself for Merryn."

"Good-bye to you," said the hedgehog. "Don't be so sad. Next time we meet, I'll bring you some bugs to eat!"

Merryn returned to her room, where she set Drelli on the floor. The draenog didn't move. Had she died? Merryn nudged the spiky mound with her foot, but nothing happened. Then the prickly creature relaxed her spines and slowly opened.

"Ah, this is more like it!" grunted Drelli. "I've been banging around in that no-spiner's pocket for days on end." The draenog scuttled about on hidden feet like a spiny crab on wheels.

"Where did you learn to talk?" Merryn asked.

Drelli skittered back to her. "All 'nogs can talk, you ninny! I've never met a no-spiner who could understand our speech, though. Maybe you're a big 'nog whose spines have fallen off. Say, you've even got the scars to prove it. I saw them on your arms."

Merryn was about to explain where she had gotten those scars when the door creaked. She grabbed Drelli and shoved her roughly into her pocket just as Gwynneth entered the room.

"Hullo!" said the princess cheerfully. "I thought I might find you here. How do you like being Queen Rowena's new maid?"

"Well enough, so far," Merryn replied. She wished Gwynneth would go away; Drelli's spines were sticking her and she wanted to get to the bottom of the "talking hedgehog" mystery.

Gwynneth's green eyes roved about the austere room. "You're alone? I thought I heard you talking to someone else."

"I—well, I was talking to myself," Merryn lamely offered.

"Liar!"

Merryn flinched as the tiny voice pierced her pocket. Gwynneth stiffened and her mouth flew open.

"What was that?" she demanded, her eyes narrowing.

"Nothing. It's just the wind whistling past the window."

"Liar! Liar! Liar!"

Gwynneth was choking, though whether with laughter or dismay, Merryn couldn't tell. She stole a glance into her pocket. Miss Beady-Eyes glared back. "Let me out, you lying no-spiner!"

"Shush! You keep quiet!" Merryn hissed.

"I have yet to hear the wind call anyone a liar," Gwynneth said, tapping her foot. "Now who—or what—are you hiding in your pocket? You can tell me. I'm good at keeping secrets."

However, Drelli had lost her patience. All at once, she swelled up to the size of a large pine cone, and she felt like one, too. "Ow! Ow!" Merryn cried and did a frantic jig. Then she tried to pry the draenog out of her pocket. More spines stuck her fingers. "Stop that, you wretched thing!" she said. "You're hurting me!" Not knowing what else to do, she tore open her pocket. Out tumbled Drelli and rolled across the floor. Merryn ran after her. "I ought to drop you out the window!" she scolded the creature.

By now, Gwynneth was doubled over and laughing so hard tears were streaming down her face. "A hedgehog!" she gasped. "She had a hedgehog in her pocket!" Thus began the popular Lucambrian proverb, "Snug as a spiny hedgehog in a pocket."

"Aren't you going to introduce us?" asked Drelli.

Merryn sighed. "This is Gwynneth. Gwynneth, this is Drelli."

"Charmed, I'm sure," said the draenog. "Now, how about a scratch? You owe me that much at least." Merryn obliged.

"She's a feisty hedgehog, isn't she?" Gwynneth observed.

Drelli sat back and her nose wriggled. "You shouldn't call people names they don't understand. What's 'feisty' mean?"

Gwynneth took a turn stroking the draenog's belly. "It means, my dear hedgehog, that you know how to stick up for yourself!" Merryn laughed at her friend's play on words. Then Gwynneth sobered. "How long have you had the Gift?" she asked Merryn.

"What gift?" Merryn said. Did Gwynneth know about her greenstone? She felt a blush creeping up her neck.

"I mean the gift of understanding the speech of animals and other living things. Not everyone has it, you know."

"I first noticed it here, when a draig spoke to me," Merryn said. "I thought all Vineland's animals could talk but that no one knew it except me. I take it you must have this gift, too."

"I do," said the princess. "I've had it since I was a little girl. All of us Lucambrians possess this ability and Timothy, too. We don't talk about it much, especially around otherworlders."

Merryn's head hurt. "But—how did I get the Gift?"

Gwynneth regarded her with astonishment. "Now that's very peculiar. You have the Gift and you don't know how you got it?"

"No. Does it come from climbing torsil trees or eating eels?"

Stretching out on her sleeping mat, Gwynneth rested her chin on steepled fingers. "The Gift of Understanding comes only through breathing the fragrance of amenthil blossoms, but I have seen none of those trees here. You must have come across one somewhere in your travels. The flower scent is very sweet."

Merryn recalled the heady perfume of hyacinths mingled with basswood blooms. "There was one tree," she said, and she described the sapling that had sprung from the nut she planted.

"Gaelathane gave you an amenthil nut, all right," said Gwynneth. "Fortunately for you, your staff's light must have caused the tree to grow unusually rapidly. You know, in burying that seed, you ended up cultivating a personal sythan-ar."

"Sythan-ar?" said Merryn. "What's that?"

"It's a tree you plant and tend that becomes your very own for life," Gwynneth told her. "That's why it's also called a 'life tree.' All Lucambrians need one, whether they know it or not. Nowadays, the Tree of trees usually serves as our sythan-ar."

Merryn scratched herself. "Gaelathane didn't mention anything about sythan-ars or life trees. He did show me His scars and told me He had paid a price for me. What did He mean by that, and how did He become so terribly disfigured, anyway?"

Gwynneth described Gaelathane's love for His fallen creation and how He had reconciled all worlds to Himself by tasting death through His Tree. Merryn wept. The King had borne her sores and scars in His own bleeding body, even before she knew Him!

"Thank You, Gaelathane!" she murmured.

"Don't stop scratching!" Drelli said to Gwynneth.

Laughing, Merryn told the princess, "You'd better let me have another turn," and she scooted closer to the hedgehog. At that moment, a shadow fell into the room. Looking up, Merryn saw a dragon's snout at the window, and she screamed.

"Merryn! Your lightstaff!" cried Gwynneth.

Merryn's fingers frantically searched her shift, but the staff wasn't tucked in her belt where it belonged. She went numb. Andil's gift was gone. "It's not there!" she wailed. "I've lost it!"

Now she couldn't breathe. The draig was sucking all the air out of the room to feed the fires in its belly. Just as the first tongues of flame licked from its jaws, Merryn came to her senses. Throwing open the door, she launched Drelli through it, dragged Gwynneth into the corridor and slammed the door behind them.

"Run!" she screamed. Kicking Drelli along like a ball, the two girls were racing down the hall when the door exploded in a torrent of fire. Flaming cinders and blobs of burning iron flew after them, igniting small fires of their own.

Dewi's head poked out of the queen's study. Taking in the scene, he popped back inside, returning with a water bucket. This he shoved into the inferno with a long pole. With the draig's next breath, the water flashed into steam, and the flame died away.

"Dreigiau don't like steam," he told the girls as calmly as you or I might say, "Boiled eggs need salt." His gloomy face lengthened. "We don't often see attacks of this sort on the Keep, since the beasts know that whatever they cook, they can't eat!"

After the mist-men had finished putting out the fires, Merryn dropped Drelli back into her pocket and dashed down the scaffolding to the bottom floor. No lost staff lit up the darkness. Then she felt her way into the dungeon, where Cari lay curled up on the cell floor, covered with a tattered blanket. The wall torch furnished the only light in the smelly, cobwebbed space. Yet, Merryn was sure that was the last place she had seen her lightstaff.

She raced back to the scaffolding and pulled herself up the metal framework with aching arms. Upon reaching the queen's study, she flung open the door. Rowena, Dewi and Merryn's smooth-skinned friends looked up at her in alarm.

"My lightstaff—" she blurted out. "I can't find it!"

The Greencloaks groaned and exchanged horrified looks. "It's got to be somewhere around here," Opio declared. "We'll search this tower from top to bottom if need be. Lightstaffs are hard to hide, especially after dark. Believe me, we'll track it down."

Merryn felt miserable. "I've already searched. It's gone."

Dewi leaned against the wall and wept. "Who will save us now? Without that staff, we cannot collect more greenstones. Without the stones, the People of the Mist shall all wither and perish."

Watering Day

S ince the draig had made their room a smoking shambles, Merryn and Gwynneth bedded down in the library that night. The chamber was crammed from floor to ceiling with bookshelves and gave off the musty odor of mildewed parchment. Worrying over Cari and the lost lightstaff, Merryn couldn't sleep.

Everyone except Queen Rowena spent the next day scouring the Keep for the lightstaff, but all in vain. The rod had apparently returned to the Tree from which it had been taken. Gloom settled over the Castell Mawr like a thick, black blanket.

For the second night in a row, Merryn was too restless to sleep. Without her lightstaff, she could never return to her father and the other Greenies, nor could the Greencloaks go back to Lucambra. She must have dozed off, because when she opened her eyes again, a waxing moon was peering through the library window.

Tap-tap. Rolling over on her mat, Merryn looked through the doorway. Across the Keep, someone was knocking from inside one of the rooms. Then Dewi appeared with a pitcher and rapped on the washroom door. After waiting a few seconds, he entered and set the pitcher on the floor. Next, he unlocked the door connecting the washroom with the Protector's chamber. Finally, he left the room, quietly closing and locking the door behind him.

Puzzling over the bailiff's strange behavior, Merryn fell into a jumbled mosaic of dreams. In one, she was lying in the washtub, unable to move. Then Dewi unlocked the connecting door, and to Merryn's horror, a dragon emerged from the Aberth's room to devour her. In a later dream, another dragon was sitting on her chest, crushing the air and life right out of her. Her eyes flew open. Preening herself with her tongue, Drelli was comfortably splayed out like an unruly pincushion on Merryn's chest.

"Good morning!" chirped the draenog.

"Good morning!" Merryn mumbled back. "Would you mind getting off me? I don't want to be pricked again if I can help it."

"I was protecting you," Drelli retorted and scuttled onto the bed. Merryn yawned and sat up. Remembering her staff was still missing, she flopped back onto the mat. By all accounts, she had let everyone down. Couldn't she ever do anything right?

"Hello, there!" said Gwynneth to no one in particular. The princess was standing at the window, braiding her long, golden hair. "How is our hedgehog this fine morning?"

"I am getting along famously," said Drelli. "However, I'd be better if one of you no-spiners would take me outside for a decent breakfast. I've a hankering for some grubs this morning."

Merryn's stomach lurched. "Hanker away," she said, combing the rats' nests out her hair with her fingers. Since the staff had disappeared, she had lost her appetite and most of her patience as well. None too gently, she dropped Drelli into her pocket.

All at once, a jangling noise broke out in the hall, as if someone were banging on a brass bedstead. Merryn and Gwynneth rushed out the door to find Dewi flailing away on the sgaffaldwaith with an iron bar, making such a clangor that Merryn was sure every draig in Vineland was awake. Doors up and down the corridor flew open and half-dressed sleepers shuffled toward the scaffolding. In quick order, Timothy and the Lucambrians gathered around, attempting both to plug their ears and rearrange their rumpled, slept-in clothing at the same time.

"What is the meaning of this?" Bembor bellowed over the noise. "Is the Keep on fire? Have dragons broken down the gates? Are we under siege? STOP MAKING ALL THAT RACKET!"

Dewi's arm paused in mid-stroke. "Sorry!" he said. "I couldn't hear you. What was that you were saying?"

Bembor rubbed his stubbly face. "I was asking you the meaning of this—this clamor! Are you trying to wake the dead?"

"Oh," said Dewi, and he lowered his arm. "Didn't anyone tell you? Today is Watering Day. Hammering on the sgaffaldwaith is the easiest way to roust out the sleepyheads in the Keep. We need all able-bodied hands at the walls, you see."

"No, we don't see," said Opio irritably. "Is this any way to treat your guests? And what is 'Watering Day,' anyway?"

"Yes, don't you mean 'Opening Day'?" Marlis asked.

"No, no," said Dewi. "Opening is tomorrow."

"It all makes perfect sense to me now," muttered Gemmio. "I'm going back to my bed to get some more shuteye. Good-bye."

By then, however, Dewi had resumed his rattling and banging, so no one could get any further sleep. Instead, Merryn and Gwynneth fetched breakfast for the condemned prisoners.

In the dungeon, they found Cari huddled in a corner of her cell, glazed eyes staring blankly from under her tangled hair. Since she acknowledged neither her visitors nor the food they proffered, Merryn divided the dollops of porridge and beans between Lemmy and Welt, who were all too glad of the larger portions. After praying for the three prisoners, Merryn and Gwynneth took their leave of them and of the Carreg Keep.

Outside in the early morning sun, they were swept into the crowds of people swirling about the tower. Men, women and children were working together to lower the dragon poles and stack them in piles, while others had formed a bucket brigade at the brewery. Merryn had just sent Drelli scurrying off in search of breakfast when she heard a couple of familiar voices.

"There you are!" called Timothy and Elwyn, and they ducked through a thicket of dragon poles to join the two girls. The young men were fairly glowing with anticipation.

"Isn't this some holiday?" Elwyn shouted. "It looks as if they're making room for games and dances here in the courtyard. We've already breakfasted on dragon stew in the meeting hall. You ought to try some. The boiled cabbage is excellent as well."

Gwynneth turned a pasty white. Wrinkling her nose, Merryn wondered how the Vinelanders killed dragons for meat. "No, thanks," she told Elwyn. "Lizard doesn't agree with me, especially the fire-breathing variety. Say, what's going on over there?" She pointed to the bucket brigade. Yeomen using ropes and windlasses were hauling the buckets to the top of the walls, where other men dumped their contents into long wooden troughs.

Just then, Merryn spotted Brynnor's stout, aproned figure and waved him over. The brewmaster waved back and forged toward her through the crowd, which obligingly parted for him.

"Well, well! Here for the festivities, are we?" he said, beaming as if he were Watering Day's official host. "Could I offer you all a pint of my finest? I save only the best for my guests!"

When Merryn and her friends politely declined his offer, Brynnor acted as though they'd slapped him. "This isn't the same stuff they're serving up on the walls," he told them indignantly.

"But what is in those buckets?" Merryn asked.

Brynnor gave her an astonished look. "Didn't Cari tell you?"

"She's been banished," Merryn replied, a lump growing in her throat. Fighting back tears, she told the brewmaster what had taken place in the Hall of Meeting two days earlier.

Brynnor rubbed his hairless head. "Well, I never! To think I should live to see Queen Rowena banishing such a faithful servant. No wonder her son hasn't come by this morning." His voice dropped to a whisper. "Mark my words, if the queen does exile that poor girl, she'll lose Prince Huw and the kingdom, too. I fear her illness is affecting her judgement. It won't be long now."

"It won't be long until what?" Timothy asked.

The brewmaster wiped his eyes. "In time, our sores become gnawing ulcers that ravage the mind and body until only a raving husk is left. My own parents died that way. I hope the queen has the sense to let Huw take the throne before it's too late."

Sploosh! Someone dropped a bucket near the Keep, spilling its contents. "Watch what you're doing!" Brynnor scolded the man. "I spent all month making that!" Merryn dipped her finger in the pool of liquid spreading over the ground and tasted it. Her eyes watered. It was ale, but the flavor was ranker than old socks.

"Ugh!" she said. "This tastes terrible! How can you drink it?"

Brynnor's whole head flushed. "We don't! You just sampled the dregs. I wouldn't serve that garbage to my worst enemy."

"Is that why you're going to dump most of it over the walls?"

"Just listen to the Watering Chant!" Brynnor replied. As the windlasses groaned under their burdens, the yeomen sang,

> Up to the top, don't let it drop,
> Hoist with a will, heave-ho!
> Into the trough, splatter and slop,
> Haul with a will, heigh-ho!
>
> Dragons will dine, all in a line,
> Up on the wall, slip-slurp!
> Sweeter than wine from the budding vine,
> Sit on the wall, sip-burp!
>
> Slobber and swill, drink your fill,
> Fly to the wall, flip-flap!
> High on the hill, where dreams distill,
> Fall from the wall, split-splat!
>
> Wallow and weep, outside the Keep,
> Dizzy green snake, don't snore!
> Slumber and sleep, all in a heap,
> And when you awake, drink more!

The last bucket was winched up the wall and its reeking brew tipped out. Silence fell over the courtyard as every hand ceased its labors. Then four figures appeared, one at each corner of the castle battlements. Raising curved rams' horns, they blew a long, rising note that echoed harshly across the marshes.

The air began to thrum. Though the day was clear and bright, a chill shadow fell over the castle. Then with a thunder of wings, hordes of marsh dragons descended on the walls.

Merryn screamed and reached for her lightstaff, forgetting it was gone. Before she could blink, four or five scaly dragons had hunkered around each trough, their heads deep inside. When one left, another flew down to take its place. Fights broke out, usually ending when one of the beasts chased off another.

Their paunches bulging, the sated dragons would fly away or fall off the walls. Some stayed to hover around the castle, evidently hoping for another turn at the troughs. Still others flew mad-dash around the Carreg Keep and down into the courtyard, speeding recklessly between walls and buildings. One draig failed to make a turn and smacked headfirst into the Keep, collapsing in a bloody heap at the bottom. Mist-men with long knives and saws ran over and began butchering the carcass.

"'Dregs for the dreigiau!'" Brynnor chortled. "That one will stew up nicely. My ale softens and sweetens the meat." Other thuds outside the walls signaled the demise of more dragons.

"Very clever," said Elwyn. "So that's how you bring down your dinner. But isn't this a lot of work for so little return?"

Brynnor straightened his apron. "You would be right, if draig meat were all we wanted. However, Waterings are much more than a chance to fill our larders. Dreigiau will come from miles around to swill themselves silly. It's almost comical to watch. You see, strong drink makes every draig a draenog. That's why we always have a Watering the day before each Opening. If the *bragwr*—the brewer— has done his job, when those dragons have licked up the lees to-night, they'll be as docile as kittens."

"How did you learn in the first place that your dragons have a taste for liquor?" Gwynneth asked. "Surely one of them didn't just fly down and politely ask for a keg of your ale!"

The brewmaster smiled ruefully. "One did, once, but he asked for more than ale. Anyway, we have King Rhynion to thank for Watering and Opening Days. One evening, he'd had a bit too much to drink and somehow got out of the castle. As the story goes, he was staggering about with a pint of bitters, singing dirges, when a draig swooped down and swallowed him whole."

"How perfectly dreadful!" Merryn exclaimed. "Why was he singing dirges? Had someone died?"

A pensive look softened the brewmaster's pocked face. "He was mourning the loss of his only daughter, who was taken by a draig. The poor man never quite recovered from the shock."

"I should think not," said Merryn. She had seen many a drunk in Beechtown who had lost a loved one to accident or illness and was trying in vain to drown his sorrows in a mug of beer.

"At any rate," Brynnor went on, "after swallowing the king in his cups, the draig showed up again the next day, roaring drunk, and it tried to break into our distillery. Word must have gotten around the swamp, because dozens of dreigiau started hanging about the castle, just waiting for some poor sod to take his glass of ale in an unprotected spot. We lost many fine mist-men that way until someone deduced what the dreigiau were really after. Then we hit upon the idea of using their weakness against them by keeping them soused, senseless and silly."

As the brewmaster spoke, a draig dropped to the ground by the Keep. Smoke curling from its jaws, it stupidly stared at Merryn and her companions, who all scrambled to get out of its way. Unfazed, Drelli kept nudging Merryn for a tummy scratching.

"Not now!" she whispered to the draenog.

"Easy there, Mr. Draig," said Brynnor soothingly. "Go to sleep and dream of eating sheep. Lots and lots of sheep." Reaching out, he stroked the beast's snout just between its eyes. The dragon's eyelids drooped. Then the befuddled draig ponderously rolled over on its side and began snoring. Brynnor rubbed its belly.

"You see?" he said. "You could stick a knife in this one and it wouldn't feel a thing. Now it's your turn, Merryn."

Merryn touched a wing. It felt smooth and rubbery. Emboldened, she tugged on a wing claw. The dragon's eye snapped open, burning red with an inner fire. "Thief!" hissed the beast. Then the eyelid closed and the drunken draig resumed its snoring.

CHAPTER 17

Dragon Races

Why would that draig call you a thief?" Gwynneth asked. Watching dragons soar with deadly grace against a backdrop of dark, scudding clouds, she and Merryn were standing on the rooftop of the Carreg Keep, where they had retreated to escape the mad revelry in the courtyard below. A few dragons still vied for places at the troughs, but most lay wallowing on the ground beside equally drunk mist-men. The shrieks and laughter of merrymakers carried faintly up to the top of the tower.

"I really couldn't say why," Merryn airily replied. "My, don't you love the view up here? See how the shadows chase the light across the marshes! At times like this, it's difficult to believe Ifan son of Ifor could have brought a curse upon this land."

"Let me out!" squealed Merryn's pocket.

"Oh, very well," she sighed. Slipping her hand beneath Drelli's soft underbelly, she drew the draenog out of her pocket.

Once outside, Drelli swelled, her spines bristling. "I can tell you all you want to know about Ifan the One-Armed," she said. "He was my great-great-great-great grandaddy's no-spiner."

Merryn stared at the talking pincushion. "He was what?"

"I think she's trying to say in a backward way that her ancestor was Ifan's pet," said Gwynneth.

"'Draebold the Draig-Slayer,' they called him," Drelli continued. "He would crawl along the back of a sleeping draig and drop into its breathing hole. Then he'd stick out his spines. The dragon would go half-mad with pain, but it couldn't dislodge him, no matter how hard it tried. Eventually, it would suffocate.

"After losing his arm, Ifan took to drinking heavily. When he was in an ill humor, he also took to bouncing Draebold off the wall. Thanks to his springy spines, my ancestor suffered no serious injury, but one day, Ifan missed the wall. Draebold flew out the window and was swallowed by a passing dragon, putting an end to both. That was the forty-ninth draig to die by Draebold's spines, a record no 'nog before or since has matched."

"A very admirable feat," said Gwynneth dryly. "However, you still haven't told us what became of Ifan himself."

Drelli's spines rippled irritably. "What does it matter? He was a no-spiner, after all. I believe he died in this very tower, and his bones still lie buried somewhere in the castle."

"Then he didn't lose his other arm?" asked Merryn. "The riddle he wrote says, 'Another life the king will slay upon a stake; *another arm will fall.*' Doesn't that mean Ifan himself?"

"Why would we call him 'Ifan the One-Armed' if he'd lost both?" Drelli retorted. "Then he'd be 'Ifan the Armless'! Honestly, haven't you no-spiners any common sense?"

Gwynneth laughed. "Her wit is as sharp as her spines!"

Undaunted, Merryn demanded, "Then what does the first part of that verse mean? Queen Rowena wouldn't tell us about the 'stake' or the Aberth, either. Can you, dear draenog?"

"No!" squealed Drelli. "You mustn't ask! You mustn't ask!" With that, she rolled off Merryn's hand and into her pocket, and nothing Merryn could do would coax the draenog out again.

The roof hatch's metal cover rattled, and Dewi's head poked through. "Excuse me," he said in a worried tone. "Have you seen Prince Huw? He is supposed to preside over the draig races, but he's not in his room. Nobody knows where he is."

The girls glanced at each other. "We haven't seen him," said Merryn. Thinking back, she realized she'd last seen Huw in the dungeon two nights before. Cari had asked her to look after the prince, but how could she, when he had made himself scarce?

"Draig races?" Gwynneth asked. "What are those?"

Dewi's face wrinkled in disgust. He spat on the stones. "Watering Days always bring out the worst in our people," he said. "When the dreigiau have filled their bellies with ale, the castle riffraff climb on their backs and hold races, if you can call them that. A drunken draig can barely crawl, let alone fly. When he sobers up, though, watch out! There's nothing so foul tempered as a draig with a hangover, as you'll soon see for yourselves."

Having nothing else to do, the two girls decided to take in the races. Just beyond the gates, they found hundreds of belching dragons lolling on the ground, their webbed feet sticking up. However, some of the beasts still stood bleary eyed and more or less upright in the hot sun. Five or six bore motley riders upon their humpy backs. One of the drunken men fell off his mount.

"Ugh!" said Gwynneth. "I don't know who is more soused, those dragons or their riders! They smell awful, too."

Sickened, Merryn looked away. Her parents had sheltered her from Beechtown's seamier side, especially the dock district, where drunks abounded. Was this what Hamlin's brew did to men? For the first time in her life, she felt ashamed of her father.

"Let the races begin!" cried a yeoman dressed in a bright blue tunic, and he sounded a trumpet. The spectators cheered as the cursing riders kicked their mounts and goaded them with sticks. With protesting honks and bellows, the dragons lurched off. One of them craned its long neck back to snap at its tormentor.

"Watch out, Dyllo!" barked an old man standing nearby. "That un's got a nasty hangover already." Flicking his thumb at the lumbering dragons, he wheezed at the girls, "I ain't never seen a race where everybody finished in one piece." He took a pull from a jug that hung from a cord around his neck. With hairy arms and callused knuckles that hung to the ground, the old-timer couldn't have been over four feet tall in his boots. His pasty eyes floated like lumps of lard in his mottled, pea-soup face.

"Er, are you a dragon-rider, too?" asked Merryn.

"Not on yer life! Garrick o' the Gate I am," the man slurred, and he bowed with elaborate courtesy. The bow continued until Garrick had toppled over, his jug lying beneath him. The girls ran to his side and tried to help him up, but he waved them off.

"I ain't so old I can't keep me pins under me!" he muttered, clutching the jug to his chest with a suspicious glare.

Suddenly, a shriek rang out, and one of the dragons staggered away riderless. Garrick toasted the draig with his jug. "Fare thee well, Dyllo! Shwallowin's quicker'n roastin', or so I've—urk!—heard. Either way, you're dead as dead." Bobbing his head to Merryn, the gatekeeper tottered off toward the castle.

"Girls! What are you doing out here?" Queen Marlis was steering a course for them with jaw set and green eyes flashing.

"We were just watching the races," Gwynneth mumbled.

"Well, this is a disgraceful spectacle!" Marlis returned. "You'd better come with me. Prince Huw has disappeared, and the queen has asked us all to help her find him."

Merryn and her companions searched the Keep the rest of that day, without success. Rumors abounded: Prince Huw had been snatched away by a draig; he had gone off on his own to bring back more greenstones; he had climbed a hudo to take a bride from another world. In the end, all agreed that something terrible must have befallen the prince. Dread seized the Castell Mawr's occupants, and Queen Rowena mourned alone in her bedroom.

That evening, Merryn stood at the library window, gazing out at the bloodstained remnants of a rich summer's sunset. As the light surrendered to darkness, she whispered a prayer from the heart: "Gaelathane, please help us find Huw, wherever he is!"

"He does know where the prince has gone, my dear." Queen Marlis was standing in the doorway, beckoning to her. "You must be hungry. Why don't you join us in the kitchen? Dewi has prepared us a late supper of smoked muskrat and wild *reis*."

"I would love to—" Merryn began, when a searing flash lit up the velvet sky. As she shielded her eyes against the blinding brightness, another burst of light stabbed the marshy gloom.

"Lightning!" said Marlis, joining Merryn at the window. "I just love summer lightning storms, don't you? Let's wait for the thunder to sound. It shouldn't take long. Those strikes were close."

As more tongues of light silently beamed and faded, a horrible suspicion reared up like a hydra in Merryn's heart. "No!" she wailed and rushed out the door and down the hall.

"Listen for the thunder!" Marlis called after her. Merryn paid her no attention. Flying up the iron-meshed pillar and through the roof hatch, she braced herself against a freshening wind that moaned over the dusky marshes and howled across the ramparts. *There.* White light lanced the sky again, illumining a dark, hideous shape that plunged earthward. All doubt fled Merryn's mind. Someone was petrifying dragons with her lightstaff!

After tumbling down the hatch, she raced along the corridor to the kitchen, where her friends were quietly finishing their suppers. Picking at a piece of meat, Queen Rowena lay on her cot, her eyes sunken pools of shadow above gaunt, lined cheeks.

"Sit down, child, and have something to eat," she murmured. "Oh, dear. Oh, dear. What has become of that son of mine? Did a draig slay him? Is he lost in the swamp? The pox take us!"

Huw. Merryn's mind whirled back to the night when she had first visited Cari in the dungeon. The prince had brushed past her on his way out. Could he have stolen her lightstaff then? Yearning to scratch herself silly, she announced, "I think I know where Huw is. He's outside the walls using my lightstaff!"

Food-laden forks and spoons froze midway between mouths and plates as Merryn described what she had just witnessed from the Keep's rooftop. The Greencloaks nodded knowingly, while Rowena wilted on her cot. "How could my son stoop to thieving from a guest?" she cried. "Has he gone completely mad?"

"As Ifan's heir," said Dewi, "he may have taken it upon himself to fulfill Ifan's riddle; he has threatened as much before. I mean my queen no disrespect, but if I may say so, you have driven him to this desperate act by banishing your maidservant, Cari."

"Send out a search party!" the queen commanded.

Dewi rushed out the door. While the Greencloaks prayed, Merryn helped herself to the muskrat and dark-grained wild rice. Hardly had she cleaned her plate when a knock came at the door and three tall yeomen entered, their hooded cloaks dripping.

"Your majesty, we found this on the road," one of the men said, and he handed the queen a muddy, rumpled garment.

With infinite care, Rowena examined the cloth, and a shudder ran through her frail frame. "It is as I feared!" she declared. "This cloak belonged to my son, who is no more. Prince Huw is dead."

"Prince Huw is dead; may he rest in peace!" cried Dewi, and he pulled his hood over his face. Merryn and Gwynneth wept.

The queen bowed her head and said softly, "Bailiff, bring me Cari." Dewi snapped his fingers, and the yeomen disappeared. They returned minutes later with the haggard, hollow-eyed prisoner. Cari swayed on her feet as she stood before the queen.

"Cariad," Rowena began in a cracking voice. "Your name suits you well, for you have ever been my beloved servant. Yet, I have unjustly shamed you. Please accept my humble and sincere apologies, such as they are. I do not wish to go to my grave with your blood on my conscience. Dewi, help me up, please."

Leaning heavily on the bailiff, the queen rose from her cot. From her cloak pocket she removed four black stones. Making her way around the kitchen, she placed a stone in each corner. Then she faced Cari and intoned, "A stone for every wall, a wall for every stone. Our walls have turned their faces and their favor toward you. Let all present witness this Turning of the Walls."

"We are witnesses!" said Dewi, grinning. A guarded hope flickered in Cari's eyes, and she stood a little straighter.

"You will no longer serve me as my maid-in-waiting, however," the queen went on. "Instead, I offer you a place in my heart more befitting your years of service and the love I have for you."

Rowena nodded, and Dewi brought forth a folded black garment. Taking it from him, she placed the cloak around Cari's shoulders and drew the hood over her head, saying, "This day I name you Cariad, heir of Rowena and princess of Vineland."

"But . . . but . . . why?" asked Cari, tears filling her eyes.

The queen embraced her. "Today, I have lost my only son, but I have also gained the daughter you have always been to me. I see now that Huw loved you more than life itself. I did not realize when I banished you that I was banishing him as well."

The blood drained from Cari's face. "How so, m'lady?"

Rowena sagged back onto her cot. "It appears Huw has gone beyond the walls of this life. A draig has carried him off. I am sorry, daughter. This loss must be a grievous blow to you."

A sigh that might have been a cry escaped Cari's lips, and she gracefully collapsed to the floor.

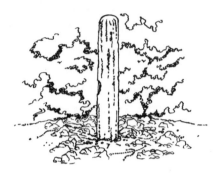

CHAPTER 18

Ifan's Heir

Earlier that very day, Huw had slipped out of the castle gates. Uncovered like one of the servants, he trusted that in the pre-dawn's half-light no one would recognize him. He stiffened as a *Clang! Clang!* rang out from the castle, but it was only the Watering summons. He couldn't have picked a better day. Watchmen and dreigiau alike would be steeping themselves in Brynnor's brew. He smiled grimly. For once, he was glad the Castell Mawr had let its guard down, if only for a few hours.

Following the road, he dashed from boulder to boulder until he had put the castle and its prying eyes out of sight. Then he removed a coil of rope from his knapsack. Using a special knot, he tied one end of the rope around a sturdy scrub oak and lowered himself over the edge of the road, much as he had done years before using his own vines instead of a rope. He reached the road's next level with only two feet of rope to spare. Tugging on the end, he loosened the knot some sixty feet above and repeated the process, this time using a rock as an anchor. In this way, he rapidly rappelled down the mountain's west face.

The sun's disc had rolled halfway above the steaming horizon when Huw coiled his rope and struck out for the causeway. The dreigiau would be watching that elevated road, but it was the fastest and most direct route to Split-top Mountain. As Ifan's heir, he was about to "confound the king," though the thought of it set his knees to knocking. When he returned in triumph with a sackful of greenstones, his mother would surely release Cariad from that disgusting dungeon cell and let him marry her.

Gaining the causeway, he pulled the shining rod out of the scabbard he had strapped to his waist inside his cloak. As Gwinwydden's next king, he was the staff's rightful owner, not some scabby gwas girl from a backward, mistless world.

"Come and get me, dreigiau!" he yelled, waving the staff. However, nothing disturbed the placid, frog-plopping surface of the great green marsh. With so many dragons swilling at the ale-troughs, perhaps he wouldn't need Merryn's staff after all.

Barely a hundred yards from the hill, he spotted telltale ripples in the swamp and slowed his pace. Sure enough, a draig was lifting out of the water. In moments, it was soaring overhead, spitting flames and smoke, its red eyes glaring down at him. Huw pointed the staff at it and a shaft of light sent the petrified beast hurtling into the marsh. He hardly had time to congratulate himself before another draig swooped down on him. Again he aimed the lightstaff, and again, lizard flesh froze like flint.

Shaking the staff, he performed a victory dance. "Tremble in your marsh, O dreigiau!" he shouted. "The staff king is your new lord! Flee my wrath, or I shall turn the very blood in your veins to stone. Gwinwydden belongs to the People of the Mist now!"

And so it went. With each fallen draig, Huw roared out his triumph and his challenge. Slowly but steadily, he advanced along the causeway until he was about halfway to the twin hills. Then the dragons fell upon him from all quarters like a horde of angry hornets. Hours later, he was still defending the same rocky piece of road, hardly able to raise his aching staff arm.

"Begone, you scaly devils!" he shrieked. "I'll kill you all if I have to, but still you cannot stop me. How many more of your stinking kind must I strike to stone before you leave me be?"

Thousands, came their silent taunt as the sun's eye shuttered, closing over the earth. Darkness oozed out of the marsh and flooded the causeway. Changing arms, Huw aimed the staff at sunlit dragons still diving on him from the indigo sky. Sweat poured in rivulets down his body, and he shed his cloak.

Whump. The biggest draig Huw had ever seen landed squarely in front of him and furled its wings. Up came the staff to petrify the beast, but no light beam shot out of it. In a panic, Huw shook the staff and aimed it again, but nothing happened. *These lightstaffs have a mind of their own,* Bembor had said. *They may do what you wish them to, and then again, they may not.*

The draig made throaty sounds like garbled speech. "So this is the new king of dragonkind!" it said with a mocking dragon grin. "We'll see about that. What a whelp you are! You and your shining stick are powerless against me, for I am Drundaig!"

"Get away from me, you filthy draig!" Huw shouted, but the beast seized him in its steely talons. In his terror, he dropped the lightstaff and it rolled off the causeway and into the marsh.

"Nooo!" he screamed as the draig tore him from the earth.

CHAPTER 19

Noni

S tars and fire. Merryn was floating along the causeway, dressed in a white linen gown. A fickle breeze had sprung up, driving rain-heavy clouds across the shrinking sky. The air was so sticky warm that even the fat raindrops spattering out of the gloom felt like grease hot off a griddle. Rolc's whip cracked over the sleeping swamps. Thunder boomed. *Where is my staff?*

Now she stood among rain-drenched rocks before a tall finger pointing accusingly at the drowning sky. Lightning crackled all around her, dancing on the stones and shattering boulders with ear-numbing explosions. *What is this place? Why am I here?*

Lightning flashed again, and in its garish light, the finger leapt to life. A dragon pole it seemed, though stouter and shorter. Dark streaks ran down its lightning-scarred length. Seized by a nameless dread, Merryn fell to her knees before the post and wept.

KROOM! A thunderbolt struck the pole, setting it afire and throwing Merryn on her back. After she had picked herself up, a white wisp fluttered out of her pocket and sailed into the fire, where it flared into flame. Merryn recognized it as Cari's note.

She awoke soaked with sweat, her heart racing. Gwynneth's snoring had mercifully called her away from the charred pole and the horror behind it. The wind moaned through the window, bringing with it sudden sprays of rain. Merryn tried to collect her senses. Realizing that further rest was out of the question, she set out for the washroom to refresh herself.

The corridor lay silent and empty, basking in the wavering light cast by the smoking wall torches. Inside the washroom, Merryn found some water in a pitcher to splash on her face. She was about to leave when—*Rap! Rap!*—someone knocked on the outer door. Squeezing into a closet, she pulled its door partway shut behind her just as boot soles scraped against stone. Peering out, she saw Dewi place something on the tub. Then he unlocked the connecting door, knocked on it and left the washroom.

Cautiously, Merryn pushed open the closet door and stepped out. A white linen dress lay draped over the tub. Merryn held it up to herself. The frock might have been made to fit her, and with a shock, she recognized it as the gown she had worn in her dream. She was about to try it on when the side door opened, and out stepped a maiden of about her own age and frame with raven-black hair and vaguely familiar features. Seeing Merryn, the girl put her hand to her mouth and blanched.

"Who are you, and what are you doing in here?" she gasped. "Don't you know your life is forfeit for seeing me?"

Merryn's heart faltered. "I'm sorry," she said. "I've been wanting to meet you, so I hid when Dewi came in. I suppose he brought this for you." She handed over the frock. "My name is Merryn, by the way. What's yours?"

"I am the Aberth," replied the girl bleakly. "Isn't that enough? You should go before Dewi catches you here. Just count yourself fortunate that I came in before you put on my gown, or you would be wearing it in my stead tomorrow. Now please leave."

Recalling the words she'd once heard through the door, Merryn said, "You'll be wed in that dress tomorrow, won't you?"

The Aberth shuddered. "In a manner of speaking, yes. But you should already know that, being a gwas. Have you come to torment me on the eve of my passion? If so, get out now!"

"I only wanted to know why you're always cooped up in that room. Have you done something wrong? If so, maybe I can help."

"You cannot help me," said the Aberth. "Nobody can. My fate was sealed long ago, and I must meet it on the morrow. Unless you wish to take my place, leave while you still can, gwas."

"But—what is your fate?" Merryn asked. Before the other girl could answer, knuckles drummed on the washroom's outer door. Sharply drawing in her breath, the Aberth seized Merryn's wrist and dragged her into the next room, slamming the door behind her. Then she knocked on it three times. Immediately afterward, Merryn heard the deadbolt drive home with a 'click.'

"Fool!" hissed the girl, turning on her. "I told you to leave when you had the chance, and now you're trapped in here with me! What am I going to do with you?" She began pacing about the room, wringing her hands and weeping softly.

The Protector's room was nearly as spare as Cari's dungeon cell. No paintings graced its bare walls; no carpet covered its cold stone floor; no curtains softened the barred window nor blocked the fierce, rain-laden breeze. Its only furnishings were a wooden table and chair opposite an iron bedstead—the first Merryn had seen in the Castell Mawr. At least the Aberth slept in comfort! On the table, a brass lamp splashed spooky, long-necked shadows across the walls and ceiling, as of light-devouring dragons.

Ignoring Merryn, the other girl cast off her shift and shrugged into the lacy gown. Then she threw herself on the bed and with short, furious jabs, began sewing on a dress similar to the one she already wore. After pricking herself, she dropped the needle and thread and broke into sobs, burying her face in the gown.

"What's wrong? Don't you like to sew?" Merryn asked.

"During her last year in office," said the girl dully, "an Aberth must sew a gown for her successor. This one is nearly done."

Merryn said, "If you don't tell me your name, I'll have to call you 'Miss Aberth,' and I don't think you'd like that very much."

"It's Noni, if you must know. Not that it matters."

Like a dove's wing, the dream-note fluttered before Merryn's eyes and burst into flame. Digging into her pocket, she drew out the folded parchment and handed it to Noni. "Cari, the queen's former maidservant, asked me to give you this. I almost forgot."

With fevered haste, Noni opened the note and read it. Then she closed her eyes and held the paper to her breast. "*Fe'th garaf hyd byth.* 'I will always love thee.' Thank you for giving me this message. I am content. My sister Cariad has not forgotten me."

"Your sister!" Merryn exclaimed. "Cari is your sister?"

Noni went to the window, where the wind blew her hair back in feathery black wings. "My true name is Noniad, sister of Cariad. She is two years older than I, although I have already aged a lifetime sitting in this miserable cell. How I miss my Cari! If you should see her again, please give her my love."

"Cari told me her sister was dead. Was there another sister?"

"No, she was speaking of me. From the hour an Aberth goes into seclusion, she is mourned as one dead, for no one may see or speak with her save Dewi son of Dylan, upon pain of death. Would that I could fly away from this place! Would that I could cast myself off the Keep and end my bitter life, for I dread the coming of the dawn. So speaks the Song of the Aberth:

> Oh, how I yearn to kiss the rising sun,
> To feel its warmth upon my feathered breast;
> To ride the wind before my race is run,
> To find true love before my final breath.

"Why don't you wish to wed?" Merryn said. "Is it the groom?"

Noni forced a laugh that came out as a sob. "Of course it's the groom! He's as ugly and wicked as they come, but he's also the king, and no Aberth has ever refused him and lived. Who are you that knows not of these things? A simpleton, perhaps?"

"I am a foreigner," said Merryn quietly, and she explained how she and her friends had come to the Castell Mawr.

Weeping, Noni collapsed on the bed. "I am sorry," she said. "I thought everybody knew. Cari should have told you."

Merryn came over and sat beside her. "How did you become an Aberth in the first place? Did the queen appoint you?"

Noni held out her arms. Her skin was smooth and clear, free of the pocks and cankers that plagued the other mist-people. "The king requires an unblemished, smooth-skinned maiden," she said. "In the days when the niwl gwyrdd still flowed from Split-top Mountain, only the very young looked as I do. After a child was weaned, her parents would take her down to a stone hut by the marsh for the Rites of the Mist. All night they would remain together during the child's blaguryn—her 'breaking out.'

"All that changed when the king came, demanding that we bring to him a fresh-skinned maiden once every year as tribute. From that day since, every mist-mother has lived in constant fear until her female child is weaned and the stones are thrown."

"Do you mean they throw stones at the children?" Merryn asked, horrified. What a savage world Vineland was!

"No, though that would be a kinder fate. In the month of *Ebrill*, the name of every newly weaned girl in the kingdom is written upon a stone. The stones are collected, and the day after Protector's Day, the bailiff scatters them from the top of this tower. The girl whose stone falls the farthest from the Keep becomes the newest Aberth, and her relatives are richly rewarded, for there is no higher honor in the land than to be chosen Aberth. The maiden is imprisoned in a room like this one until she comes of age, when she is presented to the king as his bride.

> A king he was, in search of one to wed;
> He promised peace but brought us blood instead;
> With armored might, he shed our puny spears;
> His price for peace has cost us all our tears.

"There are more of you in the castle, then?" Merryn asked.

"Sadly, yes. Twelve is the usual number. Sometimes the stones are thrown twice a year, in case an Aberth falls ill or dies. When I'm gone, another girl will occupy my room, and so on."

"How awful!" Merryn cried, clenching her fists. "Who would serve such a cruel king? You have a secure fortress here; resist him! Throw off his yoke and pay him tribute no more!"

"We cannot. He has threatened to destroy the source of the niwl gwyrdd if we rebel against him, and all our people with it. His is the chief law that hangs over our kingdom like a spear."

"What law is that?" asked Merryn.

Noni turned to stare at her. "Have you not read what is written above my door? *Rhaid rhoi eu haeddiant dyledus i'r dreigiau.* 'The dreigiau must have their due.' It is a consequence of the curse that Ifan son of Ifor brought upon us."

"Why should you also pay tribute to the dragons?"

Noni sighed heavily. "You do not understand. The king whom I must meet tomorrow is the king of all the dreigiau, and he shall slay me upon the stake, as he has slain many another maiden:

How soon I must embrace the dreaded stake,
That stands between the heavens and the earth;
Though men might say there must be some mistake,
For this, I know, my mother gave me birth.

'Aberth,' you see, means much more than 'Protector,' although that is my purpose. The word really means 'Sacrifice.'"

"You're a sacrifice?!" gasped Merryn. "If only I had my lightstaff, I'd petrify that dragon king from head to tail!"

Noni smiled thinly. "So you're the one! Dewi told me of the strange maiden who was one of us yet not one of us. 'She has a wondrous, shining rod that can change a draig to cold stone,' he said. 'Let her turn it upon the dragon king, and we would be rid of him and his tyranny. I would gladly set you free then.'"

"Alas, the staff is lost, and my hopes with it," said Merryn. "Still, we must find a way to keep you from your date with the stake. Perhaps I can speak with the queen on your behalf."

"She would not listen," said Noni, shaking her head. "For generations, the Aberth has gone to meet her doom, and neither the queen nor her people will brook any interference with that custom. Now, how does my dress fit? Tomorrow will be my first and last public appearance, and I want to look my very best."

"It becomes you nicely," Merryn absently remarked. She wasn't about to give up on Noni yet, though the Aberth had surrendered to her fate. Escape was impossible, but perhaps another means of rescue was not. She walked the floor, noting how the feet of so many desolate maidens had worn the stones smooth.

"What if you smeared yourself with mud or dirt?" she suggested. "Maybe then the dragon wouldn't want you."

Noni snorted. "Marsh dragons live in the mud, and everything they eat is mixed with mud. For them, it's like a garnish. The dragon king would no doubt like me better that way."

Merryn considered other possibilities, but none seemed any more likely to succeed than mud. "Gaelathane," she said, "please help me to save Noni's life. I know You can deliver her, but I'm fresh out of ideas. Thank You for hearing my request. Mae'r Goeden yn fyw!" Peace began crowding fear out of her heart.

The Aberth eyed her suspiciously. "'The Tree lives'? What is that supposed to mean? And why are you talking to yourself?"

"Never mind. I'll explain later." Merryn gazed out at the gray rain streaming past the window. If only she had skin as smooth as Noni's! With that thought, the barest seed of a plan sprouted in her mind. It was risky, but if all went well, Noni would live.

"Has an Aberth ever budded out and remained an Aberth?" she asked. "I mean, would the dragon king still take her?"

Noni's face froze in a shocked expression, as if Merryn had suggested that dragons be kept as pets. "Of course not!" she said indignantly. "That's one reason Protectors were once confined to the tower's upper floors, to keep them above the swamp mist. Nobody could risk an Aberth sprouting, for fear of displeasing the dragon king. There's no telling what he would do."

"I think it's high time the dragon king suffered a little displeasure," Merryn declared. "And I know just the thing that will stick in his craw, too. Now hop off the bed, please."

Grumbling, "It's my bed, you know, at least until tomorrow," Noni did as she was asked, taking with her the gown she had been sewing. Merryn stripped the bed of its sheets and blankets, which she stuffed between the window bars until all the spaces were plugged. The room suddenly seemed to shrink.

"What are you doing?" Noni demanded. "I like the fresh air, and now I'll have nothing to sleep under! Really, I'm beginning to think you came in here to play cruel practical jokes on me."

Merryn gave her no answer. Casting about the room, she found a pitcher by the door and gave it a shake. Water gurgled inside. Now she needed only a few more items. "Do you have such a thing as a metal pan or dish around here?" she asked.

"Will this do?" Noni fished a tin pan from under her bed. "Dewi lets me use this to eat out of, but only with a spoon. We're not allowed to have sharp objects such as knives or forks. An Aberth might hurt herself, especially on the eve of her Opening."

"Your pan will do very well, thank you," Merryn said. "All I need now is a way to support it." Glancing around the room, she saw nothing that would suit her purposes. Then she noticed the bed. Throwing off the mattress, she found a set of rusty springs on the frame beneath. With savage twists, she wrenched off four of

the springs, which she fastened to the handles of Noni's pan and then joined at their tips, forming a springy tent.

"Bring me your pillow, will you?" she asked the Aberth.

Rolling her eyes, Noni tossed her the pillow. Merryn slipped off the pillowcase and tore it into strips, which she knotted together to form a cloth rope. Under Noni's puzzled gaze, she then searched the shadowy ceiling. "Ahh!" she breathed. From its center jutted an iron hook for hanging a lamp or torch. On her third throw, she managed to fling her pillowcase-rope over the hook.

Noni made a face. "If you were thinking of hanging yourself with that, I doubt it will hold your weight—or mine, either."

"That's not what I had in mind," Merryn said. After setting the lamp beside her on the floor, she tied one end of the cloth rope to the top of the spring tent. Pulling on the cord's opposite end, she hoisted the pan and springs off the floor and suspended them there by tying the rope's free end around a bedpost.

Curiosity softened the suspicion in Noni's face. "What's that for?" she asked, pointing to the pan-and-bedsprings contraption.

"You'll see," said Merryn, filling the pan with water from the pitcher. Next, she dropped her greenstone into the water. Finally, she slid the lamp underneath and adjusted the cloth rope until the pan hung just above the lamp's smoking chimney.

Through the blocked window came the muffled whuffing of dragons' wings. The lamp sputtered and its flame shrank. "It's almost out of oil," Noni said. "I forgot to refill it yesterday."

Merryn sputtered, too. If the flame died untimely, Noni could die with it. "Do you have any more oil?" she asked the Aberth.

"Dewi keeps a jar of it in the washroom," Noni replied. "After I refill the lamp, I have to return the jar. I wouldn't want that stuff in here, anyway. Rendered dragon fat stinks!"

Rendered dragon fat. The Vinelanders feared and hated the dreigiau, yet they also relied on the creatures for food, oil and goodness-only-knew what other necessities. "Then you'd better call Dewi to unlock your washroom door," Merryn said grimly.

Noni knocked on her outer door. Minutes later, a knock came from the washroom and following that, another at the side door as Dewi unlocked it. Noni waited a few seconds before opening the door and disappearing into the washroom. When she reappeared, she was holding a glass jar filled with a yellowish liquid, which she poured into a hole in the lamp's base. The flame leapt up and the water began to bubble and froth. After returning the jar of oil to the washroom, Noni asked Merryn, "Now what?"

Merryn edged toward the door. "Now it's time for me to leave. Don't let the pan boil dry, and whatever you do, don't open either door or unblock the window, or you'll regret it!"

Tears spurted from Noni's eyes. "But why are you leaving? I thought you would keep me company a few more hours at the least. And how long must I tend the pan?"

"Until you've fully broken out," Merryn replied. She pointed at the pot. Clouds of green steam were boiling out of it.

"What is that?" Noni gasped, her eyes bulging.

"The niwl gwyrdd," said Merryn. "Breathe it in! The sooner you begin your blaguryn, the better." Closing the door behind her, she left a terrified Noni with her hands clenched beneath her chin, as though she feared losing her head to the green mist.

Saying a prayer for the Aberth, Merryn knocked on the outer door and hid in the washroom closet. After all the knocking and re-locking was done and Dewi had departed, she crept out again. Her hair stood on end. Green fog was billowing under the door and flowing across the floor. After stuffing a couple of towels beneath the door to block the fog, Merryn fled the washroom.

CHAPTER 20

The Dragon King

erryn awoke to a gray dawn. Silence drummed inside
her head as she stole down the hall and left Drelli in
Cari's room. The former gwas was still asleep. Then
Merryn went to the Protector's chamber. Putting her ear to the
door, she heard only the pounding of her heart and the rushing of
blood through her veins.

"Somebody must have told you."

Dewi was standing over her holding a pitcher of water. Sorrow
furrowed his face and dark half-moons hung under his bloodshot
eyes. Every muscle in his jaw stood out in rigid relief.

Not trusting herself to speak, Merryn nodded. She felt her body
falling, falling onto a forest of murderous dragon poles.

"I daresay she hasn't slept a wink," Dewi went on. "I haven't
slept, either. How could I, the night before another of my daughters goes away? Knowing my duty doesn't ease the ache."

"Your daughter—?"

Dewi graced her with a half smile. "Since I am the only living
soul these girls ever see until the day of their death, they naturally
become attached to me, as I to them. They are the daughters I
never had, for I have no children of my own, and I love and grieve
over these girls as their families cannot." A tear squeezed from
under his eyelid. "Noni especially I shall miss. May her death be

mercifully swift! I fear Cari will never be the same without her sister. Loyalty to an Aberth is wasted loyalty, for in the end, it too will die. 'The dreigiau must have their due,' though I would as soon ride the cart myself to let an Aberth live. Now you'd best run along before the queen sees you here."

Merryn was only too glad to leave Dewi. She didn't wish to be anywhere near the bailiff when he opened that dreaded door and discovered what Noni had become—with Merryn's help.

Swinging down the scaffolding to the bottom, she noticed several yeomen rolling a compact, long-tongued black cart toward the door. Slipping outside ahead of the men, Merryn found herself hemmed in by hundreds of mist-people under a lowering sky. In memory of the lost prince, black banners hung from every wall and window, making the dismal day even more somber.

Merryn broke through the crush of bodies just as the cart rattled into the courtyard. A sigh rose from the expectant crowd. Following the cart, Merryn's companions spilled out of the Keep. Waving and shouting, they hurried over to meet her.

"These mist-people surely picked a gloomy morning for their festivities!" Gemmio remarked as he brushed raindrops off his cloak. "The next time, I hope Gaelathane sends us to a dry, sunny world without any marshes or dragons or foggy drizzle."

"Do you suppose they're serving breakfast in the dining hall?" asked Opio. "I'm starving! Even dragon sounds good to me."

"I doubt you'll find anything to eat at this hour of the day," said Rolin. "Besides, everybody is out here waiting for the gates to open. After that, I'm sure they'll stoke the cooking fires. You'll just have to cinch your belt a little tighter until then."

"I've already cinched it up as tight as I can," muttered Opio.

"Maybe no one is eating today in honor of Prince Huw," Elwyn suggested. "The queen is still mourning in her room."

"Poor Queen Rowena," Marlis murmured. "It's a pity Huw is gone. His death must be awfully difficult for his mother to bear."

Gwynneth pointed out the black cart, which now stood midway between the Carreg Keep and the gates. "What are they doing with that? If it's to be used for children's rides, I don't see any horses or donkeys to pull it. And why is it painted black?"

"It looks like a little vegetable cart to me," said Scanlon.

Alas, to ride the cart my destiny, in satin white to stand before the king. "I think it's for the Aberth," said Merryn. "She—"

A mighty roar cut her off as the swelling crowd greeted Dewi son of Dylan at the door of the Carreg Keep. Fear, relief and fury all fought to rule his features. He raised his fist over his head.

"People of the Mist!" he cried, and the milling spectators fell silent. "We are ruined! We have lost our eldest Aberth to the niwl gwyrdd. She has suffered a blaguryn." Dewi opened his fist and displayed the leaf he had been holding. "If you do not believe me, here is one of her leaves as proof. We are undone!"

Angry, confused murmurs ran through the crowd. "How could this have happened?" some cried. "Where is the wretch?" shouted others. The tumult ceased when Queen Rowena emerged from the Keep, supported by two servants. A third hastened to set a padded chair against the tower, and the queen was gently lowered into it.

Bang! The door flew off its hinges and a couple of brawny yeomen hurtled through it, sprawling into a mud-puddle.

"What's the hurry, gentlemen?" crooned a young woman's voice, and a mass of vines filled the doorway. "I don't like being manhandled, especially when there's no need for it. I was on my way down here, anyway. This is my first Opening since becoming an Aberth, and I don't want to miss it." With her whips, she deftly tossed Merryn's greenstone into the air and caught it.

"Noni!" Merryn exclaimed, and she hopped up and down for the sheer joy of seeing her new friend in Greenie form.

"Kill her! Kill the traitor!" roared the mist-people. "Seize her; burn her with fire!" The crowd surged forward, but with her vines, Noni tossed her would-be assailants aside like so many straws. The mob drew back, only to gather around Dewi.

"This is all the bailiff's fault!" cried the ringleaders. "He must die for neglecting his sworn duties! Death to Dewi son of Dylan!"

Queen Rowena slowly rose from her seat, feverish eyes burning with an unquenchable fire. "Silence!" she commanded. "I and I alone will decide who shall live and who shall die in the Castell Mawr. Dewi son of Dylan has served me faithfully these past forty years, and he has never yet betrayed my trust." She motioned to the bailiff, and he came to kneel before her.

"Dewi son of Dylan, tell me the truth," she said with a pleading look. "Did you or did you not take my greenstone and give it to the Aberth for her own use? Ponder well your answer."

Dewi raised his head, devotion shining in his eyes. "No, m'lady," he said. "I would never do such a thing, not even for Noniad. Let me prove my innocence to you, once and for all!"

With the queen's leave, Dewi disappeared into the Carreg Keep. He returned a short time later and laid Rowena's greenstone at her feet. "Here is the stone, your majesty. I found it in your study lying in the same drawer where you left it last night."

"Then you are not to blame for this blaguryn," said the queen, and she held up Dewi's hand. "Do you hear me, my people? I absolve Dewi son of Dylan of all guilt in this matter!"

"Then who is to blame?" cried a bystander.

"Yes, who is to blame?" the crowd echoed.

Queen Rowena turned to Noni. "How came you by that greenstone? Tell us the truth, and it will go the better for you."

Noni's vines drooped. "I cannot say, m'lady."

"Cannot or will not?" growled Dewi. "You may have escaped the black cart, but the penalty for refusing the queen's command is death by impalement. Is that what you wish?"

Her own heart impaled on pangs of guilt, Merryn drew near and cried out, "The stone has been mine since childhood! I am to blame for Noni's blaguryn. Let her punishment fall upon me."

"You should have kept silent, my friend," said Noni. With a leafy tendril, she dropped the greenstone into its owner's hands. Merryn caressed it lovingly before returning it to her pouch.

As the Greencloaks gaped at her, Timothy gripped Merryn's arm. "What are you doing?" he hissed. "Keep out of this! Do you want to be impaled? These people are clamoring for blood!"

Merryn shook him off and approached the queen. "Please let Noni go," she said. "She's done nothing wrong. Hasn't she already suffered enough as an Aberth? I am sorry for deceiving you, but I could not sit idly by and let Noni go to her death."

"Then you shall go to yours!" snarled Rowena with white-lipped fury. "Since you care so little for our laws and customs, you shall wear the dress and ride the cart instead. Dewi, let the sentence be carried out before I strike this gwas dead myself!"

"No!" From the crowd darted a slight figure that threw itself at the queen's feet. "Please, Mother!" Cari cried. "Do not send Merryn to the cart! She is your maidservant and my friend, and she has saved my sister's life. Is that not worth your mercy?"

Seeing the queen was unmoved, Cari stabbed a finger at Gwynneth and Marlis. "Look! Here are two women with skin smoother than Noni's ever was. Take one of them instead. The dragon king won't have Merryn anyway, pocked as she is."

Rowena's face was chiseled stone. "Enough! I have decreed that this one will take the other's place and die the death of an Aberth, and so she shall. Let the Protector's Rites begin!"

Cutting off Merryn from her friends, the howling mob seized her, and carrying her to the cart, tossed her in. Rough hands clamped chain-linked iron cuffs on her wrists, shackling her to the cart. Then other hands pulled the unfinished Aberth gown over her body, splitting seams. Next, a lane opened in the throng, allowing Queen Rowena and the bailiff to approach the cart.

Leaning on Dewi, the queen laid her hands on Merryn's head. "May the curse of Ifan son of Ifor rest upon you as you go hence," she said. "Let it pass from you to the king. May he be cursed in his swamp; cursed in lying down and cursed in rising up! May the curse enter his bones and melt them like wax. You are the Aberth. Carry now the curse of our people far from us."

"Carry now the curse far from us," the mist-people echoed. Rowena raised her hands and face to the sky, crying,

> Reverse the curse! Return the stolen stone, or worse
> This world befalls, when drunken dragon creeping crawls
> Into the crack, to make a mist, to hatch a batch
> Of burning brood, where other ancient spawn has stewed.
>
> And there remain, your bones to fall among the slain
> Beyond the gate; before the dragon king your fate
> Is to be killed, for curse is calmed when blood is spilled
> With none to mourn, for then will Vineland be reborn.

"Let her go! Let her go!" shouted Merryn's companions from the back of the crowd. "She has done nothing to deserve death. Let her go!" Their protests were quickly silenced.

Merryn's head reeled as Garrick of the Gate laboriously raised the iron portcullis and cranked open the gates. Surely it was all a dream! But no, she was still sitting in the black cart, wearing the gown, *the* gown, and she had a date with the dragon king.

Tramp, tramp, tramp came the sound of Merryn's doom as two drummers marched up at the head of six black-hooded yeomen. "Stations!" one of the drummers called out. Seizing iron rods set in the harnessing tongue, the men lifted it and at a second command, set the cart in motion. Men shouted, women wept and children jeered as Merryn rolled through their ranks. Overcome by the noise and the horror of her fate, she swooned.

She came to just as the portcullis slammed down behind her, cutting her off from the Castell Mawr and from any remaining hope of rescue. Trumpets blared, and when Merryn looked up, she saw tall, winged figures standing on the walls, blowing on silver clarions. When she looked again, the figures were gone.

Rocks crunched beneath the cart's creaking wheels as the trudging yeomen chanted to the cadence of the drums,

> Pull with a will to the top of the hill;
> No slackers here! No dragons to fear!
> Sharp are the rocks, but no one talks,
> Up near the top of the hill!
>
> Steady that wheel lest it wobble or reel;
> Mind you the cart! Brace up your heart!
> As we are bade, we are bringing the maid
> Up to the top of the hill!
>
> Dreadful the stake that for us awaits,
> Blackened and charred! Bloody and scarred!
> Be not afraid, for the price must be paid,
> Up on the top of the hill!
>
> Bind on the rope with last words of hope;
> Struggle and scream! It's not a dream!
> Soon he will come with the beat of the drum,
> Onto the top of the hill!

At a snail's pace, the rumbling cart rounded the road's last bend and rolled onto the causeway. Yet, all during the trip from castle to marsh, Merryn hadn't seen a single dragon. Leaning forward, she spoke to one of the yeomen toiling in front of her.

"Where are all the dreigiau? They should have come around by now. How will we defend ourselves against them?"

The man turned his hooded head. "They're still nursing hangovers! Besides, on Protector's Day, no draig may taste flesh until dusk, by the dragon king's decree. By then, begging your pardon, my mates and I will be back behind the castle walls."

Merryn fell backward as she collapsed into the cart. "Poor little waif," the man muttered to his neighbor. "I hope *he* doesn't toy with her the way he did with the last one, bless her!"

Then the clapping began. Out of the marsh rose thousands of hydras, snapping their tentacles together as they had done when Merryn had first entered Vineland. The drummers picked up their rhythm: *Slap-clap-drumbeat-slap-clap-drumbeat*. Merryn covered her ears. "Why are they making that noise?" she cried.

Sighing, the yeoman replied, "It's the hydras' way of alerting the dreigiau to prey that is out of tentacle reach."

"Please—make them stop!" Merryn pleaded with the soldier, but he only snorted scornfully and turned away from her.

"Can a man muzzle a draig or put a bit in its jaws?" he said. "Can anyone call forth the rain and wind? Nobody has ever tamed a draig or hydra, nor ever will. Fear not, for all will soon be over. If you wish me to deliver a message to a loved one—"

"Quiet back there!" barked a yeoman at the front of the line. "Put your shoulders into it, men. We've had a late start, and you know what that means. If we're not back by sundown . . ."

Defeated, Merryn sank into the cart again. How had she gotten herself into this fix? By all rights, she belonged in Thalmos with her father and the other Greenies. Instead, she was jolting toward a tryst with death. "Gaelathane, please help me!" she cried.

Ahead loomed Split-top and Ifan's Hill, both wreathed in a sickly, greenish light. The air grew hot and sticky. As in Merryn's dream, black clouds were stacking up all around, and rain slashed the sullen sky. Fat raindrops pelted her, soaking the white dress. Still no draig assailed the plodding train, which groaned along the crumbling causeway until it reached the land bridge.

Left across the bridge they clattered and up the narrow track that led to the summit of Split-top Mountain. The air sizzled as if alive, and blue flames danced among the rocks. An eerie twilight cloaked the mountain. *Crash!* Lightning shivered between sky and earth, splitting light from darkness and sound from sense. Merryn moaned. Her dream was becoming a waking nightmare.

Onward the men pressed, their rain-drenched backs glistening black in the lightning flashes. The cart slipped in the mud, nearly skidding off the road and onto the cruel rocks waiting below. Finally, the wheels ground to a halt. A yeoman removed Merryn's clinking shackles and dragged her to a wooden post jutting from the earth. The Stake. Darker than dripping death it was, more hideous than any night horror. All Merryn's strength left her.

Another man bound her to the stake with ropes, cutting off her breath. *Bam! Bam!* Someone hammered a red-lettered wooden sign into the post over her head. It read, *Rhaid rhoi eu haeddiant dyledus i'r dreigiau.* The dreigiau must have their due.

Doom dah-dah doom, rolled the drums, and the yeomen fell back, leaving the tallest of their number near the foot of the stake holding a spear. Hefting his weapon, he said, "Though the king prefers his victims alive, I can offer you a quick end now. Most of the girls beg for death. Believe me, it's better this way."

Merryn shook her head, and the man shrugged. "As you wish," he said. Pulling out a leather flagon, he forced its contents into Merryn's mouth. She coughed and gagged as the fiery liquid burned its way down her throat and into her stomach. A gray fog gathered in her head and shrouded her teary eyes.

"Courtesy of Brynnor," said the spearman. "He asked me to be sure to give you a swig. You'll need it." Shouldering his spear, he tromped back to rejoin the others. After turning the cart about, the men took their places at the harness-tongue again.

"Back to the castle, and make it quick!" cried their leader. "The night and the dreigiau wait for no man." At a quick jog, the soldiers set the cart rattling down the mountainside.

Wind drove the rain against Merryn's face in stinging pellets. Never had she felt such loneliness or terror. "Gaelathane, save me!" she screamed against the lightning-forked sky. There was no answer but the thunder-fist that pounded her throbbing head against the unforgiving stake. Tears tumbled from her eyes. She would never see her father again, or the other Greenies, or the Greencloaks, or Beechtown, or the Vinelanders, or—

To Merryn's right, a blacker shadow emerged from the storm's darkness. Taller than the Carreg Keep and twice as broad it seemed, and it was coming for her. With a voice to drown the thunder it bellowed, and with its every step, the death-stake shook at Merryn's back. The dragon king in all his awful splendor was stalking toward her, his glittering green scales throwing back the lightning in a million stars. His bulk blotted out earth and sky, and in his fiery red serpent's eyes, Merryn saw the death of worlds written. Now she understood the merciful spear, and with her last full breath, she shrieked out her despair.

"Thief!" The dragon's roar rumbled out of the mountain, from the sky, from the very belly of the earth. "You will return what you stole from us, or I shall take it from you by force. Either way, you shall die in fire and blood with none to save you."

Return the stolen stone.

Rocks rattled. "Hello, Drundaig," spoke a still deeper voice. A tall, shadowy form was standing beside Merryn's stake.

"YOU!" thundered the dragon king. "How dare you come between me and my prey on this day of all days? Have I not warned you not to interfere in my affairs? The female two-legs rightfully belongs to me, and you cannot stop me from taking her!" In reply, the stranger played a merry fiddle tune that seemed entirely out of place on that dark, savage mountaintop.

"You're the Fiddler!" Merryn gasped, and she began to laugh hysterically. Here she was about to be devoured, and the Fiddler was sawing away on his instrument's strings as if he were in Beechtown's dance hall performing before an admiring crowd.

"'Meddler' is more like it," growled Drundaig. "He's always sticking his puny nose where it doesn't belong." Slaver dripped from the dragon's grinning jaws. "What do you want, Meddler? Don't think you can put me to sleep with your songs, either."

The fiddling stopped. "My life for hers, Drundaig."

Flames licked from the dragon's mouth. "Hsssss. Why would you trade your life for such a pitiful scrap of flesh? Give her to me. I will have my vengeance upon her and all her sniveling, thieving kind. Besides, fresh meat has been hard to come by since you blocked up the other entrances to my kingdom."

The Fiddler now stood between Drundaig and Merryn. In the high, wet wind, his dripping rags streamed out like weeping willow leaves. "As you say, she is a mere 'scrap of flesh' who wouldn't make a mouthful for you. I am still offering my life in place of hers, because she belongs to me and has called upon me in her time of trouble. I cannot and will not refuse her."

Drundaig's head lowered, a scaly green mountain dwarfing the Fiddler. "Step aside, muck-man, or I'll have you both!"

The Fiddler pointed a scarred arm at Merryn. "Think about my offer. The girl will return what is yours, and in exchange for her life, you shall have me. I don't need to remind you that if I wished, I could banish you from this world forever."

The dragon king hooded his eyes, and smoke curled from his nostrils. "Very well. I accept your offer. How can I know you will do as you say, Trickster-of-the-Marsh? Perhaps you will hide yourself in some mountain cave where I cannot find you!"

An impossibly high note floated off the violin, and Drundaig shrank back. "I always keep my word," said the Fiddler. "After I release the girl and she has given you what you want, she will bind me to the stake with her own ropes. Then I am yours."

"I will watch," said the dragon king, and his red tongue flicked out to tickle Merryn's face. She couldn't scratch herself.

The Fiddler untied her ropes and caught her as she collapsed. Drundaig stared at her greedily, smoke coiling from his snout and breathing hole. Numbly, she removed her greenstone from its pouch and tossed it to the dragon. With surprising gentleness, Drundaig scooped it up in a webbed claw. Then Merryn turned to the Fiddler, who was already standing with his back to the stake, hands at his sides, fiddle at his feet.

"Who are you?" she asked him tearfully. "Why are you sacrificing your life for me? Isn't there some other way?"

The man shook his shaggy head. "No, there is no other way. Just bind me to this stake. When the dragon-dust flies, however, you must flee to Ifan's tree and climb it!" Merryn wondered how any tree could have survived on that fire-ravaged hilltop.

Under Drundaig's watchful eye, Merryn tightly bound the Fiddler to the stake with soggy coils of rope. Flames now freely poured from the dragon king's jaws, lighting up the whole ghastly scene. The air reeked of brimstone and blasted rock.

"Move away from here," the Fiddler told Merryn. The earth shook as Drundaig approached the stake.

"What you do, do quickly," rasped the new Aberth.

The dragon king bellowed to split the sky. "Now I'll be rid of you for good, Marsh-Meddler! What fools and weaklings you puny two-legs are. After I have killed you, I shall finish despoiling this pitiful land, as I have many others. Before any world was, I ruled the darkness, and now the watery worlds are also mine. Despair and die, Fiddler!" Webbed claws flashed past Merryn, and the Fiddler groaned as his right arm dropped onto the rocks.

Merryn screamed and fell to her knees. "Please, oh please, don't kill him! Take me instead. Let him go, just let him go!"

"As I did to Ifan son of Ifor, so I have done to this pretender!" Drundaig growled. His claws swung down again, snapping the ropes. The Fiddler sighed and fell forward, blood gushing from his gashed body. *But on that day, another life the king will slay upon a stake; another arm will fall to make our people free . . .*

Merryn shrieked as Drundaig crushed the Fiddler's violin to splinters with his massive foot. Then he turned a cold, slitted eye upon her and gnashed his saber teeth. "The penalty for stealing is death!" he roared, and he seized her in his claws.

Fully expecting to be swallowed on the spot, Merryn cried out, "Gaelathane, take me to Your kingdom!" and closed her eyes. She felt a bobbing, swaying motion. Drundaig was loping along on his hind legs, clutching her in his webbed fist. Lightning crashed around him, but still he hastened on. Merryn felt sick.

At last, Drundaig stopped before a contorted tree. Merryn had never seen such a pathetic specimen of the tree tribe. With charred, broken limbs, it clung to life amidst the rock-strewn graveyard of rotting cedars, firs and pines that had succumbed to lightning or dragonfire. Drundaig lightly ran a curved claw down the tree's trunk. A lightning bolt was arcing toward him when the mountain bucked and Merryn tumbled into darkness.

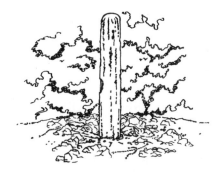

Chapter 21

Dragon Dust

Merryn was swaying in a hammock, so tightly bound she could scarcely breathe. Something was squishing in rhythm with the hammock's swinging, like this: *Squish-swing-squish-swing.* Opening her eyes, she discovered Drundaig was still clutching her in his clammy claws as he squished his way through the stinking swamp. Some of those claws were drenched in blood—the Fiddler's blood. Merryn wriggled and squirmed, but the dragon king's grip only tightened, cracking her ribs.

The sun beat down on her from a mirrored green sky. Everything else was green, too, a putrid shade of green that turned Merryn's stomach. Then a horrible certainty hooked its claw into her. Through Ifan's torsil, Drundaig had taken her back to his own marshy world, the source of all Vineland's scourges.

The last words of Ifan's riddle came to her: *And there remain, your bones to fall among the slain beyond the gate; before the dragon king your fate is to be killed, for curse is calmed when blood is spilled with none to mourn, for then will Vineland be reborn.* Ifan had written of this very day and hour, when Merryn would pass the torsil gate into a world not her own, with none to mourn her passing nor mark the resting place of her bones.

Drundaig raised his massive head and thundered to the sickly sky, "He's dead! At long last, the Marsh-Meddler is dead! Rejoice with me, brothers and sisters, for I have slain our enemy!"

All across the swamp, dragons rose out of the watery muck and stamped their feet in a ponderous dance, shaking the marsh and spattering Merryn's gown with mud. As they danced, the beasts sang, if their grating grunts could be called song:

Down with the Meddler, the puny little Peddler;
We've murdered that Meddler, who said he'd never die!
Now we're free of the Meddler, that scrawny little Riddler,
The falsifying Fiddler, that irritating fly!

Death to the Meddler, that merrymaking Muddler,
The smooth-tongued Befuddler, who claimed to be the King!
Now our two-legged Troubler, that swamp-singing Swindler,
That moralizing Idler has felt the dragon's sting!

Drundaig and his friends were still singing when a stiff breeze sprang up and the sun dimmed. The dragons stopped dancing.

Crick. Cracking stone broke the silence. Drundaig grunted. One of the bloody claws gripping Merryn had turned gray, and stone-like scales were flaking off it. He clenched his foot tighter, and the claw broke off. *Crickety-crick-crick.* The dragon howled as ashen streaks ran up his scaly foreleg. He was shaking Merryn like a rag doll when with the sound of sleet blowing against a brick wall, the entire limb dissolved into gray powder.

Merryn fell—*plop!*—into the swamp. Drundaig began hopping about, bellowing madly as gray stripes streaked up his torso and down his legs. He unfurled his wings to fly, but they dissolved into dust. Seeing Merryn, he snarled and opened his jaws to spit fire at her, but a grainy fountain shot out of his mouth. Then the king of the dragons disintegrated in a boiling cloud of sand.

Now the ashen runners were snaking through the swamp, reducing marsh plants and dragons alike to heaps of fine gray silt. *When the dragon-dust flies, you must flee to Ifan's tree and climb it!* Merryn struggled back through the knee-deep muck. Strogarns sprouted in her path, only to dissolve into writhing dust-tentacles.

Scant yards away, a green hill collapsed with a hissing sigh, a sandcastle felled by invisible waves. Another green knoll loomed ahead, its top crowned by a broken tree.

I'll never reach it before I'm turned to dust! she thought.

Roll.

Startled, Merryn glanced back but saw no one. Who had just spoken to her? The voice resembled Gaelathane's, but—

Roll! Dropping to the mud, Merryn began to roll sideways toward the hill, dodging the sand-fingers burrowing through the marsh. Free of the clinging ooze, she moved quickly, despite the water and mud that clogged her mouth, eyes, ears and nose.

After slogging the last few feet on foot, Merryn clawed her way up the knoll. Below her lay a sea of seething gray. Dust spouted and spewed from every hole and hydra burrow. The fine stuff swirled on the rising wind and fell from the sky as a gritty rain. Shot through with silvery streamers, the sun darkened.

Quick as a whip, Merryn nipped up Ifan's torsil. As she descended, a hail of pebbles peppered her. Had she failed to make passage? But no, below her tree lay the stones of Split-top Mountain. Dropping out of the torsil, she plastered herself against the ground. Dawn's watery light was filtering across the landscape, softening the starkness of the fire-blasted hilltop. Although the storm had passed, leaving a few frothy clouds in its wake, a high wind had sprung up, moaning among the rocks and stirring up puffs of dust. Merryn wept in relief. Against all odds, she had safely escaped the dragon world—thanks to the Fiddler.

The Fiddler. Surely she could not leave his body exposed to the elements, a prey for the birds and wild animals! Intending to erect a cairn of stones over her rescuer, she made her way across the rocky, uneven ground to the stake, which still stood pointing defiantly at the heavens. However, the Fiddler's body was nowhere to be seen. Thinking a wolf or mountain lion had carried him off, she searched a wide area around the post but found no bloodied rocks or drag marks in the dirt. Had the whole horrible night been nothing more than a bad dream?

Returning to the stake, she found its wood still glistening wetly with fresh blood. Below it lay the smashed violin. She hadn't been dreaming after all. What had happened to her friend? If she couldn't give him a decent burial, at least she could tear down the hideous instrument of his death. She shoved on the stake, but the thing wouldn't budge. It was driven too deeply into the ground. Weeping, she tore at it with her fingers.

Snap. Merryn froze and the hairs rose on the back of her neck. A monstrous dragon was heaving itself onto the hilltop, belching smoke and flames. Merryn had forgotten that although Drundaig and his fellows were perishing in their own world, plenty of their relatives still roamed Vineland—and this one looked hungry.

Leaving the stake, she ran until a yawning chasm blocked her path. A stinking, sulfurous cloud poured out of the gulf, along with tapping, rattling sounds that reminded Merryn of hail bouncing off the slate roof of her former home. Lying on her stomach, she held her nose and peered over the edge.

At first, the pall was too thick to make out much of anything. Then the haze briefly cleared away, revealing tens of thousands of greenstones, all packed tightly together along the ravine's walls like the cobbles on Beechtown's narrow streets.

The stones were rocking in place as if jostled by an unseen hand. Quite a few were already split open, and green shapes were emerging, spitting puffs of black smoke. Dragons. Baby dragons, all noisily pecking their way out of their . . . *eggs.* The greenstones weren't stones at all. They were actually dragon eggs.

Like a cloud of locusts, the hatchlings boiled out of the chasm and fastened onto Merryn's body. Some bit her exposed skin. Others burned holes in her dress with tiny jets of blue flame.

"Get away! Get off me, you fiends!" she screamed, batting at them with her hands. They only attacked her more ferociously.

Suddenly, the hatchlings scattered. Merryn shook herself. Then she saw what had frightened off the pesky creatures: The snorting female draig was crawling toward her over the rocks.

Merryn knew it was a she-dragon by the size of its belly, which dragged along the ground, swollen with ale and eggs, if Ifan's riddle was any clue. *When drunken dragon creeping crawls into the crack, to make a mist, to hatch a batch of burning brood, where other ancient spawn has stewed.*

The truth seized Merryn like a spasm. Somehow, the dragons sensed when their "ancient spawn" was at the point of hatching, and another female would climb Split-top to line the crack's rocky walls with a fresh batch of "burning brood."

She yelled at the dragon and waved her arms, but the beast kept coming with single-minded determination. While Merryn helplessly looked on, the draig climbed down into the ravine and half-slid, half-flew into its dark depths. Merryn threw a rock after it. "May you and your eggs rot down there!" she screamed.

Now the hatchlings returned in force, swarming over her like enraged bees. Swatting at the frenzied creatures only seemed to excite them, and she couldn't outrun them. She fell to the ground and covered her face, curling up to protect herself.

Thunder shook the ground. Peeking through her fingers, she saw a dark cloud of dust and debris sweeping across Split-top. Instantly it was upon her, stripping the hatchlings off her back. Onward rolled the cloud, plucking up the death-stake like a straw before funneling itself into the top of Ifan's torsil, which sucked down the lot. Merryn ducked as more squealing baby dragons whizzed by, mixed with marsh plants and hydra tentacles. Then a full-sized dragon sailed past and disappeared into the torsil.

Everywhere Merryn looked, the marsh was convulsing, yielding up its deadly denizens. Shrieking dragons, flailing hydras, squirming snakes and assorted other creatures went whirling into the torsil, swallowed up as if they had never been. And they created their own wind, a hurricane that threatened to tear Merryn right off the hilltop and carry her back into Drundaig's world.

From the chasm beside her spewed a green geyser, a stew of eggs hatched and unhatched, thickened with countless baby dragons and the remains of dreigiau long dead. When the torrent thinned, Merryn crawled over and looked down. The rock walls had been scrubbed bare as if by a gigantic wire brush. Then she saw a great green whale rising out of the ravine. The she-dragon! Limbs and wings windmilling, the bloated beast rushed by and was caught up in a greenish-black cloud that was bearing down on Split-top from all sides like a monstrous tidal wave.

In a flash, Merryn understood. *Reverse the curse.* When she had returned the greenstone to the dragon king, and the Fiddler had shed his blood in her place, Ifan's curse had been reversed.

Now a world's worth of accumulated evil was being sent back whence it had come, and Merryn stood squarely in its path.

The towering wave crested and fell upon Split-top in all its green fury, sweeping Merryn over the edge of the abyss. *Into the Hole you go, you go, into the Hole you go; over the brink, down you sink; into the Hole you go!*

Falling, falling into the earth's dark womb, she thrashed the blackness with her hands, drawing forth the inky blood of lightless places. "Gaelathane!" she screamed into the echoing void.

Splash! Water hit her like a block of river ice. Down she went, though "down" and "up" were all the same to her. Like so many other hapless victims, she had fallen into Stygweth's pool.

For time out of mind, Stygweth had lain at the bottom of the pool—*her* pool, she liked to think it—drawing the dregs of the upper world into her many mouths. Dragon hatchlings, insects, snakes, rock rabbits and other sick or careless creatures rained down into her pantry, quickly drowning in the chill water.

Here was something different, though. Such a struggling, such a thrashing and a splashing she was sensing in the pool above her! Any prey too large for her small mouths to take in was worse than useless, for after drowning, it would bloat and float and taint the water until she sickened for months at a time.

She had to cleanse the pool of this intruder before it perished, a task she had not undertaken for many waxings and wanings of a moon she had never seen. Tiny twitchings ran through her bulk, which smothered the bottom of the pool from edge to edge like the round, rotting hide of some eyeless sea creature. Her margins lifted and rippled, setting off a wave of motion that broke the suction mooring her to the mud. Stirring up clouds of silt, she flapped off the bottom and rose toward the surface.

Merryn had run out of air and out of time. She could no longer move her cold-numbed limbs. Bubbles trickled from her mouth and nose as she yielded to her fate. Gaelessa's bright lights were dancing before her eyes when something slick and rubbery bumped her from beneath and buoyed her to the water's surface. Coughing and gasping for air, she weakly wallowed on a gray, slippery mat pocked all over with teacup-sized holes.

"Ow!" Something had nipped her thumb, drawing blood. Her ear was next. Poking her pinky into one of the holes in the cushiony raft, she felt the prick of needle-sharp teeth. She was lying on the back—or was it the belly?—of a floating nightmare! The mouths began to open and close, forming whispered words:

"Go . . . away. Go away and leave us be. You are unfood."

Fearful that the beast was about to fold up around her, Merryn skittered over its gently rolling surface until she reached the safety of the rocky shore, where she collapsed in tears. With a gurgling sigh, the mouthy monster sank beneath the water, creating dark waves that lapped loudly against the rocks.

Pebbles rattled nearby. "Who's there?" someone called out.

The hollow sound broke upon Merryn like shattering stone. It was Huw! She dragged herself toward his voice's dying echoes.

"Who's there? I can hear you," he cried again through waves of hysteria. "I have a sword; come out or I shall stab you!"

"It's me, Merryn," she replied in a stranger's hoarse tones.

"Merryn! What are you doing down here?"

"I fell into this place," she said. "What are *you* doing here? Did you fall, too?" She couldn't imagine anyone surviving such a drop, unless Huw had fallen into the pool. Perhaps he had used a rope. A horrible thought wormed its way into her mind. Maybe this wasn't Huw at all. Maybe some fell beast had found his broken body on the rocks and was borrowing it to trick her.

"Where are you?" cried the Huw-brute.

Rocks clattered. Merryn pictured a loathsome stone-beast dragging its bulk toward her. If only she had so much as a stick or a lightstaff with which to defend herself! "Stay back!" she squealed. "Don't come any closer, or I'll—I'll—!"

The footsteps stopped. "Very well. I'll sit right here. We can still talk without seeing each other. It's so dark I'd probably trip over you anyway. Is Cari with you, or did you come alone?"

"I'm alone," Merryn replied, and she related what had taken place at the castle in Huw's absence. Recalling the horrors of the stake, she exclaimed, "Why did you steal my lightstaff? I could have petrified the dragon king with it! Now the Fiddler is dead, and it's all your fault! You ought to be ashamed of yourself."

Huw let out a deep sigh. "I am very sorry. The rod is lost now. I dropped it on the causeway when a draig waylaid me."

"A draig! Why didn't it swallow you right then and there?"

"I don't know," Huw replied with such misery that Merryn almost pitied him. "I wish it had. After grabbing me, it flew me into this pit and left. I've been down here ever since. Today, another draig arrived, but it disappeared just before you showed up. I don't know which is worse, being devoured or starving."

Merryn said, "Now I know why the first draig didn't eat you! It was leaving you for the brooder. After she lays her eggs, the brooder stays here, feeding on whatever her friends bring her."

"Eggs?" Huw said. "What eggs?"

"The greenstones are actually dragon eggs," Merryn told him. "I saw them hatching today. The babies even attacked me."

"You don't say!" Huw exclaimed. "That explains why the dreigiau appeared after Ifan threw his stone in here. But why couldn't the brooder just lay her eggs and move on? Why does she hang around this miserable hole instead of flying away?"

"Dragon eggs must need lots of warmth to hatch, so the brooder remains behind to breathe on them. As you know, when the eggs are heated or boiled, they also give off the green mist."

Huw groaned. "So that's why the mist ceased to flow! When I disturbed the greenstones—eggs, that is—the brooder came out to investigate, leaving the other eggs in here to cool."

Merryn took up the tale. "When she swallowed the pilfered eggs, her mothering instincts took over and she left to find a safe place to rear her young. The remaining eggs have taken longer to hatch because they had no heat." Suddenly, a long-neglected book opened in Merryn's mind as she chased a draig through sharp-bladed swamp grass. At last, she *remembered*.

"We'll have plenty of heat down here when that brooder returns and makes us its next meal," said Huw sourly. "Face it: This is the end of the causeway for us. And I lied. I don't have a sword."

"Your brooder won't be returning, nor any other draig, either," said Merryn, and she told Huw how the Fiddler's sacrifice had led to the torsil storm still raging above. "That thundering noise is the sound of all the cors dreigiau and their eggs being drawn back into their own world, and the hydras with them."

"Oh, no!" Huw said. "Without those eggs, our people will perish within a generation! In the meantime, what will we eat instead of dragon meat? We are all doomed to starve or rot!"

Merryn heart went hollow. No dragon eggs meant no marsh mist. The Vinelanders would gradually die out, leaving their castles as monuments to a vanished tribe of lost Lucambrians.

"I'm sorry," she said. "I was only doing what Ifan's riddle had predicted. Your ancestor brought a curse on this land when he climbed the hudo tree and stole that egg, and I was merely setting matters straight. How was I to know what would happen when the curse was 'reversed'? Would you rather be sitting in the brooder's belly while it hatched another batch of eggs?"

Huw grunted. "I suppose you're right. However, we're still stuck down here without any hope of rescue."

"With Gaelathane there is always hope," said Merryn softly. "In case we're not found in time, though, there's something I want you to know. Your sister—the one who disappeared—" The words stuck in her throat and dammed up her tears.

"What about her?" said Huw irritably.

"She didn't die."

Floop! A stone plopped into the pool, sending ripples mincing musically among the rocks. "Then what did happen to her?"

Words and tears flowed from Merryn like waters long pent up. "She—she followed you when you sneaked out of the castle that night to visit Split-top. I believe she wanted to help you."

"Even if she had," Huw said, "I would have spotted her in the moonlight. Anyway, I saw her torn, bloody sash lying in the grass. One of those accursed beasts snatched and devoured her. She's dead, and don't try to convince me otherwise, gwas girl!"

"She tore her sash in strips to wrap her feet after the marsh grass sliced them to ribbons," Merryn persisted. "And you know very well how cunning she was, crafty enough to creep through the swamp without being seen. Didn't she use to spy on you by hanging from the wall outside your window?"

Huw let out a choking gasp. "You—you're just grasping at leaves. I don't remember any such thing."

Merryn pressed on. "She was watching when you threw those eggs into the brooder's mouth, and assuming the beast was carrying you off, she trailed it to Ifan's Hill, where it burrowed under the roots of the hudo tree that grew there. Following the draig, she made passage into my world. As she was leaving the burrow, however, a great stone fell from the tunnel roof and struck her head, wiping away all memory of her former life."

"What an amusing cellmate you are!" said Huw. "If you keep this up, I'll forget all the meals I've missed. How many more tall tales can you tell to help pass the time until we die?"

"It's not just a story," said Merryn, her face aflame in the darkness. "It's the truth! That draig didn't eat your sister."

"Then why didn't she return to Gwinwydden?"

"Weren't you listening?" Merryn flared. "She lost her memory! The poor girl didn't know who or where she was. She couldn't have returned home if she'd tried." Merryn racked her brain for some detail that would persuade Huw his sister was still alive.

"You once had a draenog named Miniog," she began.

"What of it? You could have learned that from anybody in the castle. Now leave me alone. I want to get some sleep before that brooder returns to put us out of our misery." He sighed. "If only I could have said good-bye to Mother and Cari."

"As I was saying," Merryn went on, "Miniog was your pet draenog, and your sister was very jealous of you, since she had no pets of her own. One night, she crept into your room and took Miniog from his little basket in the corner. She kept him in a wicker cage in her closet until he escaped by squeezing through a hole in the wickerwork. A couple of days later, someone found him swimming in a rain barrel and returned him to you."

"Drat that girl!" said Huw. "She was into mischief more often than she was out of it. It's a wonder she lived as long as she did. Since you seem to know so much about her, why don't you speak of her by name? I'll tell you why. You've concocted this tale out of the bits and pieces you've gleaned from my mother and the servants. Nobody would tell you her name because the queen has forbade anyone from speaking it. She doesn't want to be reminded of her only daughter, and I don't blame her. That girl was more trouble than a hundred other mist-maidens her age."

"You're wrong about me, Huw," said Merryn. "I learned a little about your sister from others. The rest I . . . remembered."

"Remembered?" said Huw scornfully. "How could you remember anything about a dead girl you've never met?"

"I know her well. I *am* your sister, and those eggs you filched are still in the draig's belly, just waiting to hatch in my world."

CHAPTER 22

The Water Tree

Stop it!" Huw roared. "Enough of these lies! G—my sister is dead and gone, and that's that. Nobody can bring her back."

"You never found her body."

"Of course not! The draig ate her! Now go to sleep!"

Seeing no use in pursuing the subject further, Merryn felt her way to the pool and dipped a finger in its frigid water. No prickly teeth seized her, so she ladled water into her parched mouth.

Refreshed, she curled into a ball for warmth, murmured a prayer and was nodding off when a string of high, sweet notes wafted down into the darkness, weaving a melodious tapestry of word and thought that settled over her like a soft blanket:

> Over the marsh I seek for you;
> Be not afraid; gone is the draig!
> Into the deep, I sing to you;
> Hearken unto My song!
>
> Out of the wind I call to you;
> Rescue is nigh; you shall not die!
> Hearing your heart, I cling to you
> With cords that My love made strong!

Over the storm I fly to you,
Bringing a rope that's spun of hope!
Calm lies the land when I am through
With purging it of all wrong!

Out of the gloom I cry to you,
Be not dismayed! Death is betrayed!
Following Me, you have subdued
The beasts that do not belong!

Merryn awoke to find sharp stones poking her back and sides. Judging from the gray light, the torsil storm had passed in the lands above. *I saw the Fiddler fall, and the rocks dripped red with his blood. Who then was singing to me before I slept?*

Then the same Voice spoke again, its words thundering into the chasm. "I am the light of every world; he who believes in Me shall not walk in darkness but shall have the light of life."

"Someone's come to save us!" Huw shouted. "Help! We're down here! Hey, lower us a rope with some food and ale!"

However, no rope came uncoiling into the chasm. Instead, a lofty light appeared above the pair, brighter than the morning star that shines in all torsil worlds, and it was falling.

"What is that?" cried Huw. Light filled the dragons' rookery like water, devouring shadows that had long bred unhindered in the cliffs. This was not a glaring light, such as a burning torch throws off, nor yet a wan, yellowish candle's light. It was a living rainbow-light, and it pierced Merryn's soul to the core.

Swiftly the star dropped until every rock and ridge stood out starkly in its brilliant light. Then there came a soft splash, and as suddenly as it had appeared, the light vanished, plunging the ravine into a darkness thicker than curdled stone.

"Merryn, where are you?" Huw hollered. "What's happened?" As his voice echoed recklessly off the rocks, a softer light shone out of the depths of Stygweth's pool, whose waters began bulging in the center like an enormous, swelling bubble.

"The pancake-beast is coming for us!" Merryn cried.

However, Stygweth still lay at the bottom of her pool, blind to the light that had spread across her bosom like the first blush of dawn. Now the water shrank back from the shoreline as it mounded higher in the middle, making a bulbous, shining shape like the smooth, featureless head of a hulking water beast. Eyeless fishes and other odd creatures swam in its transparent depths.

"What's going on?" said Huw hoarsely. "Is that a water dragon? We'd better get out of here!" He edged away from the pool.

Climb on. Startled by the Voice, Merryn stared about. What was there to climb? She tested the pond with her foot. It was as solid as the crystal lake she had trodden in Gaelessa. She took a cautious step forward, then another. The water held.

"How did you do that?" Huw exclaimed.

"I just put one foot in front of the other," Merryn shot back. "Come on; I think we're supposed to climb that thing growing in the middle of the lake, whatever it is."

Stepping gingerly, Huw followed Merryn to the swelling bump, which was sprouting knobby side shoots like stubby clothes-tree arms. "Maybe we can hang onto one of those," Merryn suggested. She shinnied up the water-hump and settled on a thick nub.

Grumbling, Huw joined her. "Now what?" he said. "Do we sit here until we turn into tadpoles? What are we to do for water, now that it's all gone stiff? Honestly, you've been nothing but trouble ever since you showed up and broke down our gates."

"That proves I'm really your sister," Merryn retorted.

The tree-like lump grew so rapidly that before the two knew it, the pond below them had shrunk to a mere puddle. "Help!" cried Huw. "Where is this thing taking us? I want to get off!"

"I'm afraid it's too late for that now," Merryn said as she clung to the frozen waterspout. Rock walls silently blurred by and the daylight grew steadily stronger as she and Huw were lifted out of the ravine. Then the cliffs fell away and the world unfolded like a rose under dewy skies. Stripped clean of its former corruption, the dreary landscape stretched out gray, moist and still.

"We're out!" Huw whooped.

As the water tree rose above Split-top, Merryn glimpsed a man fiddling away, his lilting music floating skyward like spent cherry blossoms carried on the wind. Cloaked in mist, the Castell Mawr swam into view, still perched on its lonely prominence despite the torsil storm's ravages. Swamps and hills shrank together as the tree passed through a layer of wispy clouds that shrouded the earth in a feathery haze. The air snapped like a frozen twig.

Still the shining water tree grew. As its stubby arms lengthened, side and tip branches budded out, dividing into fine, flat sprays of water-filled foliage. This was the same Tree Merryn had once climbed to reach Gaelessa, and she wept over it in love.

At last the Tree's growth slowed and stopped. The pair sat clinging to its swaying top as the wind roared through its limbs. Then another branch budded from the trunk, shooting out farther than the others. At its very tip, a bright spot appeared and rapidly grew. Dazzling light poured from the opening, and then a figure flew out that Merryn recognized as one of the castle's winged trumpeters. He wore a linen robe that shone like quicksilver, and his kindly face radiated the love of the King.

"Who are you?" asked Huw, his eyes as big as barrel tops.

"I am the angel Melchandor, and I have been sent to give you these." Holding out his hands, the angel showed Huw and Merryn five smooth stones. Greener than dragons' eggs, they were round and flat, like the stones Merryn used to skip across the Foamwater. They glowed fiercely in the Tree's light.

Handing the stones to Merryn, Melchandor said, "The Fiddler will tell you what to do with them." Then the angel spread his magnificent wings and flew back into the shimmering hole.

"Wait!" cried Merryn. "Take me with you!" But then it was too late, for the light-gate had already dwindled to a speck and disappeared. Choking back tears, Merryn pocketed the five stones. They seemed a poor trade for the glories of Gaelessa.

"We'd better climb down now," said Huw. "Just watch your step; it must be a very long way to the bottom of this tree."

Before they could move, however, their perch shuddered and began to shrink. Merryn's stomach heaved as the world rushed up like a broad-rimmed bowl overflowing with gray mud. When Splittop drew near, the Tree's earthward retreat slowed, allowing the two adventurers to hop onto the hilltop. Music sounded as a fiddling figure strolled over to meet them.

"Welcome back!" said the Fiddler with a twinkle in his eye.

Hands on hips, Huw shot Merryn a reproachful look. "I thought you said the Fiddler was dead!"

"He was! I mean, I thought he was," said Merryn, confused.

"Dead?" The Fiddler laughed. "Oh, no. Death mired me down once, but never after. As you saw, Drundaig sorely wounded me. However, after you left, I quickly recovered. I hold the keys to Death and Gundul, so neither power has any grip on me."

Merryn eyed the Fiddler's well-worn instrument. "Your violin recovered quickly, too, I see. Thank you for saving my life, by the way. My blood should have been spilled at the stake, not yours. Tell me, though: Whatever happened to Drundaig's world?"

The Fiddler played a lament before answering. "As Drundaig showed no mercy, no mercy was shown him. Shennis, Land of Mist, is no more. From dust it was created, and to dust it has returned. All that remains are the stones Melchandor gave you—the Shennis Stones. For centuries, my name was scorned in that world. Now Shennis has passed into the Outer Darkness, whence there is no returning. Another limb has fallen from the Tree, never to grow again. I do not wish for even the least of my worlds to perish, but my creation often chooses to go its own way."

Huw took a step back. "Who *are* you?" he demanded.

Light burst through the Fiddler's rags as Gaelathane revealed Himself in splendor, and Huw son of Rhynion fell on his face, trembling from head to toe. Merryn bowed before her King.

"I am your Maker and the King of the Trees," said Gaelathane, raising Huw to his feet. "All that exists was conceived and created by Me, and apart from Me, there is neither life nor breath, love nor light, hope nor help. No person or thing that rejects Me can long survive, whether it be a proud heart or a stubborn world."

Merryn gazed into Gaelathane's sorrowing eyes. "But why did I have to return my greenstone—the egg—to Drundaig?"

"In My kingdom," He said, "justice must be served, even where dragons are concerned! If what is stolen is not restored, the land will languish under the weight of its rebellion." Raising the fiddle to His shoulder, He played a series of falling notes. With the last note, the Tree dissolved in a deluge of water and spray. A huge gray umbrella landed on the rocks and feebly flopped about before lying still. Stygweth of the many mouths was no more.

"Look at this!" Merryn cried. She picked up a lightstaff that looked remarkably like hers and stuck it under her belt. "It must have gotten caught up in the Tree, and the water left it behind!"

"My staffs can transform whatever they touch into the essence of the Tree," Gaelathane explained. "In unbelieving hands, however, they eventually lose their powers. That is why the stolen staff betrayed you, Huw. Will you now betray Me?"

Huw's eyes widened. "Betray You? How?"

Gaelathane laid a scarred hand on the prince's arm. "When you live your life as though I do not exist, that is betrayal of the worst sort. Long have I sought entrance to your bitter heart, Huw son of Rhynion. Will you now let Me in of your own free will, or do you wish to continue walking in darkness?"

Huw knelt before Him. "I will walk with You always in the light," he said fervently. "Who could have guessed the Fiddler was actually a King? Wait till my mother hears about this!" He frowned and bit his lip. "What if she doesn't believe me?"

"Once she sees you, she'll believe you," Gaelathane said. "To that end, we must first enter into the miracle of Ifan's Lake."

"Ifan had a lake?" said Huw. "I've never heard of it."

"That is because it has just been born," said the King, and He pointed to the ravine where dragons had once hatched. The chasm was brimming over with limpid, shining water.

"Where did all that water come from?" Merryn puzzled. Even if the water tree had drawn up every last drop in Stygweth's pool, it would still not be enough to fill the canyon to overflowing.

"Whatever I touch, I also multiply and cleanse," said Gaelathane. "These are the same Waters of Life that flow from the Tree in Gaelessa to fill the Lake of Love, and they will fill this cleft in the rock until the end of time. The lake lacks but one thing."

"What is that?" chorused Huw and Merryn.

"The Shennis Stones," Gaelathane replied. "When these healing and purifying waters have passed over the stones for a period of seven ages, they shall be fit for My service again, and I shall make of them a finer world than the one that perished."

"Passed over?" asked Merryn. "Does that mean—?"

"Yes, My dear child. You must commit them to the deep."

From her pocket, Merryn took one of the Shennis Stones. How like a dragon's egg it looked, and yet how unlike! Cupping it in her hand, she sent it skipping over the lake—Splish! Splish! Splish!—

until it sank. So clear were those waters that she could follow the stone's fluttering course nearly all the way to the bottom. The other four stones quickly joined the first.

Gaelathane clapped His hands. "Very good!" He said. "Now we have only to watch and wait for the stones to awaken."

Bubbles began breaking on the lake's unruffled surface. Green bubbles. Bursting, they released puffs of greenish gas, which swiftly spread across the teardrop-shaped body of water.

"I don't understand!" Merryn said. "I thought all the eggs went back to Shennis. Are some of them still left down there?"

"Not a one," said Gaelathane. "Nothing of the dragon kind remains in this world. What you are seeing is the Shennis Stones at work. In water, they throw off the same green fog that the eggs did, but this mist will not burn off in the sunlight."

To Huw and Merryn's astonishment, Gaelathane then stepped onto the lake and began walking across it. Turning, He smiled at them and beckoned, and they followed on shaking legs.

"This lake must be hundreds of feet deep, and I can't swim!" muttered Huw. However, he and Merryn joined their King in the middle of the lake without so much as wetting their feet.

"Now for your leaves," Gaelathane announced. He took up the fiddle again, playing dulcet, drawn-out notes that coaxed the wispy mist around the three until they stood in a green pool.

"I don't want to become a Greenie!" Merryn cried.

Love and sympathy mingled in Gaelathane's eyes. "If you wish, you may depart this place and return home leafless, but if you do so, you must not delay, or it will be too late. However, if you remain, you will fulfill your life's destiny as My servant."

Merryn hung her head. "I will stay here with You and Huw."

Then the itching began, and it was all Merryn could do to stay put. Realizing that if she lost her nerve, she could also lose her life, she closed her eyes against the rising tide of green, as a captain hides his face from the sea that claims his doomed ship.

She wept. She wept for her skin, for beauty lost, for the flawless reflection in Gaelathane's lake that she could never be on earth. She wept for her mother, for her brother and for every other smoothskin who would never recognize or accept her clothed in leaves. *Perhaps a partial outbreak would be better.*

Following the mist, the itching worked its way up her body, and its torment consumed her. Screams raked her raw throat, accompanying Huw's groans. She ripped at her pocked skin until her nails and fingers ran red with blood. Still the green itch-gnats swarmed over her, biting and stinging her without mercy.

"Gaelathane," she sobbed. "Please help me. I can't bear it any longer. Please make this agony stop before I—"

"Peace, little one," He said. Strong arms encircled her beneath the green blanket, and the itching subsided. Merryn opened her eyes to find that the fog had risen above her chin.

Still, she could not surrender to the mist. She stood on tiptoe, and as the green covered her nose, she gasped, "I can't breathe! Please make the mist go away or take me to Gaelessa!"

"It will not harm you, child. Breathe. Yes, that's right. Relax and breathe, and all will be well. Your sufferings will end soon, for the second blaguryn is always shorter than the first."

Merryn held her breath until the blood roared in her ears and her heart hammered. When at last she drew in a draught of burning ice, the mist muffled her screams. Struggling in Gaelathane's embrace, she took another long, shuddering breath, and a hundred spikes began working their way through her flesh with piercing, sweet pangs. Never had she known such torture, but as the skewers broke out, they soothed away her itching.

"I, too, once was pierced," said the Champion, cradling Merryn's limp form. Sagging in His arms, she looked down at herself. Vigorous, blue-green vines were breaking through her skin, reaching for the light as the green mist dispersed.

"Glaslyn!" Cloaked in his own vines, Huw was struggling to his feet, a look of bewilderment spreading across his face. "Glaslyn!" he repeated. "It really is you. I never would have believed it possible after all this time, and yet here you are!" His whips shyly touched Merryn's, and then she knew: She was Glaslyn, princess of Vineland, daughter of Rowena and Rhynion.

Huw wryly smiled. "Glaslyn means 'blue.' You were still a toddler when we exposed you to the niwl gwyrdd. Mother held you all through your blaguryn. We marveled at the bluish tint to your leaves, and that's how you got your name. I'm sorry I didn't believe you, and I'm sorry for stealing your staff, too."

"Glaslyn." She rolled the name over her tongue, liking the familiar feel and sound of it. Throwing herself on Huw, she embraced him with arms and vines and together, they wept and laughed themselves hoarse, their voices ringing over the lake.

"Now for some real fun!" said Gaelathane with a wink, and He took Glaslyn and her brother to the brow of the mountaintop. Fitting the fiddle under His chin, He began playing a merry tune that set Glaslyn's vines to dancing.

The marsh mud quivered and green lumps sprouted from it. Some rapidly grew into swamp oaks and sycamores, poplars and tulip trees, while others became frogs and turtles, salamanders and snails. Then ducks and geese appeared, along with eagles, swans, jays, woodpeckers, wrens and a host of other birds unknown to Glaslyn. Fur-bearing creatures followed: There were scampering squirrels, slinking minks and frisky otters, among others. Like a green flood, the fiddle-forest rippled across the mud flats in all directions. Vineland was being reborn.

"Just look, Huw!" Glaslyn cried. "No more hydras or dragons or swamps, just real forests and real birds and animals! Let's go down and see them for ourselves. Are you coming with me?"

Gaelathane stopped His fiddling. "You may explore later," He said solemnly. "You two have much work to do before the night falls." Setting the bow to His violin, He began playing again.

"But it is just past noon!" Huw protested.

"That's right," said Glaslyn. "There's plenty of time until dark. Besides—" Her vines tugged at her. Bobbing in time with Gaelathane's music, the whips were weaving in and out as if possessing a life all their own. Ever more spiritedly the King's fiddle sang as back and forth, up and down the vines wove, gradually forming a leafy mesh that quivered and snapped in the wind.

"Hey!" cried Huw. "What are You doing?" But Gaelathane played on until the pair's every vine was intertwined with its neighbor and every tendril plaited into place. Last of all, Glaslyn and Huw's leafy mats were joined together to create a solid sheet. The violin bow slowed, wailing across the shining strings.

"Really, this will never do," Huw announced in his most princely tones. "Glas and I may be sister and brother, but that's no reason to sew us together like a couple of carpets! Why—"

A howl from behind the hill drowned out his next words as a dust cloud boiled up and swept toward the three. When the gale struck Huw and Glaslyn, their woven vines billowed and bellied out like a leafy sail, dragging them across the rocks.

"Run!" Gaelathane cried after them. "Run for it!"

Run or be dragged, thought Glaslyn as she and her brother half-ran, half-slid toward the mountain's brink. Then the ground fell away and their flailing feet found only empty space.

"Help!" Glaslyn cried, but instead of falling, she and Huw lofted higher into the sky, swept along by the shrieking wind. Huw's legs pumped, and he waved his arms excitedly.

"We're flying!" he shouted. "We're really flying!"

"But where are we going?" Glaslyn shouted back. Her answer came in the form of the Castell Mawr, which was looming before them with terrifying swiftness. Glaslyn screamed.

"We're going to crash!" Huw yelled as they sailed toward the castle. "Can't you do something to slow us down?"

To her surprise, Glaslyn found she could control their flight merely by tightening or loosening the weave of their shared sail. Working together, the two rapidly descended until their feet were skimming over the mountaintop where the castle sat.

"Look out for that rock!" cried Huw, and they both raised their legs just in time to avoid smashing into a boulder.

Glaslyn was wondering how they were to set down without injury when the wind gentled, and she and Huw hit the ground running. After a few yards, the pair separated their vines and unraveled the rest of the sail. Gasping and laughing, they rolled on the dirt, letting their whips wriggle like long, leafy fingers.

The wind sprang up again, and Glaslyn felt cold, wet drops pattering on her leaves. Still laughing, she told her brother, "Hurry! We've got to reach the castle before we're drenched!" As the rain drummed down in earnest, she arranged her vines to form a leafy parasol to fend off the worst of the downpour.

The torsil storm had thoroughly scoured the mountain, plastering the castle's walls with marshy debris. The portcullis, inner and outer gates had been neatly plucked from their places. Glaslyn and Huw stopped dead outside the entrance. "Where are the gates?" Huw rasped. Passing through the paved archway, Glaslyn shuddered as she recalled how the black cart had trundled her out of the castle over those very stones.

Inside the walls, the two found scores of dazed Vinelanders milling about. Not a single dragon pole cluttered the courtyard; all had apparently been swept away along with the new gates and portcullis. No one took notice of the two mulberry bushes shuffling toward the Carreg Keep, nor did anyone raise the alarm when those bushes squeezed through the Keep's door.

Blinded by the darkness inside, Glaslyn unleashed her supple fronds. *Rough. Cold. Smooth. Slimy. Bitter.* Vivid sensations of flavor and texture, warmth and odor came back as her tendrils probed the place. Then she tasted a sharp tang. *Iron.* She had found the sgaffaldwaith, and she finally knew its purpose.

Glaslyn flittered across the floor and ducked inside one of the scaffolding's portals. Hurling whips into the blackness above, she hauled herself up through the cage's center, just as generations of mist-people had done before they lost their leaves. At the top, she curled her vines around the ceiling latticework and swung down the corridor to the queen's study. The door was ajar, and voices were murmuring inside. Glaslyn threw open the door and flounced in, leaves and vines all a-quiver.

Cari, Noni (still in her vines), Dewi, Timothy and the Lucambrians were gathered around the queen's cot. Seeing Glaslyn, Opio and Gemmio drew their swords, while Elwyn grabbed an iron poker and held it at the ready. Then Huw burst inside.

"You should have waited for me!" he told Glaslyn.

Dewi's eyes flitted between the two. Then his face went slack and his jaw sagged. "By the queen's greenstone," he gasped, "it's Prince Huw and Princess Glaslyn, returned from the dead!"

With a squeal, Cari smothered Huw in her arms. Queen Rowena sat up, and seeing the two visitors clothed in leaves, fell back in a faint. While Dewi revived her, the questions flew like fury. Where was Merryn's lightstaff? How had Huw survived outside the castle walls? When had his vines grown back? Where had Glaslyn been all those years everyone had thought her dead?

Leaving her brother to parry the questions, Glaslyn turned to the queen, who had come around again. In the short time Glaslyn had been away, Rowena had shrunken to a dry shell of her former self. Her translucent skin stretched tautly across her sharp jaw and cheekbones like strings over a fiddle bridge.

"Mother, it's me, Glaslyn," she said, weeping.

Eggshell lids fluttered open, and bleary, yellowed eyes stared up at her. Waxen lips formed the words, "Glaslyn is dead."

"No, she's not. I'm right here, Mother. Can't you see that it's really me? I've come back to you, and I'll never leave again!" Enfolding the dying queen in her vines, she kissed her cheek.

Rowena's eyes focused. "The voice is the voice of Merryn, but how could I forget my daughter's fronds? Like new grape leaves kissed by the sun they were, with the sweet odor of summer fruits. Have I truly lived to see you again, my dear Glas?"

"You have, Mother!" Glaslyn cried. "The niwl gwyrdd is back, too. Huw and I will take you to the lake where it flows, and you will be made well. All our people will have their leaves again!"

Tears rolling down his face, Dewi took her aside. "It's too late for that now. She wouldn't survive the blaguryn. Now it's time you told us who you really are, imposter!"

Glaslyn's friends were staring at her dubiously. "Yes, who are you?" Rolin said. "From what we have heard, Princess Glaslyn was carried off by a dragon many years ago. Now she reappears, speaking with our friend Merryn's voice. How can this be?"

Starting with the night she had followed Huw to Split-top, Glaslyn related how she had ended up in Beechtown as Merryn, the pockmarked girl without a past. "Now I not only have a past but also a future," she said. "If you'll all have me, that is."

Dewi said, "We would, if only we knew how Merryn—or Glaslyn—escaped death at the stake. No Aberth in all Gwinwydden's long history has ever returned alive from Split-top."

"The Fiddler took my place," said Glaslyn, and she relived the terrifying events that had led to Vineland's deliverance.

"What a dreadful ordeal you've had!" said Gemmio. "Yet, it's just like Gaelathane to sacrifice Himself to save another's life."

"A torsil storm," murmured Bembor. "I have heard of such a thing, but never have I seen one before. We thought the Carreg Keep itself would be uprooted and carried away!"

"I never want to see another hydra fly by the castle windows!" said Cari, and shivering, she pulled her cloak around her.

"You weave a convincing tale, stranger," said Dewi. "However, I find it remarkably coincidental that a long-dead princess should appear at her mother's deathbed in time to contest the crown."

"I make no such claim!" Glaslyn snapped. "Let my brother take the throne, as he ought." She uncovered her face and drew out her lightstaff. "Look at me!" she cried. "It is I, Merryn, and this is my staff. Merryn and Glaslyn are one and the same, if you care to accept it. If not, then look beyond the four walls of this castle, and you will see for yourselves the rest of my story is true."

The others rushed to the window and looked out. When Dewi turned back, his face was gray. "My eyes have beheld the salvation of Gwinwydden," he said. "Forests wave where dreigiau once flew; all has been restored, just as was foretold." The bailiff fell to his knees. "Welcome home, Princess Glaslyn!"

Tears streamed down Queen Rowena's sunken cheeks. "Woe is me! I condemned my own daughter to ride the cart, when she was the 'heir' that was to save us all! Now the blood of every Aberth is on my hands." Exhausted, she fell back against her pillow.

"You couldn't have known who I was, Mother," said Glaslyn. "Not even I knew. You mustn't blame yourself, for it was not you who sent me to the stake, but Gaelathane. He planned all this from the beginning so that no more of Vineland's maidens would have to die. The King does love you, and so do I."

"Don't exert yourself, Mother," Huw said, smoothing her hair with a tendril. "It is time for you to rest from your labors."

The queen's eyes flashed. "I'm not dead yet! I have something to say to you and your Cariad." She motioned weakly to her adopted daughter, who edged closer, her hands clenched.

"Forgive me for all the grief I've caused you both," Rowena said. "If you still wish to wed, you have my permission and my blessing. I am sure you will be very happy together."

Tears sprang to Huw's eyes. "Thank you, Mother! Your blessing means more to me than any crown or title." Weeping, he and Cari kissed her on the forehead and caressed her hands.

"She who loves much is forgiven much." Dressed in soiled rags, the Fiddler stepped into the light, bow and violin in hand. Elwyn snatched up his poker, and metal rang as the sons of Nolan drew their swords again, fell purposes written upon their faces.

"Who are you, and how came you here?" they demanded.

"I am that I am," said the Fiddler. "I have been here all along, hoping to be invited into your conversation." His ragged guise fell away, revealing him as Gaelathane, robed in glory.

"It's the King!" Marlis gasped, and everyone but Queen Rowena bowed to Him. Laying aside His fiddle, He took Rowena's pale hand in His own and asked, "Do you recall the day you wandered off from the castle and lost your way in the swamp?"

The queen's eyelids slowly raised as if straining against great weights. "Why, yes! I had almost forgotten about that escapade. I believe I was five at the time. How did You know?"

"I was the stranger who saved you from the draig and brought you back home," said Gaelathane with a tender smile.

Rowena's eyes sparked. "That was You? Twice You've saved me now. Thank You, my Lord." Her eyelids and head drooped.

"You are welcome," said the King. "Now I must take you home again." Raising His fiddle, He played a soothing melody until the Tree of trees appeared, its graceful branches splaying into the study. Then He bent low over Rowena. Straightening, He raised a radiant maiden from the cot, and together, they climbed the Tree into eternity. The Tree disappeared after them, its light fading slowly from the room, a sunset reluctant to leave this world.

White clouds chased red ones in Dewi's face. "Is she—?"

King Rolin glanced down at the cot and then at Dewi, Cari, Noni, Huw and Glaslyn. "I'm sorry to have to tell you this, but—"

"Our mother is gone, isn't she?" said Huw, his eyes brimming. He stroked the queen's cheek, but her smiling, serene face remained unchanged. Noni and Cari burst into tears.

"The queen is dead; long live the queen!" murmured Dewi.

"Don't you mean, 'long live the king'?" asked Marlis.

Dewi said, "By our traditions, the one who fulfills Ifan's riddle shall inherit Ifan's throne. Moreover, any Aberth who survives the stake is promised the crown after the death of the reigning monarch. Glaslyn has earned her title on both counts."

Glaslyn threw herself on Rowena's still form. "Mother, don't leave me! I so much wanted to know you better. Why did you have to die now? Oh, whatever am I going to do without you?"

Bembor's hand found its way through her vines to touch her shoulder. "You'll take up where she left off, as she would have wanted you to," he said huskily. "I know it's small comfort, but she's much happier now with Gaelathane in Gaelessa."

Glaslyn wiped her eyes with a leaf. Bembor was right, though sorrow's keen edge still stung her heart. She and Huw wrapped their mother's body in a shroud that Dewi furnished. Then they lowered her down the scaffolding and placed her in the black cart, which their friends rolled through the doorway.

A hush fell over the crowd outside at the sight of the leafy figures and the queen's shrouded body. Taking her stand beside the cart, Glaslyn announced, "Today we rejoice that the dragon king and all his ilk are dead!" At this, her hearers cheered and threw their cloaks and scarves into the air, and the children danced with delight. Glaslyn was trying to restore order when Dewi appeared with a bevy of smooth-skinned, chattering girls.

"Do you see these fair maidens?" he cried. "Thanks to Glaslyn and the Fiddler, no Aberth will ever again ride the cart or face the stake. Now welcome back your daughters from the dead!"

Amidst much weeping and shouting, the crowd rushed forward to embrace the bewildered girls and restore them to their families. Dewi reentered the Keep, returning shortly with Lemmy and Welt, who stood blinking in the glaring summer sunshine.

"Blimey, Welt!" said Lemmy. "Ain't a one o' them draig poles out here in th' yard. That means there's no impaling fer us!"

"We could still drop you off the top of the Keep if you'd like," Dewi said darkly. Taking the hint, the two men disappeared.

Glaslyn motioned with her vines, and the hubbub died down. "We sorrow—" Her voice broke as a sob forced its way out. "We sorrow that Queen Rowena has died this day." A groan went up from the throng, and many wept, tearing their garments.

Composing herself, Glaslyn continued. "Because of what the Fiddler has done, you no longer need to cower in your castle behind closed gates. Do you understand me? You are all free!"

Silence greeted this proclamation, as if the bare suggestion of spending a single unguarded minute outside the walls was unthinkable. Then a lone voice spoke up. "Who are you and how did you come to be clothed in leaves as we once were?"

"I am the Aberth!" she cried. "Glaslyn daughter of Rowena and Rhynion is my name. The niwl gwyrdd has returned!"

"Long live Queen Glaslyn!" someone shouted, and others took up the cry. "Long live Queen Glaslyn! May her vines grow long!"

Glaslyn turned to her brother and pleaded, "Tell them that as the eldest child, you are next in line for Vineland's throne!"

Huw smiled. "Didn't you hear what Dewi said? After braving the stake and fulfilling Ifan's riddle, you are the rightful heir." He waved his vines and shouted, "Long live Queen Glaslyn!"

As the multitude roared its approval, Cari came forward with a bag and shyly touched Glaslyn's leaves. "I never had a chance to thank you properly for saving my sister's life," she said. "As a small token of my gratitude, I'd like you to have this." She dug into her bag and brought out a beady-eyed, spiny ball.

"You want to give me Drelli?" Glaslyn exclaimed.

"I've never seen anyone handle that draenog the way you do," Cari said with a laugh. "It's almost as if she talks to you."

"Thank you!" said Glaslyn. Curling out a whip, she gently picked up the hedgehog and enclosed her in a nest of leaves.

"Eh! Unhand me! Let me out!" came Drelli's muffled voice.

Glaslyn retorted, "Scissors cut vines, spines break scissors, vines cover spines," adding a new twist to the age-old game.

"I'll give you spines!" sputtered Drelli. Hearing the hedgehog, Timothy and the Greencloaks broke into peals of laughter. When Huw, Noni and Cari traded puzzled looks, Glaslyn winked at them.

"Draenogs really can talk!" she said.

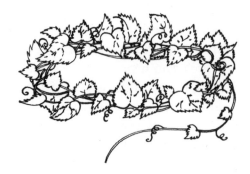

CHAPTER 23

Beer and Greenstones

Glaslyn crouched on the Greenies' hill, looking out over their camp. On this lazy, hazy September afternoon, she had returned to the Forest of Fellglade, hoping to dispose of the brooder and her eggs before they hatched. The campsite looked deserted. A solitary frog sang, but otherwise, the swamp was eerily quiet.

Then a tendril snaked across the ground and touched one of her own. Fear! Loneliness! Anger! A host of raw passions stormed up Glaslyn's vine like wildfire climbing a tall fir.

"Hello there, stranger! Who are you?" a man's voice hailed her. Once again, the Greenies had caught her off guard.

"It's me, Gl—Merryn," she called out, her heart hammering.

Mulberry bushes emerged from the trees fringing the hill. "Merryn? Ye're a Greenie now, too? We thought ye were dead! Where have ye been? When did ye have yer outbreak?"

With many such questions the Greenies plied Glaslyn, who told them the flood had forced her out of the Grotto after dusk, when she had encountered the marsh mist. Then she had gone in search of her father. Had they seen him?

The Greenies hadn't. Moreover, they had no interest in discussing his whereabouts. Instead, the bushy men fell over another telling Glaslyn their latest news.

"It's time! Bart says it's time!" Ramble said.

Glaslyn's head whirled. "Time for what?"

"Time to make Bart king of Beechtown!" they all declared.

"But why? Beechtown's already got a mayor," Glaslyn said. She recalled the blind bandit's boasting of his plans for seizing the town but had dismissed his talk as a lunatic's ravings.

The Greenies snapped their whips. "We're sick of this stinking swamp. Town life suits us much better. Bart has it all figgered out. He's a clever one, that Bart. Follow us, and we'll show ye."

Seeing she had little choice in the matter, Glaslyn reluctantly traipsed down the hill after the gabbling mulberry-men. At the bottom, King Bart shuffled out of the Grotto to greet them.

"What have you dunderheads been up to this time?" he demanded as he settled on his throne. His whips played over the men, drawing the truth from them. Then a tendril brushed Glaslyn, and she recoiled at the raw hatred surging through it.

"My, my," the marsh king said. "What has the green fog brought us today? And who might you be, young thing?"

"It's Merryn!" the other Greenies exclaimed.

Bart gasped. "Merryn! You have more lives than a cat! Somehow, I knew you'd be back. You've grown yourself a mess of healthy vines. I think we'll call you 'Beauty' from now on."

"I'm afraid I can't stay this time," she said in a small voice. "I'm looking for my father. Do you know where he is?"

The marsh king grunted. "He blew away in the storm, and we haven't seen him since. I reckon the gale wrapped him around a tree somewhere. You'll never find him, not in a hundred years."

"I still have to look," said Glaslyn resolutely.

"As you wish, but you're wasting your time. Join up with us, and you'll have your chance to pay back Beechtown's mockers."

One of the king's whips snaked into the cave behind him, returning with a shiny, emerald-colored object. It was a greenstone, the largest Glaslyn had ever seen.

"A pretty little bauble, isn't it—or so I've been told," King Bart remarked. "My men found it in the mud after the flood. Now I can easily spread the green breath through Beechtown's houses and hedgerows. You see, left in the sun, this rock gives off the green fog. Boiled in marsh water, it produces clouds of the stuff. I don't often bring it outside because an animal might steal it."

"That's no rock!" Glaslyn cried. "It's a dragon's egg, and it will only make enough mist for a partial outbreak, which is fatal. You must destroy it before it hatches, or we'll all be sorry!"

The mulberry-men hooted. "A dragon's egg?!" snorted Bart. "Why, let's make an omelet of it, then. Before that, we're going to initiate everyone in sleepy old Beechtown with it. Afterwards, you and my trusty men will reign with me as lords—and lady!"

"Three cheers for King Bart!" shouted the Greenies. "Hoorah! Hoorah! Hoorah! No more sleeping in caves and trees! No more drinking swamp water! No more snakes and mosquitoes!"

"You see?" gloated the marsh king. "With followers like these, I'll make Beechtown a steppingstone to greater things. Now if you'll excuse me, it's time for us to board our ship and set sail."

Sunlight fell upon the egg, producing wisps of greenish gas. "Put it away!" Glaslyn begged Bart. "Put it back in the cave before it's too late! You don't know what's out in that swamp."

"It's already too late," sneered King Bart. "Too late for your Smoothie friends, too late for my enemies, too late for Beechtown!" His cackling laugh sent shivers up Glaslyn's vines.

The green mist fell off as a cloud obscured the sun, cooling the egg. By then, though, it truly was too late. From the swamp came the sucking sound of a giant boot being pulled out of the mud. The marsh hummocks flew up as a gigantic form rose flapping into the air and landed heavily among the terrified Greenies.

"What was that?" Bart cried, his whips squirming.

Glaslyn screamed, "Get rid of it! Get rid of the egg!" The mulberry-men scattered, leaving their leader to fend for himself. Bart disappeared inside the Grotto and took the egg with him. As fire spurted from the brooder's nostrils, Glaslyn frantically fumbled for her lightstaff, knowing that when she brought the rod to bear on the beast, the toppling stone dragon would crush her.

All at once, the draig snorted and greedily licked its jaws, reminding Glaslyn of the drunken dragons on Watering Day. With a roar, the beast beat its leathery wings and launched itself skyward. Flinging a whip after it, Glaslyn caught the coiling tail and was jerked into the air. She had hoped the draig was returning to its marshy bed, where she could easily petrify it. However, she quickly realized the dragon had other plans of its own.

"Eeeeeeekkk!" Glaslyn wailed as forest and marsh rushed by below her and the wind roared in her ears. Twirling behind the monster like a kite caught by its string in a tree, she narrowly missed clipping the Beechtown bell tower and smashing into the chapel steeple. Then the dragon swerved and made a low pass over the brewery, sending screaming ant-people scurrying for cover. Glaslyn released her whip and dropped into a nearby tree. After catching her breath, she discovered her lightstaff had fallen out during her short but harrowing hitchhike into town.

Meanwhile, the brooder was snuffling around the brewery. Not finding a ready entrance, it flew up and with a blow of its massive tail, smashed a hole in the west wall. Alighting again, the draig stuck its snout inside and began making gulping noises. A few heads poked out of windows or from behind bushes, but no one appeared anxious to evict the dragon from the premises.

While the beast was thus occupied, Glaslyn lowered herself to the ground. Without her lightstaff, she couldn't hope to take on her foe, but something had to be done. Mincing up to the drinking draig, she peered around its scaly side. The thing's head filled her father's largest beer vat, which held five hundred gallons. That much beer would addle any dragon's brains and give it a terrific hangover to boot, spelling havoc for Beechtown.

She was about to retreat when Drelli fell out of her waist-pouch. The dizzy draenog staggered in circles before regaining her balance. "Where are we? What's happened?" she squeaked.

"Shush!" Glaslyn told her. "We're at my father's brewery, and this dragon is drinking all the beer. There's nothing I can do; I lost my lightstaff, and I haven't got a sword or a spear."

"You still have me!" said Drelli brightly. "A draig can't drink if it can't breathe." Before Glaslyn could stop her, the draenog had scurried up the dragon's tail and along its ridged spine.

"Drelli! Come back!" she cried, but the draenog had disappeared behind a hump. Glaslyn's stomach knotted with dread. Would she ever see her spiny, sharp-tongued friend again?

The dragon snorted, spitting sparks and flame. Then it backed out of the brewery. Glaslyn backed with it, hoping to avoid being stepped on. She was trampled instead by some rash spectators, who stampeded over her and one another trying to escape. Roaring in distress, the draig waggled its enormous head and clawed the ground, the beer in its belly sloshing noisily.

When the dragon's shoulders hunched and its eyes squeezed shut, Glaslyn plugged her ears. *ACHOO!* Sneezing, the draig ejected a small, smoking missile from its breathing hole. Then it turned on Glaslyn, its eyes reddening with a murderous rage.

"Thief!" the serpent snarled as it stalked toward her, sucking a hurricane into its maw to stoke the fires within.

Just then, the smoking ball dropped to earth and rolled into harm's way. Planting a webbed foot on Drelli, the draig shrieked to topple towers and shot into the air, sending Drelli bouncing across the dirt. After swooping in to scoop up the scorched draenog, Glaslyn retreated to her secret glen and peered out.

The beast that landed beside the brewery again was in a very sorry state. Its armored stomach was swelling, and it was burping up puffs of green smoke. Queen Rowena had once said that ale made her greenstone froth—and beer was beefier than ale.

Writhing in agony, the dragon tried to relieve the pressure in its bloating gut, but to no avail. Its belly grew until it resembled a scaly green balloon. Green mist spurted out of the draig's breathing hole and from its ears, nostrils and fanged jaws.

PLOOMPH! The brooder exploded in a blast of green fire that knocked down the already damaged brewery wall. Ducking flying dragon parts, Glaslyn crawled deeper into the dell, where she examined Drelli. The squashed draenog's spines were burnt and broken, and she whistled wetly with each labored breath.

"Thank you for saving my life, Drelli," Glaslyn told her.

The hedgehog whimpered, "What happened to me?"

"That draig sneezed you out its breathing hole. Then it stepped on you." Glaslyn wept as she stroked Drelli's scorched belly, her tears falling freely. "You'll be all right now. Once we've patched you up, you'll be as good as new." Privately, however, she doubted the draenog would survive the night.

"Sneezed out and stomped by a dragon, was I? If only I were a little larger, I could have finished the job, Draebold-style!"

"Do all dragons have such a taste for beer?"

Whirling, Glaslyn found another Greenie behind her, vines dancing. "Marsh dragons do," she said. "Who are you?"

"It's me, your father," said Hamlin. "I never thought I'd see you again! The marsh mist finally caught up with you, did it? I can't say I'm sorry. It's lonely being Beechtown's only Greenie."

Glaslyn felt faint with relief. "I thought you were—I mean, nobody has seen you since that day the wind carried you off."

"I was blown quite a distance, all right. I woke up in an oak some twenty miles northeast of here, completely lost. It was a grueling trek back to our hill, I'll tell you. I'd have died if I hadn't stopped to sun myself now and again. I hid out watching the camp until I overheard that the others had given you up for lost. After that, I wandered aimlessly, grieving for my Hoppy, until I found my way to Beechtown. Now I understand why Bart told us to forget our former lives. There's nothing left for me here."

"What about Mother? Have you tried to speak with her?"

"I did once, but she drove me off," said Hamlin gloomily. "Lately I've been watching the comings and goings at the brewery. Someone should go in there and straighten things out! By the smell alone, it's obvious those dimwits have forgotten everything I taught them about ale. The stuff they roll out of there now isn't fit for pig slop. And such carelessness! Someone left a spigot open last night, and all the ale ran out of a vat. You could smell it for miles. It's no wonder your dragon came sniffing around here."

All at once, screeching broke out beside the brewery. Glaslyn and Hamlin climbed higher and peeked over the valley's lip.

Milly stood before a crowd of crestfallen brewery workers, waving her arms and pointing. Though Glaslyn couldn't hear what her mother was saying, she could easily imagine it: *Just look at this mess! It will take a month of Sundays to clean it all up! Don't stand around with your mouths hanging open; get back to work!* As the cowed brewery crew began picking up after the dragon, Milly stormed into her house and slammed the door.

"We'd better go before someone spots us," said Hamlin softly. Linking whips, he and Glaslyn climbed down to the stream, where their leaves served as drinking cups and framed their reflected faces in viney foliage. Gray alders leaned over them as if eavesdropping, casting their old cones into the quick currents.

"Maybe it's time we started a new life together—as Greenies," Glaslyn suggested. "I know of a place where—"

Before she could finish, shouts rang out on the river. Following her father, she vined down the valley and perched in a poplar that overhung the shore. Moored in the midst of the Foamwater sat Rolc's battered ship, green fog billowing out of every hatch and porthole. Under the creeping shadow of the Tartellans, the mist was spreading across the water toward town.

The fog dropped off as greenery plugged the ship's hatches. Hollering mulberry-men were crawling out and frantically throwing themselves over the ship's side into the frigid water.

"What's gotten into those fellows?" said Hamlin.

"I don't know," Glaslyn replied. "But if we don't help them, the silly creatures will all drown." Dropping out of their tree, Glaslyn and her father anchored themselves to its trunk with their whips and took turns throwing out vine-lifelines to the Greenies.

"Heave ho!" cried Hamlin as he dragged the first man ashore. Shortly, fifteen piles of coughing, sputtering foliage lay flopping feebly on the sand. King Bart was the last to be rescued.

"Drat that blasted boat!" he groaned.

"I thought you were going to take over Beechtown," said Glaslyn archly. "What went wrong with your plan, anyway?"

"The fog," Bart choked out. "I forgot it will make dead wood sprout like a willow in spring. We were brewing up a nice thick batch of mist in the galley when the ship started growing shoots. We were lucky to get out of there when we did."

Sturdy oak switches were breaking out of Rolc's ship on all sides, creating a floating jungle. Planks popped and seams split as the craft tore itself apart. In its final agonies, the vessel settled by its stern and sank beneath the waves with a gurgling sigh. A bubbling green froth briefly hissed over the ship's grave.

"What we gonna do now, boys?" whimpered Molt. "Our boat's gone, the stone's lost, and we're miles from home!"

"This is all Bart's fault," grumbled Droopy.

"That's right. Into the water with him!" cried Bern.

"Yes! Into the water for Bart the Rat!" they all chorused.

Over their leader's protests, the Greenies trussed him up in his own vines and tossed him back into the river, where he promptly sank. Glaslyn's heart sank with him. Much as though she disliked the blind highwayman's ruthless ways, she couldn't bear to see him drown. "Gaelathane!" she cried. "Please save him!"

Where Bart had gone down, bubbles boiled and broke on the river's surface. Then a green, sodden mass bobbed up and awkwardly dragged itself across the water toward shore.

"Great leaping toadfish!" cried Ramble. "He's a-walkin' on th' water! We're in fer it now, fellers!" The mulberry-men fell on their knees and prostrated themselves before their king.

On reaching dry ground, Bart promptly collapsed in a tangled heap. Behind him stood another Man garbed in a white robe.

"Hey! Where did You come from?" the Greenies demanded. They joined vines to form a solid hedge, barring His way.

A faint smile lit Gaelathane's lips. "Aren't you going to thank Me for saving your friend?" Receiving no answer, He strode forward and effortlessly passed through the leafy barrier.

"How did He do that?" the Greenies asked one another. "Wait up there! Where are You going? What's Your name?"

Gaelathane turned back. "I never stay where I'm uninvited. And why do you ask My name? I am Who I am."

Puzzled, the Greenies broke ranks to gather around the King and touch Him with their whips. Gasping and wheezing, Blind Bart let Glaslyn and her father help him to his feet.

"What do you wish of Me, men?" asked the King of the Trees.

The Greenies shuffled their feet. "Some of us got wives and young 'uns in town," said Stumpy. "We cain't go back as we are, or folks would set their dogs on us. We've no company but our own to enjoy, and we're sick to death of each other and of our swamp. If we could jest get a glimpse of our kin . . ."

"I can do better than that," Gaelathane said. He opened His mouth and a river of white mist poured out. The Greenies shrank back, but the fog quickly surrounded and engulfed them. Oddly enough, Glaslyn and Hamlin were left standing in the clear.

"What are You doing to us?" the men cried. Bart shivered, his vines restlessly seeking out what his eyes could not fathom.

Singly at first and then in clumps and clusters, the Greenies' whispering whips dropped off and withered where they lay. When the white mist drifted away, it left behind a pitiful band of half-naked men clothed in filthy rags and festering sores.

Sitting on the ground, Bart clawed at himself. "Where are my vines?" he screeched. "Don't leave me like this! You've made me Bartholomew the Blind again! I would rather die than beg."

"Your name is Bartholomew son of Bertrund, and you shall not beg," said the King. He laid His hands on Bart's white-filmed eyes. When He removed His hands, those eyes shone a clear ice blue.

Bart blinked. "Why, I can—I can *see!*" Pointing at his companions, he exclaimed, "Look at that! Walking trees with noses!"

His men stared at him. "We're not trees, Bart; it's us, your mates! This is how we really look." They crowded around him and shook his hand and pounded him on the back.

"Some 'mates' you turned out to be," said Bart. "First you throw me in the river and then you congratulate me." He gazed at Gaelathane. "Your voice is familiar. Have we met before?"

"We have. In your begging days, I sometimes stopped to lend you a helping hand, although I did not appear in this guise."

Bart's eyes lit up. "Yes! I remember now. You would bring me piping hot bread from the bakery and cheese from the dairy. Thank You!" His brow furrowed. "But who are You?"

"I am Gaelathane, and I made you. Dying for you, I earned these scars." He showed the men His hands, arms and feet.

"That's all very well for You," said Bart. "But we can't go into town looking this way. Folks will think we've got the pox."

"Well, *I* once looked like you, and I lived here," said Glaslyn.

The Greenies turned puzzled looks on her and Hamlin. "Why didn't You strip off their whips, too?" they asked the King.

"I have prepared fruitful work for them where they will need their leaves," He said. "In the meantime, you follow Me!"

The men scratched their sores. "How can we do that?"

Waving a scarred arm at the Foamwater, Gaelathane said, "First you must bathe in this river, and you will be cleansed."

The men's faces fell as Bart explained, "Sir, none of us knows how to swim. Besides, we just came out of that river, so we should be plenty clean already, if You don't mind my saying so."

"I'm not asking you to swim, just to bathe," the King came back. He laid a reassuring hand on Bart's bony shoulder.

"Oh, all right," the Greenies said. Following Bart, they trooped down to the dark, rushing waters and waded in up to their waists. Then they began splashing themselves and each other, whooping and shouting like small boys on a summer's swimming lark.

"What about Drelli? Will she live?" Glaslyn asked Gaelathane.

"You mustn't worry about her," He replied. "When I made hedgehogs, I wrapped spines of steel around the heart of a lion. Those little fellows are tougher than they appear."

"Hey! Hi! Look at me!" cried one of the Greenies. He was holding his unblemished arms above the water.

"We're as fresh skinned as babies!" shouted Curly. "There's not a mark on us!" Laughing and tripping over one other, Bart and his men piled out of the river, raising a mighty racket. Smiles breaking out all over, they bowed stiffly before Gaelathane.

"You're the Boss now!" they told Him. "What You say, we will do. Just don't make us go back to the Forest of Fellglade!"

"You won't have time to return there," said the King with a gleam in His eye. He nodded upriver, where twenty or thirty people were emerging from the woods. Then He disappeared, while Glaslyn and Hamlin withdrew to the verge of the forest.

As the crowd neared, a burly woodsman stepped forward. He peered around suspiciously, fingering his ax. "We came down to see what all the commotion was about. Is everyone all right?"

The Greenies grinned and elbowed one another. "Everything is fine," said Bart cheerfully. "We just had a swim, that's all."

An old man with hair as white as his floury apron pointed a quivering finger at him. "You're Blind Bart! You used to come by my bakery for stale buns. It's me, Baker Wornick!"

Bart bowed. "I always wondered what you looked like."

"He can see! Blind Bart can see!" the crowd murmured.

Glaslyn drew her father farther up the valley. "We must return to the swamp and climb one of the trees there," she told him. She was about to explain how torsils work when Gaelathane's white mist rolled down the dale to meet them. When the fog lifted, the two were standing in their leaves before the Castell Mawr.

Embracing her dumbfounded father, Glaslyn said, "We're home now, Papa. At long last, we're truly home."

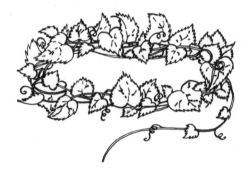

CHAPTER 24

A Crown of Leaves

A fter her people had weathered the regrowth of their vines, Glaslyn returned to the Greenies' swamp, where she found Bart's decaying throne still sitting at the Grotto's mouth. The musty scent of old leaves haunted the autumn woods as she searched among the sleepy, russet-leafed trees. Finding five or six Greenies rooted in place, she touched them with her new lightstaff, liberating the tree-men from their bondage to earth and vine. They all stretched and yawned, looked about and tottered off.

Back on the torsil hill, Glaslyn stood beside the same tree she had once climbed for firewood. Black scars ran down its furrowed, tortoiseshell trunk. With a tendril, she touched one of the torsil's supple branches, sensing the hardy spirit that had kept the tree alive through drought, flood and dragonfire.

"So this is how trees feel!" she said to herself. Sap ebbs and flows; leaves and seeds come and go; trunk and limbs gird themselves with yet another season's woody strength, all the better to reach higher toward sky and life-giving sun.

"And this is how Leafy People feel!" said the tree, whose name was Lithelimb. "Truly we are offshoots of the same Root. And yes, you may climb into my top again. Just don't break anything!"

Glaslyn smiled and patted the torsil. "I'll be careful," she said, and she took a final, wistful look at the marsh basking peacefully in the wan autumn sun. Despite the horrors of the Hole, the swamp fever and the green mist, the place would always smell of home, reminding her of Gaelathane, Gaelessa and the closely-knit Greenies. A song of remembrance sprang to her heart:

To cook and clean was once my lot, to serve an outlaw band;
The Greenies loved me as their own; I could not understand
How any heart could learn to love a face as marred as mine,
Until I met a Man Whose scars bespoke a love divine.

He sent me to a world where I would rather not have gone,
For life was grim and mist was spun of deadly dragon spawn;
But there I met the Fiddler, my faithful Champion;
Who patiently has trained my vines to seek the rising Sun.

He wanders over misty marsh and plays a merry tune,
To drive away the dreigiau and charm the laughing loon;
He walks without a track or trace to mark His miry maze;
His skin is sleek despite the reek of green and heavy haze.

In fullest time, when fickle fog and leaves of green had failed,
And broken was the castle wall where weeping women wailed;
The Champion gave up His arm to save me from the stake;
And by His blood recover all we'd yielded to the Snake.

The cheerful Champion is He, this enigmatic Man,
Whose goings forth are from of old, ere time and stars began;
When danger dogs my weary steps, my Champion appears,
To chase away the dismal dark and calm my foolish fears.

The Champion has always been, the Champion shall be;
When torsil worlds have turned to dust, He'll live eternally;
And when I climb the Tree again, I'll walk beside the Lake,
Where first I met my Champion, Who hung upon my stake.

Then came her coronation day, when the Vinelanders formed a double line and joined whips to create a leafy, high-vaulted hall. Through this green tunnel, Glaslyn floated on waves of melody to meet her smooth-skinned friends and Gaelathane, Who was coaxing joy from the strings of His old violin. Love radiated from Him like heat rising off a slate roof on a sunny afternoon.

"I have no crown for you, My dear Glaslyn," He told her as she knelt before Him. "Rather, a wreath of your own leaves shall you wear all your days." Handing her the fiddle, He said, "This is My coronation gift to you. When you play it, remember Me. Make it sing to heal wounded hearts; to restore hope and faith; to rekindle love. Play it when your spirit flags and in glad times, too."

Glaslyn ran a green tendril over the taut strings. "But I've never played a violin before! Who will teach me?"

Gaelathane showed her how to hold the instrument, gripping the broad end between chin and shoulder and the neck with her fingers. Then He gave her the bow. Stroking it across the strings as she had seen her Master do, she was astonished to hear beautiful, melodious sounds pouring from the instrument.

The smooth-skins clapped and cried, "*Da iawn!*" Well done!

"*Da iawn!*" echoed down the leafy lines of lost Lucambrians.

"I created this violin especially for you," Gaelathane said. "In a way, it *is* you, for it reflects your very soul and spirit. Its strings will respond solely to your touch and to no other." Gaelathane then laid His hands upon Glaslyn's head and said, "I name you Glaslyn the Blue, Queen of Gwinwydden. As are your leaves, so shall be your heart—full of the sap of love and life. I grant you the wisdom to rule these leafy people, but not without help."

From the Vinelanders' twin ranks stepped a pair of tall mist-people, their sturdy vines entwined. Huw and Cari bowed. "We will always stand beside you in your service," Huw said. "We'd be most grateful, too, if you would preside over our wedding—after your coronation festivities are completed, of course."

"I would be honored," Glaslyn said, and she meant it.

Huw wickedly grinned at her through his vines. "Thank you! Now you'd better let me hold your fiddle for you."

"What for?" Glaslyn asked, passing the instrument to him.

He winked at her. "You don't want it to break, do you?"

All at once, sinewy whips seized Glaslyn and hurled her shrieking high into the air. Falling, she landed on a springy hammock woven from thousands of vines. Up she went again.

"Long live Queen Glaslyn!" her subjects shouted, and Glaslyn laughed for joy. *Scabby and Merryn are gone. Long live Queen Glaslyn! Long live Gaelathane, the King of the Trees!* As Hamlin had once predicted, Glaslyn was indeed "Queen of the Greenies."

Epilogue

Because I know them best, I will first tell you what became of the Greenies. Thanks to the uproar over the dragon, they managed to slip back into town and resume their lives on an honest footing. However, it was not an easy task, especially for the long-vines. Kinfolk had moved away or died, and few friends remained who still recognized the former brigands.

Most of Bart's men returned to the river, where they distinguished themselves with ropes and sails and pulleys. Their chief sport was using bullwhips to pluck fruit growing along the riverbanks, a trick the other rivermen could never master.

Work permitting, the men often met at the "Quaffing Dragon," a pub named after the beast that had nearly drained the brewery dry. Having sworn off drinking, they reminisced over their Greenie days and amused themselves with darts and other games requiring a quick hand and a keen eye. They would also bend any listening ear with tales of a King Who cares for the likes of drunks and pickpockets, a King as close as a whispered prayer.

Bart took service with Baker Wornick, who mended his ways after hearing of Gaelathane and stopped lacing the bread with sawdust. In Wornick's later years, when he had grown as plump as a white-bearded dumpling, Bart often helped him trim the village wassail tree at Yuletide. In the wee hours after midnight, the two would hang stockings full of sweets and gilders outside the homes of the poor and needy. "Saint 'Nick," the baker came to be called, though it was Bart who stuffed the stockings.

The Greenies would have faded into the dim halls of legend were it not for the tales of "green men" hiding in the Forest of Fellglade, prompting local stonemasons to carve leafy caricatures of the creatures over doors and windows. Those grotesque faces still leer down from the moldering stones of ancient burghs, though the events behind the faces have long since passed into obscurity.

Milly never did find another husband. To her dying day, she could "make a gilder go for two," as the saying went. Still, she loved dressing in frippery and finery. Emory would have followed in her vain, penny-pinching footsteps were it not for a shining rod he found in the forest one evening. Thereafter, he saw life in a different light and apprenticed himself to the vicar.

Drelli recovered to become the royal draenog. When she wasn't eating or sleeping, she liked to join Glaslyn on trips to Thalmos collecting amenthil seeds, which the queen later planted in Vineland. Glaslyn also introduced her father to the pink-blossomed tree, launching him into an argument with a very persistent robin that was busily building a nest in his vines.

Hamlin taught Brynnor a thing or two about ale, though the brewery stands mostly idle, now that Openings are devoted to sober celebrations of the Fiddler's sacrifice. The crowning event of every such occasion is the Stake Dance, wherein young, eligible maidens intertwine their vines around a tall pole until they are tethered to it, recalling the Aberth's fate. At the end of the dance, each girl earns a kiss for her efforts. This tradition has passed into other worlds as the "Maypole Dance."

Each year, an Aberth is still chosen—not to ride the cart, which stands chained to the floor in Noni's former cell—but as its curator. The inscription over the door now reads, "Gaelathane paid our due." As the first Curator of the Cart, Noni recites for her listeners the tale behind that instrument of death and how its creaking wheels were finally silenced by the Fiddler's blood.

Glaslyn's smooth-skinned friends remained in Vineland until the rising mist drove them out. After taking their tearful leave of the new queen, they climbed the torsil Lithelimb. Rolin and Marlis had hardly dusted off their thrones before Gaelathane sent them on another adventure, which comes into a later tale.

As for me, I awaken each day grateful to Gaelathane for restoring my sight, and I'm not speaking only of my eyes, either. Now that Wornick is gone, I'm the chief baker with an apprentice of my own. When Dall can knead a decent loaf, I'll let him take over. Then I may accept Glaslyn's invitation to visit her in the Carreg Keep—but only by griffin. My Greenie days are over!

I nearly forgot to tell you: Soon after I lost my leaves, a beggar met me by the river and offered me a fiddle. It looked so worn and cracked that at first I wouldn't take it. At his urging, I put the bow to the strings. Wouldn't you know it, but that old fiddle sang to make me weep! I expect that if you asked Him, Gaelathane would give you one, too. Won't you take it up today and play?

Glossary and
Pronunciation Guide

a´menthil. Tree of understanding.

Aberth. A "Protector" of Vineland.

Andil of the Wood. One of Gaelathane's guises.

ash´tag. Torsil of Gundul; "black tree."

Awst (pr. Owst). Low Lucambrian for "August."

Bartholomew the Bold. Notorious Thalmosian highwayman.

battle´ments. Notched wall (rampart) encircling tower's top.

Beechtown. Nearest town to King Rolin's birthplace.

Bembor son of Brenthor. High chancellor to King Rolin.

blaguryn (pr. blog´-ear-in). Low Lucambrian for "outbreak."

bragwr (pr. brog-oor). Low Lucambrian for "brewer."

Brynnor of the Brew. Brewmaster of the Castell Mawr.

Cari (Cariad) (pr. Kar´-ee). Maidservant to Queen Rowena.

Carreg Keep. Main defensive tower in the Castell Mawr.

Castell Mawr. Castle built by the People of the Mist. ("Great Castle.")

Common Speech. Trade language spoken in Thalmos and elsewhere.

cors draig. Low Lucambrian for "marsh dragon."

croen-esmwyth. Low Lucambrian for "smooth-skinned."

Croeso! (pr. Kroy´-so). Lucambrian for "Welcome!"

curtain wall. A castle's defensive wall.

Dewi son of Dylan. Bailiff of the Castell Mawr.

Draebold the Draig-Slayer. Drelli's illustrious ancestor.

draenog (pr. dry´-nog). Low Lucambrian for "hedgehog."

draig (pr. drayg or dryg). Low Lucambrian for "dragon." (pl. *dreigiau*.)

dreigiau (pr. dray´-ghee-eye). Low Lucambrian for "dragons."

Drelli. Cari's hedgehog.

Drundaig. King of the dragons.

dyddiadur (pr. dith-ee-aw´-deer). Low Lucambrian for "diary."

Ebrill. The month of April (Low Lucambrian).

El´gathel. Former king of Lucambra; Rolin's grandfather.

El´wyn son of Rolin. King Rolin and Queen Marlis's son.

ffrind (pr. frind). Lucambrian for "friend." (pl. *ffrindiau.*)

Fiddler. How Gaelathane appears in Vineland.

Foamwater. Beechtown's river (Thalmos).

Forest of Fellglade. Uncharted forest northeast of Beechtown.

Gaelathane (pr. Gale´-uh-thane). King of the Trees.

Gaelessa (pr. Gale-es´-suh). Gaelathane's home, reached only through the Tree.

Gannon son of Hemmett. Rolin's father.

Garrick of the Gate. Gatekeeper for the Castell Mawr.

Garth. Timothy's father.

gil´der. Thalmosian coin, equivalent to a penny.

Glaslyn. Merryn's real name.

Greencloak. Thalmosian name for Lucambrian scout.

Gun´dul. Underworld; place of darkness and death.

gwas (pr. gwoss). Low Lucambrian for "servant."

Gwinwydden (pr. Gwin´-with-en). Low Lucambrian for "Vineland."

Gwledd Mawr (pr. Goo-leth Maw-er). Low Lucambrian for "Great Feast."

Gwyn´neth daughter of Marlis. Rolin and Marlis's eldest daughter.

Hal´lowfast. Tower of the Tree (near the Sea of El-Marin).

Hamlin son of Harmon. Beechtown's brewmaster; Merryn's adopted father.

hudo (pr. hee-do). Low Llwcymraeg term for "enchanted tree" (torsil).

Huw (pr. Hugh). Son of Rhynion and Queen Rowena, and heir to the throne.

Ifan (I´van) son of Ifor (I´vor). Discoverer of Vineland.

Ifan's Hill. Hill beside Split-top in Vineland.

inner curtain. A castle's inner (secondary) defensive wall.

King Rhynion. Former king of Vineland; swallowed by dragon.

lancet. Tall, narrow window coming to a point at the top.

Lithelimb. Torsil tree on Ifan's Hill.

Llwcym´raeg (pr. Hloo-kawm´-reig). The Lucambrian language.

Low Llwcymraeg. Ancient dialect spoken by People of the Mist.

Lucambra (pr. Loo-kam´-bruh). "Land of Light." (In the Lucambrian: *Llwcymru*.)

Mar´lis. Emmer's daughter, Scanlon's sister, Rolin's wife and queen of Lucambra.

Med´wyn. Scanlon's wife.

Meghan daughter of Marlis. Rolin and Marlis's younger daughter.

Melchandor. Angel sent to help Huw and Merryn.

niwl gwyrdd (pr. nee-ool gwirth). Low Lucambrian for "green mist."

Noni (Noniad). Cari's sister.

Opening Day. Day after Watering Day when gates are opened.

Opio and Gemmio, sons of Nolan. Lucambrian brothers; advisors to King Rolin.

Ort. Ringleader of gang of Beechtown bullies.

People of the Mist. Inhabitants of the marsh world Vineland.

portcullis. Sturdy iron grillwork protecting castle's main gate.

Rolin son of Gannon. King of Lucambra.

Rowena. Queen of the Mist People.

Scanlon son of Emmer. Rolin's chief deputy and Bembor's grandson.

sgaffaldwaith (pr. sguh-fald´-wyth). Low Lucambrian for "scaffolding."

sorc´athel. Top of Hallowfast.

Split-top. Mountain near Castell Mawr in Vineland.

Stygweth. Creature lying in pool at bottom of cleft in Split-top.

sythan-ar (pr. sigh´-thun-ar). Lucambrian word for "life tree."

Tartel´lans. Mountains west of Beechtown.

Thalmos (pr. Thall´-mose). Timothy's home world.

Timothy son of Garth. Merryn's Thalmosian friend and rescuer.

tor´sils. Trees of passage.

Vineland. Mist People's marshy world. (See *Gwinwydden*.)

Watering Day. Special day each month when dragons are "watered."

Wornick. Beechtown baker.

Yeg. Batwolf (plural—yegs or yeggoroth; adj.—yeggish).

You may order additional copies of

The GREENSTONES

from our secure server web site:
greencloaks.com

or by sending $14.95 each plus $3.95 shipping* to:

KOT BOOKS
3237 Sunset Drive
Hubbard, OR 97032-9635

Other titles in the King of the Trees series:

Book I: The King of the Trees ($11.99)
Book II: Torsils in Time ($14.95)
Book III: The Golden Wood ($14.95)
Book V: The Downs ($14.95)

Please make checks and money orders payable to KOT BOOKS.
*(Add $1.00 shipping and handling for each additional copy.)